RAISE THE STAKES

ACES HIGH, JOKERS WILD BOOK 3

O. E. TEARMANN

"Okay Aidan, I'm going to ask you to start counting down from a hundred out loud."

Aidan focused on the surgeon's eyes, crinkled in a smile above her mask. The cool weight of the micro-injector pressed against the skin of his throat.

"A hundred..."

Holy crap, this is actually happening...still can't believe it...

"Ninety-nine..."

Almost two months late, but still...holy crap...

"Ninety-eight..."

Please. Please let this work out...

"Ninety-seven..."

Aidan could barely feel his lips moving. He seemed to be drifting away from his body, only just aware of it.

God I hope there's no drone passes while they're working...

"Ninety-six..."

The world around him lost reality, growing distant. Aidan closed his eyes.

Man I hope...

this…

works…

Aidan woke slowly, letting the world fade into focus around him. Sound came first. People talking far off. Med-bay machinery, giving cheery blips and quiet whirs. Rustling cloth.

It took work to peel his eyes open and blink at the ceiling. What he could see was, mostly, white. Based on the size of the corner where the ceiling met the wall, it was a small room. He let his eyes drift closed and swallowed, trying to wet his dry mouth.

"Hey." Long, slim fingers slipped between his, squeezing gently. Aidan's heart expanded.

"Hey Kev." The words sounded odd in his ears, fuzzy around the edges.

"The medic said you'd be thirsty. Could you use some water?" His boyfriend asked quietly.

It took Aidan a few seconds to process the question. He nodded against the pillow and opened his eyes, trying for a smile. Kevin gave one of his heartbreak-sweet little smiles in reply. In the light coming down from the overhead lamps, he looked like a statue made from copper and marble. Those outdated glasses he liked so much sat on his nose like graffiti on a painting.

Kevin lifted a covered mug with a straw sticking out of it, hitting the button that sat the bed up just a little.

"Here. Just sip it, don't get enthusiastic," he murmured, pressing the straw against Aidan's lips. Aidan took a sip of the lukewarm water. It tasted odd, but he didn't know if that was courtesy of different water-recycling techniques used up here at the big Regional base, or the last of the painkillers.

Funny what your brain decided to focus on when it was free-wheeling.

Eyes half-closed, he took in the room. Small, white, sparse. A cabinet and workstation setup extruded from the far wall. A private room. That was weird. It was warm—nice change, their base was cold right now—and quiet. The beeping of the bed's sensory panel was comforting.

He shifted. He was dressed in something soft, loose and cozy. *Robe*, he decided eventually.

A holo panel gently sizzled into being, displaying his condition and full body scan in pastel colors. The sites where the slick white auto-pads were at work over the operational incisions across his chest and between his legs were outlined in soft blue.

"Good morning," the speaker above the bed intoned softly. "Your procedures of simultaneous mammoplasty with reduction, full hysterectomy and colpocleisis were performed successfully." Aidan's ears caught the pause as the automated voice stumbled, taking time to pull up his surgery record from Regional Medical's information bank. But you couldn't expect too much from the third-hand surplus tech that their Force could get its hands on. It was better than nothing.

"Your projected recovery is optimal," the program interface continued, "your current care: post-operative rest. Nerve block treatment. Delivery method: short duration nanoid conglomerate. Tissue and nerve regeneration treatment. Delivery method: Automatic Tissue Reconstruction Pads. Pertinent issue detected: slightly elevated cortisol level. Pertinent issue detected: minor dehydration. Call aid?"

"No, thank you." Kevin stated, loudly and clearly. The screen image displayed the Force star symbol as it softly dissolved.

"Your Automatic Tissue Reconstruction Pads are currently doing their work," the automated voice whispered. "Your body is processing general anesthesia. Drowsiness is normal at this time. Please relax and allow healing to proceed."

Kevin smiled and pulled his chair a little closer to the bed, brushing Aidan's hair back from his eyes. His hand cupped Aidan's cheek. "Looks like everything's squared away," the redhead remarked. "How do you feel? Or is that a stupid question?"

Aidan pressed his cheek into Kevin's hand and closed his eyes, enjoying the moment of comfort. "Feel like'm floating..."

"You look like you're high as a kite," Kevin replied gently, his smile soft. "Does anything hurt at all? I can get the surgeon..."

Aidan shook his head against the pillow. "Nah. Can't...feel much. Sorta numb."

He tried to prop himself up and take another sip of water on his own. Well, that and get a look at himself. The readout said he was in good shape, but he wanted to *see*.

Kevin's hands pressed gently against his shoulders.

"Ah, you might not want to try that. The internal tissue scaffolds and the ligatures need to be kept still if they're going to integrate with your tissues, and you shouldn't stress surgical auto-pads until they've laid down a few layers of tissue."

Aidan smiled weakly. "Guess you'd know. Help me out here?"

Kevin held the straw until he'd drunk his fill. Aidan watched as his boyfriend glanced behind him to make sure the door was closed, his body moving with a grace that was half logistics training and half crazy-good genetic tailoring. Satisfied that they were alone, the pale redhead leaned over. Kevin's lips brushed his.

"The surgeon said you might need a little more sleep; your body's cleaning out quite the chemical cocktail."

Aidan thought about protesting, but the words jumbled in his mind. So he smiled and mumbled an agreement, fumbling for Kevin's hand as he slid back into sleep.

The next time Aidan came around Kevin was reading, grey eyes intent. They softened when he glanced up. Aidan gave him a smile. "How long was I out?"

"Around six hours," the logistics officer replied with an easy smile, curled comfortably in his seat and his heavy grey sweater. "I've been getting my consultation hours in with their Logistics division and helping them out while we're here, otherwise I'll catch hell from Commander Magnum for coming along with you."

"Good plan," Aidan agreed. He started to stretch, but holos fizzled into life with the words 'please remain still, Surgeon en route,' blinking on either side. He sighed. "Information understood. Switch off."

The holos dissolved. Kevin smirked, his thin face sardonic. "They get to be quite a nuisance, don't they?"

"Yeah," Aidan agreed, trying to shift a little without setting off the holos. He turned his head as the door opened.

Slim, dark Surgeon Lawston stepped inside, smiling down at Aidan when she reached his bedside. Her white coat gleamed in the room lights.

"How're you doing this evening?"

Aidan shrugged. "I feel pretty good. How long until I can get up?"

The surgeon chuckled. "Want to get moving already, hunh? It'll be tomorrow morning before the surgical auto-pads are finished reconstructing the muscular tissues, but I'd say by lunch you should be able to move around."

She tapped the wall above his head, and four holographic screens faded into being around them.

"This is looking great." Lawston remarked cheerfully as she read through the body scans and the scrolling information, "Your body's cleared out the general anesthetics and the nerve blockers are doing their thing. In fact I'd say you're ready to start your PT regimen tomorrow. I'd like you to stay on restricted movement and nerve blockers in the general recovery ward for the next four days, but Friday should be your last epithelial auto-pad treatment; after that it's just keeping up on your PT and not stressing the internal ligatures that you need to think about. The nerve-block nanoids will run out of power by next Monday, but by then the new skin will be fully innervated and they won't be necessary. How does that sound?"

Aidan nodded, thinking. Tomorrow, he could see what he looked like without breasts. Raising his head, he gave the surgeon a smile. "Um. Thank you again. For fitting me into the Regional schedule. I'm still floored your surgical team had time for me. Thanks for...well, everything."

The surgeon smiled down at him, nodding an acknowledgment. "I don't do the actual scheduling, but I'm glad we could get you fixed up. I'd like you to wear some final epithelial auto-pads to bed Friday night and throughout Saturday, just to protect the new skin. But they'll be consumer grade; any untrained personnel can apply them. Give the muscles of your pectorals two weeks, then hit the gym and you'll look great. The more detailed care instructions are in the notes I've sent to your tab."

When she'd gone, Aidan turned to Kevin. To make his boyfriend smile, he rolled his eyes. "Four days in bed. I don't think I've held still that long in years."

Kevin leaned casually against the wall, chuckling. "You should read some of the medical history docs I have, love. Back in the 2060s Victor Cavanaugh was still developing the first auto-pads, and this procedure would have seen you in bed for six weeks at least. And they used to drown the patient's entire nervous system in opiods to suppress pain." He gave one of his showy shudders. "Consider yourself lucky on this count, at least. Those drugs were terrifying."

Aidan chuckled, his fingers absently tracing the line of a slick plastic auto-pad under the warm robe he was dressed in. "Well, hey: at least Cavanaugh left behind something that didn't totally suck."

Kevin glanced away, the muscles of his shoulders tensing. When he spoke, each word was bright and brittle as a diamond. "Yes. Too bad he didn't leave behind more technologies and fewer ideologies."

Kevin's eyes fixed somewhere on the middle distance. "Though I will say, the justice of using that rigid bigot's inventions to do things that would make him turn in his grave is something I find quite satisfying. Rather poetic, really."

Aidan shifted uncomfortably in his bed. Kevin looked distant now, hard-eyed and ramrod straight in his chair. Untouchable. He always got like that when he talked about Victor Cavanaugh, or anything else from the Corporation whose power had shaped the way he looked and spoke. His head tipped back, his vocabulary went up, and his body went rigid. It was never fun to watch. Kevin had a good reason for that anger, Aidan knew. The Cavanaugh Corporation designed the genome of Kevin and his father before him the way it would print executive tools. When Kevin's father tried to buck the way the Corporation ran, the Board of Directors had discarded the whole family like a defective product. And then there were all the other people Cavanaugh discarded; anyone who didn't meet their eugenic standards for humanity was 'aberrant' in their eyes. And they disposed of aberrations.

Aidan knew Kevin had every reason to hate anything to do with Victor Cavanaugh and the Corporation he'd founded way back when. But it was always a little uncomfortable to watch his boyfriend go cold on him.

Aidan cleared his throat and tried for a joke. "Okay Professor."

Kevin glanced down, and the cold gene-tailored Corporate scion was gone, leaving his sheepish boyfriend. The lean man lifted Aidan's hand, brushing his lips over Aidan's knuckles. "Looking forward to seeing you out of your shirt when the auto-pads have done their duty."

Aidan nodded a little, smiling. "You and me both."

"Oh, and by the way," Kevin added with a winning smile. "I landed us our ride home. An empty supply transport being sent out. All the room in the world."

"Thank god." Aidan said in genuine relief, "Coming up into the San Juans in a packed truck was bad enough."

Kevin snorted, adjusting his glasses on the bridge of his thin nose. "You think you had it bad, love? Try being as tall as I am in a well-packed truck. I'm *still* working some of the kinks out of my—"

Both men looked up at the knock on the door, watching the panel slide open. When Kevin caught sight of the woman standing on the lintel, he shot to his feet and saluted like a page out of a manual. Aidan's heart skipped a beat.

CO-WY Regional Commander Hall nodded. "At ease, McIllian. I hear Headly's awake and thinking straight?"

"Yes ma'am," Aidan croaked. He tried for a salute, not sure if it looked right from a half-lying-down position.

Regional Commander Hall nodded, lips curved in a grim smile.

"McIllian, go get chow. Take an hour."

Aidan watched Kevin glance between the door and him.

"Er, Commander—"

Commander Hall turned her head like a bird of prey. "Dismissed, Officer. Close the door behind you."

Kevin jerked his head in a nod. "Yes, ma'am."

The slide and click of the door was loud in the quiet room. Commander Hall eyed it for a moment.

"Let's get small stuff out of the way first, Headly. Commander Magnum tells me you and your logistics officer are an item?"

"Yes Commander," Aidan agreed, too numb to be worried yet.

The older woman turned her eyes on him, measuring. "Magnum also tells me it's a net benefit to your unit. And that you've been impartial in disciplinary acts when necessary. As long as it stays that way."

The regional commander stepped to his bedside, studying him.

"How awake are you, son?"

Aidan considered the question. The anesthetic drugs had worn off; he could feel his body again. The nerve blocking nanoids stopped the nerve signals at their sources around his incisions, hiding the pain like a razor blade in cotton wool. His mind was mostly clear; that was the important thing.

He cleared his throat. "Eighty-five percent, ma'am. I think."

Commander Hall nodded, pulling the bedside chair over and taking a seat. The situation was a little surreal. The CO-WY Regional Commander was sitting there, her uniform perfect from her boots to her winter-issue khaki jacket, staring at him with her rank badge gleaming on her lapel. And he was wrapped in a nice red recovery robe.

"Lawston said you'd be alert around now," Commander Hall stated. "You'll be moved into the general recovery ward by the end of the day. So we're going to talk now."

Of all things, she pulled a soundbox from her pocket, turning on the little white-noise emitter and pitching it gently. It rolled to thump quietly against the room's door.

Aidan blinked. "Commander?"

The regional commander resumed her seat as if nothing had happened, her whipcord frame relaxed. "Your orders sent you up here to get your surgeries for a reason, soldier."

Aidan repressed his reaction to that. He should have known not to trust his luck. "I understand, ma'am."

He felt his bland good-soldier persona slide into place as his commander's superior spoke.

"Tell me about the changes you've seen since The Folder was released. General impressions; you don't need to be comprehensive. Just talk."

Aidan blinked. "Um...the Corps are getting called on their bullshit I guess. There are marches, protests. EagleCorp's going apeshit. They're trying to step up security everywhere, but they're having to work at it. Their factories are turning out a ton of new drones.

"AgCo's in the biggest trouble. Their people are the ones really taking to the streets, but all the Corps are being called on their shit one way or another." He trailed off, working to focus.

A stray thought made him smile, just a bit. "Chatter says there's a huge bounty out on the team who pulled it off. Our techie said it wasn't big enough."

Commander Hall nodded. "Your people did a lot with that Folder delivery. I'm going to be blunt with you, Headly."

"Ma'am?" Aidan wasn't sure if that was a good thing or not.

Commander Hall looked him dead in the eye. "I was one of the people advocating to see 1407 disbanded after we lost Taylor. And I told Magnum he was delusional when he told me your team was ready to deliver the Folder. But you proved me wrong, son. And you impressed me. We've made more tangible wins in the past two months than we did in the prior two years. We've finally shaken the bastards' cages. And they are rattled."

The sinewy, seasoned general leaned forward. A heartbeat passed as she studied him, silent. Two heartbeats. Three. "Think your unit can impress me again?"

Aidan didn't dare break the stare-down. "How do we do that, ma'am?"

"The Corps are reeling," the older woman stated, "So we hit them again. Hard."

She nodded in the direction of the door. "Let me be clear. What I want to put you on is a national, clandestine operation, designed to be conducted by four bases across the country. You and three other base commanders will execute it. There's going to be nothing written down locally on this mission. I'm not bringing you in for a formal mission debriefing either. What we're talking about is too dangerous to put through local channels, in case it leaks. But this mission is a big one."

Standing, she paced a few steps to the left, then to the right. Aidan watched her, feeling his mouth going dry again.

He wet his lips. "Ma'am...you said too dangerous."

"Leaks, Headly. It's happened before. And it can't happen now." The Regional Commander's salt-and-pepper hair swung as she turned to face him again, unconsciously standing at parade rest. "What's the foundation of the Corporate power structure, Headly?"

Aidan blinked. Okay, maybe he wasn't awake as he thought. His brain felt like a bare room. He snagged a dust mote of an answer.

"Power consolidation, ma'am. They've got all of the resources. And the cash."

"And?"

Tension started to build in his gut. Aidan drew a long breath, let it out, and shrugged. He didn't have the brain power for this game.

"Ma'am, it's a pretty long list. They've got a lot of things on their side."

The older woman tipped her head. "As in, with respect spit it out ma'am?" she asked, eyeing him.

Aidan did the smart thing, which was keeping his mouth shut. He watched her, his attentive good-soldier expression in place.

For a moment, that flicker of a smile tugged Hall's lips, pulling at the starburst scar in her cheek.

"Now I see why Magnum likes you. Alright. I'll say it straight. The Corporations don't need to spend too many resources keeping people down. They get people to do it for them. That's what the Citizen Standing Score is for. So that's the next institution we're taking aim at."

In Aidan's chest, his heart stuttered.

"Um...ma'am?"

"You heard me, Headly." The regional commander paced easily, an apex predator on the prowl. "For the past eleven years, the National Command has run a concerted campaign to give National Banking and EagleCorp nightmares. We run exploit and intrusion hacks on elements of the Citizen Standing Score aggregation system in at least eighteen randomized states a week. All bases with a decent Technical Officer have taken a turn, but no single base has done more than a few missions in this campaign. We've been deleting information and adding errors to files. Eroding public trust in the verity of their Scores. Inserting viruses that inject garbage code. It's been a slow process intended to herd National Banking towards more and more centralization of their records. Currently, they have four sets of backups around the country and one master copy in a meshnet setup. What we have is a window of opportunity. The current unrest won't last more than a year, unless we feed it." She placed both hands on the back of her chair, fingers tapping as she stared at Aidan.

"We want your unit to head the organization and implementing of the final attack strategy. Three other crack bases around the country will be following your lead. We want an infiltration and destruction method agreed on for a Natbank backup center. We want it tested and verified.

And then we want a coordinated four-part attack implemented."

Aidan swallowed hard. When he spoke, his lips felt like wood. "And you want the Wildcards to head it."

Commander Hall nodded. "Seeing that your unit was given a suicide mission with practically no prep time this winter, and you pulled it off? I want the Wildcards to head it."

Fear built behind Aidan's eyes, tingling in his fingertips.

He drew a long, slow breath, counting to keep himself calm as he inhaled.

One

Holy shit.

Two

Can we do this?

Three

If we can do this, we can change everything. Literally. Everything...

Four

We did the Folder. We took down drones.

Five

Maybe we can do this.

Six

Hey. Worst that happens is we die.

Seven

"Headly?"

Aidan swallowed hard. "Do we have a mission start date, ma'am?"

Aidan hadn't realized the woman was tense, until she relaxed. "Second week of March. You'll be fit for duty by then?"

"Doc said so," Aidan agreed quietly.

The regional commander nodded. "Then I expect work to begin then." Pulling a data stick from her pocket, she laid it on the bed beside his hand. "This has a secured VPN program, coded to accept your biometric data as your login credentials. Add passwords to it. You and the bases you're coordinating with will use this VPN to collaborate and report your progress to me. There are also informational files to get you up to speed on the teams you'll work with. Discuss the mission at will with your unit, but it is classified. Don't discuss it in publicly accessible areas. I don't want to hear gossip anywhere. And don't discuss it with McIllian until you're off this base. Are we clear?"

Aidan nodded. "Understood, Commander."

Commander Hall nodded, acknowledgment in the gesture. Then she turned, picked up her sound-box, and strode from the room.

Aidan let his head drop back onto the pillow. He stared at the ceiling.

"Shit...here we go again..."

<u>Event File 2</u>
<u>File Tag: R&R</u>
<u>Timestamp: 12:00-2-23-2156</u>

They rolled Aidan's bed into the recovery ward around lunch the next day. He didn't feel all that into food, but he managed to get a nutrient shake down. He was happy when they left him alone to sleep.

Kevin was across the room chatting with the surgeon when he woke again. A man with a cast on one arm, skin peeling from a truly vicious sunburn across his face, and a handful of IV's going into the other arm nodded amicably at him from the next bed over.

"Shrapnel, man? That's what I heard. Me too, sucks balls donnit? Name's Jack."

Aidan nodded, lying easily about the reason he was in recovery. He watched as the surgeon showed his boyfriend a few arm movements.

Ah crap, he's learning my PT regimen. Now he'll bug me about it.

Realizing that he was being rude, he gave his neighbor a smile. "Aidan," he replied, glad to interact without rank for a little while. "And yeah, shrapnel. It's a bitch."

The wounded man glanced the way Aidan had been looking. "Yeah," he muttered in an undertone, "I been watching that guy too. Officer off one of the lowland bases is what I heard. Call me crazy, but he almost looks—" his voice dropped to a grating whisper, "—almost Citizen Excellent, you think?"

Aidan shook his head, smiling. "Chill. He's a guy off my base. And he's not CES."

The other patient gave him the fish eye. "You sure? Sure looks high-standing."

Aidan shrugged. "Nah. I know him. He's not CES. Just good-looking." That was true as far as it went. Kevin was definitely not Citizen Excellent Standing, though he had been born into that class. But this guy didn't need to know that.

The man shrugged and started to stretch, then cried out. Holos fizzed into life around his bed with warnings reminding the patient that moving was a bad idea. The surgeon was at his bed a moment later. "What is it with you logistics and requisitions guys? You really can't sit still."

Jack shrugged ruefully. "Sorry, doc. Tell me I get to eat a real lunch?"

"Yes, you get to eat a real lunch," Surgeon Lawston replied with a wry smile, "but you're going to do it in here. Food cart will be in soon."

She glanced at Aidan, and her smile grew a little more gentle. "You're in shape to have a real dinner tonight, by the way. No more nutrient shakes."

"Hallelujah." Kevin added behind her, smiling softly.

When the surgeon had gone, Kevin grabbed a spare chair and dropped easily into it beside Aidan's bed.

"The surgeon has some stretches she wants you doing right away to make sure those tissues stay supple; she walked me through it. So, what did Hall have for you?"

Aidan drew a finger across his throat in a kill-this gesture. Kevin blinked, then nodded.

"Oh, on the subject of having something for you—" Digging in his pocket, he extracted two thin wafers of black plastic. Passing Aidan his data tab, Kevin tapped his own. The holographic screen fizzed into life in the air above the tab, which Kevin laid on his lap and used as a keyboard. He drew a deliberate line upwards in the air above the screen with a forefinger, and the hologram resettled itself at his eye-level.

Aidan's tab blipped, and the holographic screen slid smoothly into the air in front of him, the keyboard projected on the device screen outlining his fingers in light. Kevin laid a pair of 'buds in his lap.

"I'm syncing you with an audio book," the logistics officer remarked, "you're going to love this. Two famous authors did this one together, and it's hilarious. It's about an angel and a demon trying to stop the Apocalypse. We'll play this new Battleship program—I finally got it to start working—and enjoy the story, shall we?"

Aidan gave him a sidelong grin, grabbing the distraction with both hands. "Kev? How old's the book? More important, how old's the game?"

Kevin blushed. Aidan had found out the man's skin was gene-modified to produce its own sunscreen, and it really showed when he blushed; he looked like he had a warning beacon on each cheek as he spluttered.

"Oh come now Aidan, it's—"

"How old?" Aidan prodded.

"A hundred and sixty for the book and a hundred seventy-five for the game. At best guess. It may be older," the redhead muttered eventually.

Aidan rolled his eyes, a smile tugging at his lips. "Knew it'd be something like that. Where'd you even dig up the rules for a two-hundred year old game to use for the program?

Kevin shrugged, wearing that eager little smile he always had when he'd found some ancient thing. "I've got my sources. And I've been wanting to test this game against a live opponent for a while. Please?"

Aidan chuckled. "If it's as bad as that *Oklahoma* thing was, I'm giving you shit."

"And the Pope's a Catholic." Kevin grumbled good-naturedly. Aidan wasn't sure what that was supposed to mean, so he let it slide.

The earbuds muted the sounds of the medical bay, closing him in a cocoon of quiet with the story for company. Kevin was right: it was a nice way to spend time.

A holographic window of blue appeared in front of his main screen, and 3-D images of a bunch of old-fashioned ships floated in the air beside it. Following the instructions, Aidan chose places for all of them and hit 'play'.

A miniature explosion symbol immediately filled one of the blue dots on a little two-dot ship. A second one followed. The image of the ship broke in half and sank.

Five minutes into the game, a side window floated up to his eye-level, showing a private message.

Shall we talk about the conversation you had with Hall like this? You're looking a little nervous.

A little nervous. Was that ever an understatement. Aidan typed quickly in reply, half trying to figure out where he should drop his next bomb. He'd tried the two top rows already.

Better not. We'll talk at home.

In fact, they both needed to get off the subject of the insanity Hall had dropped on their plate. Aidan turned to a smaller worry instead as the audio book introduced an angel and a snake.

You and Damian are sure the records on our base look legit, right?

Finally, he scored a point. Now he had to decide: was Kevin's ship going across, or down?

Kevin read, sighed quietly, and typed. Another one of Aidan's ships sank on the game screen, and a message popped up.

Yes, the records show you coming up here for a routine gallbladder surgery. We used your serial number rather than your name and rank to get you this slot, so the records won't sync. Commander Magnum signed off on it, with Commander Hall's approval. It'll never appear in the

official record at 1407. Cross my heart.

Kevin glanced up, caught his eye and smiled gently as he typed.

> But you know our crew wouldn't care in the slightest if
> they did find out. In fact, life might be easier if you let
> them know about you. It would let you relax.

Aidan's gut clenched. So much for getting off onto an easier subject.

Another one of his ships sank, one of the long thin ones. Kevin was kicking his ass at this game.

Carefully, he typed.

> I know you're probably right. I'm probably being a
> chickenshit. We could probably talk about it out loud
> here and nobody would care. But I need some more time
> before I go there. Okay?

Kevin raised his eyes, holding Aidan's for a few heartbeats. He typed something, then bit his lip. He erased what he'd been typing, wrote something else. The message popped up for Aidan to read. Well, when you're ready let us know. Damian and I will keep it under our hats until then.

Kevin shot him a sly smile as he typed.

> Besides, I rather like typing clandestine messages with
> you. Takes me back to our first proper conversation. Me,
> you, a nice quiet corner...

Aidan smiled as the quiet British-accented words of the book filled his ears. He typed.

> Yeah, and a drone over our heads ready to drop a bomb
> if we made a sound.

Kevin shrugged, winked, and typed.

> Danger adds spice to romance, they say.

Aidan rolled his eyes, lips quirking crookedly. Glancing at Kevin, he typed a few words.

> Thanks, Kev.

Kevin reached over and laid his hand on Aidan's. It wasn't the smartest thing to do in an open ward with company they weren't sure of. Even in the Dust, there were people who had problems with anyone outside their version of 'normal'. His own father had been proof of that.

But the touch was what he needed if he was going to forget how deep in the shit they were, for now. So he didn't pull away as Kevin typed one-handed.

Any time, love. Oh, by the way. I think the character of Crowley was my first crush. I assume you'd like to know about the competition.

The goofball added a gif of two cats snuggling after that. Aidan rolled his eyes. He typed for a moment.

You geek.

Grinning, Kevin shrugged. "Oh, and your last battleship just sunk."

Aidan glanced at the screen. "Damn it!"

By the time they rolled into their own base on the 28th, Aidan was feeling more energetic than he had since his op. He waved at Dozer and Topher as they walked inside. Topher grinned and dropped his oily rag, making his superior's diagnostic holos blip and shudder in the air as he jogged through them. He was halfway through clapping Aidan on the back when Kevin gently caught the boy's wrist. One copper brow quirked up.

"Surgery, Topher."

"Shit, sorry," the skinny young man groaned. He mimed smacking himself on the forehead, disarranging the bandanna holding his black hair back as he grinned at Aidan.

"It's good to have you back man. Liza about had a cow yesterday." The boy grabbed Aidan's hand and shook it instead, then froze again. "Shit, was that okay?

Aidan couldn't help but give the junior transport specialist a smile. "No worries, they worked on my guts, not my arm. It's good to be home. Anybody get in trouble?"

Topher shrugged. "Just Laz."

"Topher! Ratchet!" Dozer called under the truck he was working on. Topher shot Aidan a last quick grin and a casual salute, jogging back to his officer's side.

The two returning officers had barely stepped into the hall when Lazarus caught sight of them and hurried over, wearing a huge grin and a gorgeous black eye.

"Hey guys, thank god you're back!" Lazarus remarked when he drew level.

Kevin pointedly gave him a look from straw-blonde hair to scuffed boots, smiling thinly. "Hello to you too. What happened to you?"

"Eh." The munitions officer grinned shamefacedly, shrugging. "I kinda tried to prank Janice. Stuck a can of expanding foam in one of her water quality check valves so that it would hit the water when she opened it and started expanding and...yeah well. I didn't check the water temp. Can expanded in my face, basically." he gestured at his eye.

Kevin stared at Lazarus. Then he took off his glasses and covered his face with one hand. "Laz," he sighed, "sometimes your stupidity reaches levels of absolute perfection, you know that?"

"Yeah..." Lazarus agreed shamefacedly.

Aidan blinked at his munitions officer for a long moment. He'd tried to prank their hydroelectrics officer. The toughest, most badass woman Aidan had ever met. Never mind the fact that she'd helped bring the munitions officer up; about the only reason Laz was alive was the fact that his stunt hadn't actually gone the way he'd planned. If it had, Aidan was pretty sure Janice would've cracked the guy's skull with a wrench.

"You do know that being named 'Lazarus' won't save you, do you?" Kevin continued in that tone that made him sound like a pissed off teacher. Laz rolled his eyes. "Only got the middle name 'cause I lived through a bombing on my first day alive. Get off my ass Kev, it was just pranking Janice."

"Just?" Kevin exclaimed.

Aidan settled for allowing himself to laugh. "I guess any discipline I could dole out would be nothing compared to what Janice already gave you…"

"Yeah, Aidan. She's scarier'n you." Lazarus agreed, shrugging. "Liza wrote me up?" he added, as if that made it okay.

Aidan bit the inside of his cheek to keep from laughing about that. When he got himself under control again, he said, "Well, at least someone remembers how to do their job when I'm not here."

"Oh, she does." Lazarus agreed with a roll of the eyes. "Trust me."

A half-joking cheer sounded when Aidan walked into breakfast. Liza smiled wearily as he sat down.

"Good to have you back," the personnel officer remarked, her severe face softened with a smile. "I have a disciplinary write-up to turn into you Commander. Laz—"

"We heard," Aidan interjected.

His second in command sighed deeply. "At least he was the only one who started crap this time," she muttered in resignation. Sitting on her left, Sarah and Yvonne shared a grin that made Aidan wonder about that.

It was surprisingly good to eat breakfast in his own canteen with his own crew again; Aidan hadn't realized just how much he'd gotten used to the cheerful Wildcards banter in the last nine months.

Over the meal, Damian's black cybernetic eyes caught his, glittering.

"Let's do a clinic check before you get back to work," the doctor stated, "I want to see if I've got anyone to pick a bone with at Regional."

Damian closed the door of his examination room and turned to Aidan half an hour later. "Okay, strip and let's see how things are going."

Aidan took a deep breath and nodded. He turned away out of habit to unbutton his pants, tug off his jacket and shirt. He turned back and hoisted himself onto the exam table, glancing at the skin of his chest through the clear plastic of the epithelial auto-pad. The incisions were barely visible anymore.

Carefully, Damian pulled on surgical gloves and detached the three simple auto-pads, peeling them back. Underneath, healthy skin barely showed a sign of its new growth.

Damian checked over the sites carefully, using an electrometer to check the signals the nerves were sending as the doctor's fingers prodded the skin. "Okay, full innervation, the nipples reattached fine, and everything's good on the muscle reconstruction. How's the pain level?" he asked after a moment, looking up to gauge Aidan's reaction. His black plastic eyes reflected the overhead lights.

Aidan released the breath he'd been holding. He'd half-expected to hear that something wasn't healing right. He gave Damian a genuine smile. "Feels great, honestly. Still a little sore, but that's PT more than anything, I bet."

"You're actually doing the PT, I'm impressed." Damian remarked dryly.

Aidan rolled his eyes. "Kev won't let up on it. Keeps making me run through exercises." Damian gave a bark of laughter. "Well at least he cares when it's *your* health. Medically you're all set. Aside from the twinges, how's it feeling? Doesn't have to be physical."

Aidan couldn't hold back his grin. "Really great."

Slowly, Damian nodded. "All right then. And you ought to have fewer mood issues, now that the feminizing glands are removed and you've got fewer conflicting signals going through your brain. That doesn't mean get lazy about monitoring yourself." he added, pointing one knobbly finger at Aidan. "But it does mean things should get steadier. Other than that, we're done here. Got any questions?"

Aidan grabbed his shirt. "Any activities I should still stay away from, or am I cleared for going back to normal?"

"Don't start lifting more than fifty pounds or running marathons for another week. But yes. For everything else, you're clear. Including the bedroom." Damian agreed, his lips quirking at the corners. "Be honest, that's what you meant."

Aidan laughed as he wriggled into his shirt. The fabric felt rough against his tender chest, but it was oddly exhilarating. All he needed was a shirt. He didn't have to wear the binder any more.

He zipped his pants up. "Yeah well, I gotta keep Kev in a good mood one way or another. Part of my duty's keeping morale up, right?"

Damian shook his shaved head, working to repress a smile. "Go do your job, Headly."

That night Aidan spent way too long in the shower, admiring the work that had been done on his body. He looked so much more *right* this way. And they'd cut the three planned surgical dates down to two with all the specialists up at Regional, which was a bonus.

Things weren't perfect, not yet. But the final bottom surgery was going to take some time to organize. Right now, that didn't feel so bad: he and Kevin could use a prosthetic in bed for a while longer. Living in a body that was so much closer to right was good enough, for now.

Assuming Janice let him live after he'd spent more than fifteen damn minutes in the shower, wasting her water. "Crap," he whispered when his eye caught the hygiene room clock above the thin slat of a stall door. He hastily shut the spigot down.

He toweled off and pulled his clothes from the wash-dry unit that had used the water he had been washing with to clean his clothes before it was sent into the water-recycling system. Even getting dressed was easier now. No more damn binder to make getting dressed a fight.

Stepping into the room that had been Kevin's and was theirs now, he smiled broadly. "Hey."

Kevin sat up from his reading slouch on the bed with a smile, the light from the holo on the wall catching in his hair. "Hey yourself. So, what's the verdict from The Lord of Intimidation?"

"Well, I'm not allowed to run marathons." Aidan laughed, shutting the door behind him. He crossed the room and leaned down to kiss Kevin.

He'd intended to jump right into a talk about the new mission. But the kiss decided him. They couldn't do much work this late. All he'd manage to do was freak them both out.

He'd take one night to enjoy this. One night for some fun. Tomorrow he'd break the news.

"Who said anything about running?" Kevin asked with mischief in his voice when Aidan let him up for air, grey eyes dancing. "We can have a perfectly good marathon without leaving the bedroom." Reaching up, he ran his hand through Aidan's damp hair, trailing it down and across Aidan's chest. "Speaking of that, let's have this shirt off."

Aidan's breath caught at Kevin's touch, nervous tension spiking through him. Would Kevin be okay with the way he looked?

It was a completely stupid question, and he knew it. Kevin had seen his chest immediately after surgery. Hell, the guy had seen him with breasts. Why would this be any different?

Forcing down the nerves, he kissed Kevin again before pulling away to grab the hem of his shirt. He half-expected to get caught in it, but it slid off smoothly. He stood awkwardly in front of his boyfriend, wishing he didn't feel so unsure.

"Um. What do you think?"

Standing, Kevin looked him over with soft eyes. Then he stepped in and tipped his head down for a kiss.

"I think I love you."

Aidan smiled, letting out a breath as the tension in his gut eased. "I love you, too."

Kevin's kisses were long and slow.

"Now that your shirt's off," Kevin whispered against his skin, making his pulse jump. But the brat finished the sentence with, "let's see how your arm rotations are shaping up. And you need to stretch your pectorals."

Aidan groaned. "You're going to make me do PT now? Kev!"

Kevin tipped his head up, adopting his teasing-haughty expression. "Yes, yes I am. The surgeon told me that I was your PT coach, and I take my duties very seriously sir," he agreed in his most sanctimonious tones. "It's for your own good. Besides, God forbid I take advantage of the feeble and convalescing." He crossed himself, lips twitching with a repressed smile.

Aidan crossed his arms, playing along with a glare. "I'm looking forward to healing enough that 'fuck you' is taken literally. Because fuck you, Kev."

Kevin burst out laughing, tipping his head back. "Well fuck you too then." he murmured, leaning in for another kiss.

Once the goddamned PT was over, it was going to be a good night.

<u>Event File 3</u>
<u>File Tag: Mission Briefing</u>
<u>Timestamp: 05:00-3-1-2156</u>

"Kev? You up?"

Kevin's eyes flicked open. He sat up, blinking at the indistinct shape of his boyfriend in the gloom. The other man's face was a blue-lit blur in the dark, the light from a tab outlining his contours in Kevin's weak eyes.

With the economy born of repetition, Kevin reached for his glasses with one hand and his gun belt with the other. "I'm up. Do we need to move?"

His glasses revealed a crooked, mirthless smile gracing his boyfriend's face. Aidan waved a hand. "No, we're good. It's five-hundred. I was just...you know we said we'd wake each other up if stuff got bad at night?" He tapped the side of his head.

Kevin's shoulders relaxed. "I do. I'm glad to see you remembering. What's going on?"

Aidan dropped his eyes to his hands, fingers pleating the blanket.

"I have to give a briefing later and it's freaking me out. I woke up at three-hundred and started reading the files on it, and that made it worse."

Carefully, Kevin replaced his weapon on its hook beside the bed.

"Three hundred? Did something come up overnight?"

Aidan shook his head, brushing his wheaten hair out of his eyes. "Came up at Regional. When Hall sent you out of the room? Yeah. She had a mission briefing and a packet to give me, classified. She ordered me to wait 'til I got home to talk. That was why I cut you off about it." He drew a slow breath. "She was worried about leaks. Enough that she set a sound-box by the door of my room when she talked to me. That tells you how serious she was."

Kevin felt his brows rise. "She turned on a soundbox...at regional? Well that's worrisome." Turning his head, he raised his voice a little. "Lights low."

The scrounged strands of LED lights came slowly to life in their web across the ceiling, glowing like fireflies. The wall screen buzzed to life with a Monet painting as Kevin turned back to study his boyfriend's haggard face. "What's the mission? Does it have an execution date?"

Aidan shrugged. "Second week of March, we start working on it. We..." Aidan took three long, slow breaths. "Kev, she wants us to take point on a national op. To take the Citizen Standing system down. Entirely. For the country."

Kevin's jaw dropped open. He felt the blood leave his face.

"Say that again?" His voice emerged in a whisper.

Aidan laughed, hysteria twining through the sound. "We've been ordered to shut down the entire Citizen Standing System, Kev."

Kevin ran a hand through his hair, shaking his head. "That's not...nobody can *do* that. They have supercomputers running their data encryption. They have backups of the backups. No human could break through that."

Aidan's smile was tight. "Right. I guess she wants to see if four bases full of humans can."

Kevin gave a breath of a laugh. "Well, now I know why you were worried..." slowly, he laid himself out on the bed beside his boyfriend, hands laced behind his head, eyes staring blankly upwards.

"The entire Citizen Standing System...good God almighty."

Aidan nodded. After a moment, he lay down as well, his head pillowed on Kevin's shoulder. "I don't know how the hell she expects us to do something like this. Apparently she thinks I'm a miracle-maker, since I got this base working again. And you guys got the Folder done."

Kevin barely smiled at the remark. His brain was racing.

The Citizen Standing System. The aggregation of credit scores and Citizen Rankings attached to every citizen was the bulwark of the Corporation's hold on citizens. Few people dared to commit actions that would drop their Citizen Standing Score. It cost too much: to fall down the Citizen Standing System ladder was to lose everything. Your right to your position within the Corporation. Your right to live in the neighborhood you'd been enjoying, shop in the stores you frequented. Fall far enough down the ladder, and you lost your right to be treated as a human being. To keep their Standings, people stayed in line and didn't cause trouble. They hid what could harm them from watching eyes. And those eyes were everywhere. Automated systems embedded in the fabric of the cities recorded pedestrian infractions, from jaywalking to taking a long lunch break. Managers could drop a Citizen Standing Score for so many infractions. Neighbors could report you for everything from Standing-damaging faux pas, to what you read or who you had in the bedroom. And it all went into the Citizen Standing System, recorded and tied to every individual's genome like stones tied to a drowning man's legs. The Scores trapped people as surely as a cage.

To take the Citizen Standing System out...even the idea made him light-headed.

"If we pull this off..." he swallowed hard. "If we pull this off, everything changes. Everything..."

"I know," Aidan muttered, squeezing his eyes shut against Kevin's skin. He took a shaking breath. "Hall said that's why she wants us heading it. If we can actually pull this off...."

"Then maybe we start to win," Kevin finished in a whisper. His brain was beginning to fizz, fireworks of thought burning when he closed his eyes.

He turned so that he was nose to nose with Aidan. "Which bases are we in with on this?"

"Base six hundred way up north, they run the US-Canada border," Aidan replied quietly, "handle's Wiigit Wings. Base one-forty halfway up the East Coast. The Riptides. And Base five-thousand all the way down south, the Tearaways."

Kevin nodded slowly. "Wiigit I've worked with a number of times when I'm getting refugees out, they're leaps and bounds ahead of most bases in action. They practically run the Maple Leaf Trail. And the Riptides are legendary. I've heard of the Tearaways as well, they did more large-scale missions down south than anyone believed possible...we're working with legends and they want *us* to take point?"

Aidan shrugged. "We're probably the most expendable."

"Stop that." Kevin admonished, tapping a finger on the tip of Aidan's nose. His boyfriend gave him a crooked smile.

For a moment, Kevin stared into Aidan's blue eyes. Then he pulled Aidan into a kiss.

"We're going to change the world, Aidan my love."

Aidan sighed against his skin. "We're gonna try."

"We're gonna die." Tweak's high voice dropped into the silence of the canteen like a hailstone.

Kevin sighed. Leave it to their techie to break the ice left in the wake of Aidan's mission announcement by summing up the situation in the most tactless—and brutally honest—terms available.

Luckily, that statement was put out so abruptly that Yvonne and Lazarus both gave barks of laughter. Their reaction gave everyone else permission to breathe again. The members of the base glanced at one another with weak smiles and made variations on the theme of the 'going crazy' hand gesture.

At the head of the table, Aidan shrugged. "We could've died

putting out the Folder too. But we pulled it off. And that's why we're on this now."

"Command does love to give the man who digs the best ditches a bigger shovel, you know," Kevin remarked, doing his best to keep a little levity in the proceedings. He'd always liked that word, levity. It was from the Latin levitas, if he remembered right. The opposite of gravity. And the mood in the room was certainly heavy enough at the moment.

"So how are we doing this?" Damian asked.

Aidan shrugged. "No clue. Not yet."

The silence this time was so complete that Kevin could hear the air filtration units in the walls humming. Water gurgled in a pipe over his head.

"Wait, what?" Lazarus asked, wide eyes fixed on Aidan. The smaller man met his gaze patiently.

"We're the ones who have to come up with the plan," Aidan explained, his voice uninflected. "Turns out Command was really impressed with what we did to get the Folder out. They want our out-of-the-box thinking applied to this. We're developing the attack plan on this, not just implementing it."

"Shit," Yvonne remarked, wide-eyed. "Tweak's right. We *are* gonna die."

Kevin watched the uneasy, restless fear spread through the room. Sarah fidgeted. Yvonne chewed her cuticles. Lazarus was still staring at Aidan.

Down the table, Blake caught Kevin's eye and raised a brow in one of his signature 'well, you *are* going to do something useful?' expressions.

Kevin gave an incremental nod. Carefully, he stood. "We're not going to die."

The eyes of everyone at the long table turned to him. "We are going to do what we do best," Kevin stated. Calling up everything he knew about public speech, he raised his voice to the perfect pitch, holding the eyes of everyone in the room in turn. "We are going to do impeccable research. We're going to lay groundwork. We're going to create a plan. And then we're going to execute it, and when we do we're going to rip the rug out from under the Corporate sons of bitches and land them flat on their asses. This is our chance. We've all worked for it and bled for it. Now it's our time to take it."

The deep silence held for a heartbeat longer. His family watched him with wide eyes. Then Yvonne pressed her hand to her chest and fluttered her eyes. "My hero."

Everyone burst out laughing. Kevin rolled his eyes. "Yvonne, I hate you some days. You do know that?"

"Okay, but seriously," Janice added, tapping the plastic of the table with her calloused fingers, "this's about as easy as fuckin' a porcupine with a chocolate dong. How the fuck're we supposed to do it?"

In her corner, Tweak bit her lip, staring at her boots. Her fingers fiddled with the bandages that hid her arms.

Aidan cleared his throat. "Like Kev says, we're going to start with research. Commander Hall has given us upper-level passcodes, so we can read operational reports from around the country. We start on this on the eleventh. Tweak, you work with Kevin for two weeks learning about stuff like this that people tried in the past. See why it didn't work. Grab Billie to help when Andrea doesn't need her watching the kids."

"Don't grab *Billie*, grab *me*. I know a thing or two about older operations." Blake interjected.

Aidan nodded in the older man's direction, shoving his rich blonde hair back from his face absently. "Okay, Blake you help out with that. Thanks." He turned his eyes further down the table. "Dozer, Topher. I want you guys working on chatter and drone patterns. All those extra drones that're being produced have to be going somewhere. Laz, Sarah, I want you guys to start printing more stealth guns and explosives. Yvonne, you're going to need to run physical requisitions on your own for a bit. Stick to vetted contacts only. You'll be on getting Sarah and Laz what they need when they need it, along with the usual runs. And Damian, let's make sure the med-bay's ready for more casualties than usual. In case."

"Well that sounds *encouraging*," Blake grumbled.

Aidan gave him a long-suffering look, before turning his blue eyes back to the table at large. "We'll have another full-crew debriefing in three weeks and see where we've gotten." Aidan added, "In the meantime," he paused, meeting the eyes of everyone around the table, and gave them a crooked smile, "everybody else make sure the guys who're working hard remember to eat and sleep."

It took nearly their full allotment of two weeks, but between Tweak, Blake and Kevin they had something that actually resembled a plausible attack plan when they faced the table full of their teammates on the morning of the twenty-fifth. Everyone had decided to sit in this time; only Billie and the kids were missing among the curious faces.

"I've sent a file to everyone's tabs detailing this attack plan," Kevin stated as he brought up his own screens and moved them into place, "feel free to bring it up if you'd like to follow along."

Holographic screens winked into life around the table. Lazarus gave a bark of laughter. "Christ man, you didn't send an attack plan. You sent a *book*!"

Kevin gave his friend a small, acknowledging smile. "You'll note that there's a history section and a number of other details. We've got our reasons for decisions delineated in here as well as our plan of action. So yes, it's long. This is what we're going to send to Commander Hall, once we've refined and vetted it with you lot." He held Aidan's eyes across the table, pulling on his most confident smile. "We'll give you the bullet points in person."

His tab projected a series of boxes. He touched the first one, and it came to the fore and expanded into readability. "The first thing we've discovered is that any form of simple attack will certainly be torpedoed in short order."

"Duh," Tweak muttered under her breath.

Kevin ignored her as he continued, "A number of simpler attacks were attempted in the past, and they all failed spectacularly. So we're suggesting a layered attack."

The image walked through an animated scenario as Kevin narrated. The boxes traded places in the foreground as he spoke, showing their content as he'd timed them to do. Verbal information was always easier to retain with a visual supplement. "We'll use a large number of pre-coded false Ids—and resurrect an awful lot of zombies—in the Systems to launch a massive Denial of Service attack on Natbank as a cover," he explained as the visuals played. "It will look as if thirty million people have all decided to check their Citizen Standing Score at the same time."

"Wait, zombies?" Damian asked, his ocular implants whirring.

"*Zombies*," Blake agreed with relish, "They're profiles of people who've been dead a while. But it isn't hard to re-activate them; we do it when we're in a hurry. This time we'll do large batches over several months. And the dead will riiiiiiiiise!"

Snorts of laughter greeted Blake's theatrics.

"It won't have any particular effectiveness, given our resources," Kevin cautioned, working to choke down a laugh. "It's really only a smokescreen. Best case scenario, it overloads a number of servers, but it will at least grab some attention. While that's going on, each of our bases will initiate a virus that we've put in place prior to the big day within EagleCorp and Natbank systems. This virus is designed to quickly and efficiently wipe the Citizen Rating Files that EagleCorp keeps for the other Corporations. We won't be touching the financial element of the Scores originating in NatBank, for two reasons: we don't want complete civic anarchy, and we don't want to give the Corps an even bigger reason to crack down or—God forbid—impose martial law as they scramble to cover their asses."

"How come?" Topher asked. "I mean, debt's half the damn Score, isn't it? So it's half the problem. If we don't get people all the way free, what's the point?"

"It's tempting, but if you think it through it's a trap," Kevin explained. "It would feel like freedom for a day to be completely debt free, but you'll feel less of a glow the next day, when your bank calls to tell you that they don't have a record of what you've paid on your house loan and you'll have to start over. Or when your credit card fails to work and payday is several days away. Beyond that, let's game it out. We don't want the security and finance Corps in a position where they feel justified in taking extraordinary measures. We don't want them asking Argus Corp to turn off the power to all homes and telling citizens that they must be genome-scanned and entered into a census in order to verify the patchwork of databases from other sources they'd use to rebuild the Standing System, or some such draconian ploy.

"If we took down both Corporate records systems, that's what they'd do, and the worst of it is that people would feel threatened enough to go along. We don't want that. What we want is to put the Corporations in a position where they're internally squabbling and desperate to hide their weakness. Again," he added, smirking. "Therefore, we wipe every single Citizen Rating file that EagleCorp keeps. National Banking will pretend nothing's wrong and instruct their systems to use half the data to assign Scores. The purely financial data, that is. In private they and every other Corporation will be excoriating EagleCorp for losing the Citizen Rating data. Both Eagle and Natbank will be set back on their heels, the other five will get into a froth, a lot of people will see their scores miraculously shoot up, and it's a win all the way around. So our aim is to scrub the system of Citizen Rating Files. Thoughts?"

Around the table, heads nodded thoughtfully. "Sounds good," Aidan remarked. "So what do we do after the virus scrubs the Net?"

"It won't take them long to reload from their backup servers; about twenty seconds across the country." Kevin explained. "But here's the clever bit." He raised a finger. "What they try to reload will already be gone."

"We c-can do it l-l-like this." Tweak stated, pulling up the next holographic window. "F-first we g-get all the deets on the backup centers. Physical and tech. Take a m-month at l-least. Probably three, safe side."

"Plan A is for Tweak to hack in and snag us some schematics with those magic fingers of hers," Blake interjected, "and plan B, which everyone *hates* but we can do if *needed*, is to get ourselves some maps of the maintenance tunnels under EagleCorp and establish a hard connection that'll hack us directly into their system *that* way. Once we have the skinny, Tweak?"

"We g-get into the physical backup l-location, we plant EMP bombs all over the place," the little hacker continued with a grin. "V-virus should be everywhere by then. W-wait for the other b-bases to do their b-backup centers. Lotsa w-work. W-wait four or five w-weeks. When we're r-ready, we choose a day. Coordinate. Launch the DDOS. Set off the EMPs, r-remotely. Execute the v-virus. W-watch the firew-works." The coder mimed an explosion with a grin, the white bandages encasing her arms glimmering in the overhead lights.

Around the table, heads began to nod.

"So… we're actually gonna get this together? Regional's actually going to let us *do* this?" Lazarus asked, a slow grin unfurling across his face. He looked from Kevin to his cousin and cousin-in-law, the dawning grin spreading across all their faces. Yvonne grabbed Sarah by the lapels of her jacket and kissed her hard, then reached over and grabbed her cousin in a hug. "Holy shit holy shit this is gonna be amazing!"

"If we put in the work and the planning to pull it off," Kevin admonished pointedly, watching the Three Stooges with the most censorious expression he could manage. The last thing they needed was three enthusiastic loose cannons on something this big.

"Yeah," Tweak snapped from her cross-armed slouch against the wall, "and don't die."

Sarah shot the younger girl an impatient look. "Tweak, quit saying we're gonna die. It's depressing."

The tiny girl rolled her black eyes, giving a wordless grunt.

Aidan gave his team a patient smile. Then his eyes moved

between the screens and Kevin's face. Eventually, he nodded. "It sounds like it could work. Couple of things, though."

He ticked off points on his fingers, his tanned skin looking even darker in the overhead lights. "First thing: we're on our own schedule and we've got three other bases to coordinate with, so we do this thing slow and steady. If you don't have specs on a building, don't enter it until you do. Take all the precautions." He lowered another finger with a lopsided smile. "Second off: get me full write-ups on your plans at each stage, so I can talk to the other bases and Regional like somebody who has a clue. And third: remember we've got time. We don't get second chances. So take the time and be *careful*. Okay?"

Most of the Logistics and the Munitions team acknowledged the call on their impetuous habits one way or another: a refuel grin here, lowered eyes there. Kevin wondered if that warning wasn't aimed mostly at him, after the stunt that got their base the seeds currently sprouting in the hydroelectric maintenance room. But then again, Yvonne and Lazarus both had their own streak of impatience. They all needed the reminder, really.

Aidan let that sink in a moment, then nodded. "Okay, just remember. Last thing, if Tweak's going to be talking to all these other bases along with us, she needs a real code name."

"Oh shit, we forgot!" Yvonne exclaimed. She turned in her seat. "Janice, where's the deck?"

Janice stood. "Cool your tits, I'll get it."

Crossing the canteen, the older woman slid open an access panel in the plastic of the wall and pulled out the analog deck they always used to name new Grid-operating members. Methodically flipping through the battered deck, she extracted the cards that were already taken: The King of Hearts, Kevin's own card. Liza's Queen of Clubs, followed by the Ace of Spades came out, which Commander Taylor had held before and Aidan had inherited. The base had thrown an absolute fit when Taylor's own call sign was given to someone new, but since the other nine hundred and twenty Duster bases across the country already had that down as the handle to reach the Wildcards through, it couldn't be changed. It seemed right, these days, that Aidan held it.

The Ace of Diamonds was pulled for Blake and the Nine of Hearts for Yvonne, the Two of Clubs for Dozer and the Four from the same suit for Topher. The Seven of Spades was pulled out for Jim. Janice found the Joker card and tossed it to Lazarus, who caught his card with a grin. There was Sarah's Queen of Diamonds, Janice's own Ace of Clubs and Damian's King of Clubs. Alice's Jack of Spades was pulled. The Jack of Hearts, the Two of Spades, the King of Diamonds, the King of Spades and the Three of Hearts were pulled out last. Those cards Janice set aside with elaborate care, face down. The remaining cards in the deck were spread out in front of Tweak.

"Pick a card, any card." Kevin drawled in the tones of a Vaudevillian from a Bob Hope movie, hoping to keep things cheerful.

Tweak looked down at the cards with panicked eyes. Then she looked around the room. "Y-you all g-got one?"

"Anybody who talks to other bases does," Janice agreed quietly. "You don' wanna keep bein' who you was on Grid forever, see."

Tweak blinked at her. "Yeah. Guess not." The little coder lowered her head, her body still as a lizard on a rock. Then a tiny hand darted out and grabbed up a card. "This."

"Deuce of Diamonds." Janice observed, drawing the words out.

Kevin leaned back. "Quite apt really. They do say Deuces are wild."

Tweak actually gave him a flicker of a teasing smile as she insulted him this time. "Freak."

Two smiles in one week had to be a record for Tweak. He returned the smile, miming the lifting of an imaginary hat. "At your service."

The long needle slid down into the petri dish as Aidan watched.

"So what's the holdup?" Janice asked, glancing up from her work as Damian's careful fingers set the cell culture on its new nutrient base. "Thought we'd be raisin' hell an' takin' names on the Standing System by now. It's been a month."

Aidan let his eyes run over the other cell cultures in the chamber they'd rigged, beside the gene-editing station they'd pulled together in the last couple months using the plans and the chemical recipes Kevin had stolen. It had been a tight squeeze to get everything to fit in the hydroelectric maintenance room without making it hard for Janice to work, but apparently the temperature and humidity in here were the best thing for seedlings. Now a lot of Janice's spare parts were stored in cargo nets attached to the overhead pipes, and the back wall was given to the seedlings.

He let his eyes run over the wall behind them. He was looking at actual seedlings. The storage shelves had been retooled as a plant nursery, lights attached to the underside of each shelf shining on the tiny plants below. Thin plastic lines ran like dropped spaghetti between trays, where shoots of green rose out of the loose grey grit. They'd recycled old, shredded packing boxes for planting substrate until the plants were old enough to go into dirt. The really little ones on the middle shelf were still on blocks of stuff that looked like clear tofu.

Janice looked up from her check of the lines that fed each plant a mix of nutrients and water, face expectant. "Am I gettin' an answer?"

Aidan blinked. "Hunh? Oh. Tweak's hit a wall. Turns out Natbank doesn't have copies of the backup building layouts; EagleCorp has them all. Tweak's saying that hacking EagleCorp isn't working over the Net." He started to lean against a khaki-painted mechanical box, but he stopped himself when his eye caught the sign on the machine: Do Not Touch. Not Only Will This Kill You, It'll Hurt The Whole Time You're Dying. He stepped away from whatever that machine was and took a chair instead. "A hacker from one of the other bases is helping her on it, but if they can't get it by Thursday I'm sending Kevin on Grid to get Plan B started. He has to make a couple contact meetings anyway, so it's a good use of time. I set up a holo-meeting with the other base Commanders in half an hour to go over where we are right now."

Glancing between the two, he couldn't help but smile. "You know what's weird? This setback, it's kind of a big deal and it should be on my mind. But I keep thinking 'man, we got this to work. We really got our own gene edits on seeds to work.' If we pulled this off, maybe...I don't know, maybe the other stuff isn't so crazy."

Janice and Damian shared a look that Aidan read as 'isn't he adorable'.

"Don't start singin' Kumbaya jus' yet," the older woman drawled. "Even these seeds need some work. We cut out a lot of the shit genes AgCo put in an' got 'em sproutin', but that second-generation sterility thing..." she sucked a breath between her teeth. "I can't tell if we whacked it or not. If we didn't, we only get one season out of these babies, an' their seeds won't grow."

"We didn't," Damian stated, checking his work against the workstation's computer. "Not on this batch, anyway. What we need are more seeds from more species." He straightened, cracking his back, and shrugged. "But this is a start, and we can culture more plants from the leaf tissue once these start to grow. I'm still wondering what mistakes are coming later; I was trained to do this on animal cells."

"Don't borrow trouble," Janice scolded, elbowing the tall doctor gently. "You'll jinx this all to hell with that kinda talk."

Damian cocked a brow, his ocular implant whirring quietly as it compensated. "I don't believe in jinxes."

His brick-wall act did nothing for Janice, who smirked and crossed her arms. "I don' believe I asked your opinion. I was an AgCo kid way back when. I grew up around plants. I know a thing or two; you talk nice to them, they grow better. So don't bring them down."

Damian snorted. "Great, we're back to superstition now."

Janice tipped her head to the side. "And you're takin' up space where I work," she replied. Her tone was an invitation to shut up and get out.

Damian eyed her, but he got out of the chair at the gene station. "I want you in for your check and blood panel, you missed last month. I will come in here to get my sample if I have to."

Janice waved a hand. "For the last fuckin' time, I'll be in already! Go stick somebody else with a needle."

"Monthly blood panels?" Aidan asked once Damian had stepped out. "That sounds pretty regular. You okay?"

Janice rolled her eyes. "Do I ask you 'bout your health?"

Aidan shrugged. "You're not Commander. You don't need to."

Janice heaved a sigh. "I got some chronic shit. Who doesn't, livin' out here. Damian keeps an eye on it. Nothin' important, an' it's all under control. Ain't you got a meeting?"

Aidan glanced at the clock hung between a wide-gauge wrench and some tool he couldn't name on the wall. "Guess I do." But he lowered his eyes to hers. "Chronic conditions can get important fast. Just stay on it, okay?"

Janice rolled her eyes. "Jesus Christ fucking a flamingo, do I gotta hit you upside the head with a wrench to get you outta here?"

Aidan held up his hands, smiling. "Okay, I'm going, I'm going."

Heading down to his office, Aidan set out three holo-emitters in a semi-circle, put the last one in front of his desk and checked that their connection to his main computer was good. Then he pulled up his screen, and started the login process to get on the call.

They were really taking security on this mission seriously. In addition to his usual layer of passwords, he had to pull out the little biometric reader in his console that he almost never used and spit into the tube. But eventually, the little black hemispheres on the floor buzzed to life, and the holograms of three seated people appeared around Aidan.

Commander Hagge of the Riptides was a severe white woman a couple decades his senior, built like a crow and dressed in black. She sat—or perched maybe—bolt upright in her chair.

Commander Seattle of the Wiigit Wings was somebody Aidan would've put down for a farm hand or a hunter if he'd had to guess, not a Duster. An Alaskan native, the person had long black hair and a wide face the color of the expensive tea Kevin had brought home at Christmas. They were in a faded turtleneck and slacks, a beat-up duffel vest thrown over the top. They actually had it in their official record that they were intersex. It had to be pretty amazing to live in a place where they could be so open about themselves.

Commander Anderson of the Tearaways was somewhere in his sixties, small and grizzled and scary thin. He was dressed in something that was close to uniform, but his jacket was ragged at the hems and his boots went up almost to his knees. A huge sun hat sat on the arm of his chair.

"Is everyone online?" Commander Hagge asked, her voice as crisp as her grey shirt.

"Here," Aidan put in.

"Got you," Commander Anderson agreed, the words running together into something like 'godyew'

"You're coming through," Commander Seattle added, their accent curling their words into tight, defined pieces of sound with a little lilt.

Anderson turned in his chair, the image flickering as it followed his movement. His transmitter must be cheap. He looked Aidan up and down.

"So you're in for ol' Taylor now." He studied Aidan for a moment, looking like he was chewing on his tongue. "Little young for a spot calling the shots, aren't you?" All his words were soft around the edges, fuzzing into one long sentence in Aidan's ears.

Aidan could feel his heart rate picking up speed. He shrugged. "I go where Sector Command sends me. They sent me here. So yeah, I'm here."

The older man eyed him for another moment. Then he shrugged, and his face split in a watermelon grin. "Yeah, I guess you are, after we seen that folder go out on the Social. That was somethin'."

Aidan's gut muscles relaxed. He gave the man a quick smile. "Yeah, I guess it was. We're hoping we can get the same kind of thing done on this, but we've hit our first big snag. Our coder got into the Natbank systems, and they don't keep copies of the backup center's locations and floor plans. EagleCorp does. And they're turning out to be harder to hack."

Commander Hagge barked a laugh. "Understatement of the year right there." She dropped her R's when she talked, Aidan noticed. 'Year' came out sounding like 'yeah'. For a moment, he wondered what he must sound like to them.

He really needed to get himself calmed down and focused.

He cleared his throat. "So we've all got copies of the general mission timeline. This is our situation right now: I'm sending my logistics and requisition officer on Grid next week to trade around with contacts for plans of some of the maintenance tunnels around our EagleCorp office complex in town. We'll use those and get a hard link into the fiber-optics, that should make things easier. Our hacker will go down in person and see what she can do about getting the locations and building plans. We've got a six-hour window based on their maintenance schedule, according to her that's plenty of time. If she lands the schematics, I'll schedule another meeting. I'll send a message if we're out of luck. In the meantime we're collating travel patterns and Net chatter, trying to pinpoint enough information to find the centers that way." He glanced between the three seasoned Commanders. "Speaking of that, heads up. I don't know if National's put it out yet, but we're seeing a lot more drones being produced in our region's factory. We've got one of EagleCorp's biggest plants, so we're keeping an eye on it. And it's looking bad. Watch out for higher numbers of drones in your area; all that production has to be going somewhere."

Commander Seattle gave a tight, grim little smile. "We don't worry about drones up here. They don't last long."

Aidan glanced at the person, surprised. "You guys have windstorms like we do?"

"Nope." Their grin widened, and they crossed their arms. "We have eagles. The fish eagles and the bald eagles take them down."

Commander Anderson burst out laughing. Commander Hagge smiled grimly. "Eagles taking down Eagle. Nice trick. Send me pointers on how you trained them, will you? We got some eagles around Boston."

The Alaskan nodded an acknowledgment.

Hagge straightened. "I got my own load of bad news to drop. We've been getting word about a lot of new contract bounty-hunting crews being brought in. Eagle is farming out their dirty work. And they're using a lot more nanoid mimics. We just got faked out by an old contact. Thing was the spitting image of him too. I hate these things; fucking creeps me out, you know? My logistics girl got wise, hit the EMP in her pocket. Guy fell apart; just a bunch of nanoids on a scaffold frame. Wasn't fun. So watch yourselves. Check your people when they come home."

Aidan's heart skipped a beat. He swallowed. "We'll do that."

Commander Anderson nodded gravely. "Thanks for the tip."

Commander Seattle frowned, nodding slowly.

"That's all I've got for now," Aidan stated in the silence. "So, meeting in three weeks?"

Anderson tipped his fluffy white head. "It's a date."

Hagge nodded sharply. "I'll put it in the calendar. Hope you have some results for us then, Headly." With a quick salute, she signed off. Her image fizzled away.

Seattle shot Aidan a sidelong look. Then they smiled. "Don't mind Ingrid. She's always like that. Luck." With a quick salute, they signed off. So did Anderson, with a last tip of his head.

Aidan let out a long, slow breath.

Some results. Hope you have some results.

I hope we have some results, too.

"Getting slow, High Standing!"

Kevin glanced over his shoulder. He gave the street kid a thin smile as the boy grinned, peeling the calorie bar that Kevin had tucked in his pocket ahead of time for the urchin to 'score'.

"Slower every year, it's true," he agreed quietly. "Run and let Blucifer know I'm here, will you, Kudzu?"

"You gonna pay me for it?" The dark-haired little waif demanded, pulling fragile bravado on like a cloak. Kevin fought down the momentary urge to give the kid all the money he had or kick the wall in sheer rage at a world that would make a child so young ask a question like that. He shouldn't react like this; he'd seen street children often enough. But the sight still got under his skin. It probably always would.

For the boy's sake, he pulled on something like a haughty look and pretended to be a man getting the worst of a bargain. "I already paid you, what do you think you're eating?"

"That ain't pay," the child scoffed, "I *scored* this 'cause you're *slow.*"

Kevin grunted, keeping up his defeated-and-annoyed-about-it act. "Fine you extortionate monster. Here." He passed the boy two more calorie bars. "Happy?"

Kudzu flashed a gap-toothed grin and spidered up the nearest fire escape, clattering his feet against the metal. Kevin relaxed his stance and waited. The door in front of him sizzled now and again, the electrical current running through it zapping gnats and dust motes that touched the surface.

Plan B was looking less good all the time.

Eventually the current disengaged, leaving the door oddly still. A heartbeat later, it grated on its hinges. The eye revealed in the chink was such a pale blue as to appear white. Kevin held the man's eye patiently."Mind if I come in out of the storm?"

The door gave a moan of tortured metal as it was muscled open. Blucifer Adams gave him the usual slow once-over, icy eyes watchful. Satisfied, he tucked his hands in his pockets."Best come in."

"Thanks." Kevin agreed quietly. He schooled himself to look straight ahead as he entered the abandoned warehouse, ignoring the quiet sounds of the gunmen on either side of the door standing down. The strains from an old movie about mobsters began playing in his head, and he did his best to shove it down. The Colfax Kings were nowhere near as stylish as Don Corleone and his world, but they were every bit as deadly.

Dust puffed about Kevin's feet as he moved. The warehouse was a new one for the Kings, and apparently cleaning house hadn't been high on their to-do list. The air still smelled of closed-in rooms.

On the other hand, it didn't smell of blood. He counted his blessings where he could.

The bare wooden chair creaked as Blucifer took his seat at the rickety card table, watching blankly as Kevin sat. The white man wore his bleach-blonde dreadlocks—and his demeanor—like a crown.

Kevin held his eyes. He never exactly loved working with Blucifer Adams, High King of the Colfax Kings gang running the underbelly in the Northeastern side of Denver. But there were worse gangs to work with. Much worse.

Kevin adjusted his glasses on his nose as he waited. He rarely wore them on Grid, but this wasn't the place to be taken for the elite. He needed to show his genetic flaws in this environment. He'd contacted the Kings a number of times and they'd been cordial enough, but he had absolutely no intention of ending his life on the top shelf of a cut price organ-transplant center's stockroom in a number of jars marked 'genetically superior'. Human life was cheap in the Kings' world, and bio-printers weren't. They were known for taking the more abundant natural sources from the streets to supply clinics.

They sat in silence, breathing stale air. Kevin waited the other man out patiently. He had all day.

"Been a while." Blucifer grunted eventually, giving in.

Kevin nodded. "We've been busy," he remarked.

Blucifer actually coughed a laugh at that. "Noticed. Hear it was you people who put that info packet out on the Social."

"Always nice when our work's noticed," Kevin acknowledged with a tip of the head.

He allowed the silence to build between them again. Patience was the key.

"Hear you need something from us." Blucifer stated eventually. The words were flat.

"Information." Kevin replied quietly. "We're looking for pass codes that will get us into the maintenance tunnels under Old Union Station. And an accurate map of the area. We're paying above the going rate."

Blucifer grunted. "EagleCorp or the trains, you aiming for?"

"Just information gathering. No violence," Kevin replied, matching Blucifer's manner.

"Those tunnels are useful for those who'd rather not be noticed, you know."

The silence thickened again. No, Plan B was definitely not his favorite approach.

In Kevin's ear, the tiniest of whispers crackled.

"Give the signal if he gives you shit." Lazarus's voice hissed.

Kevin couldn't respond, of course, but the voice in his ear did help him slow his breathing.

The gang leader pulled a tab from his pocket without breaking the gaze.

"We got a map. Half a mile square of the Downtown tunnels. And we got timetables on all the maintenance crews."

"We've got those timetables too," Kevin replied in a carefully neutral tone, "but that map sounds like what we're looking for."

"What's your offer?" he asked, fiddling with the device.

"Fifteen thousand."

"Thirty," the man countered.

"Eighteen, and code that will land you secure food shipments to a location of your choice."

The gang leader sat back slowly, staring. Finally, he blinked. "How?"

"We've got quite a good team of code-monkeys these days," Kevin lied easily. "As you said, you heard about those files. That took some doing. Rerouting food supplies is child's play by comparison."

Silence.

The man had eyes like blue lasers. No wonder his nickname was Blucifer.

"Some of your kids are looking a bit thin." Kevin prompted carefully.

Blucifer's eyes narrowed. "Twenty thousand, food, and if this is a fake I'll use you for three organ swaps and a nutrient base."

Kevin held his eyes. "If I faked you about food for kids, that's all I'd be worth."

Blucifer said nothing to that, but at least some of the tension eased out of his shoulders.

Kevin held out his hand. Carefully, Blucifer took it and shook.

"The funds will transfer when the file's been run through our security software," Kevin stated, standing. He smiled, tipped an imaginary hat, and turned away.

"Wait."

Kevin froze.

Breathe. In for five. Out for five.

Relax.

Turn around.

Blucifer still sat, studying him. Kevin didn't dare to twitch. If Blucifer gave the word, he was dead.

The B in Plan B apparently stood for Bastard.

Eventually, the dreadlocked man seemed to come to the end of some internal discussion. "You know there's three bounties out on the team who put those vids on the Feeds."

"Are there indeed?" Kevin asked, holding his voice perfectly level.

Blucifer nodded, his bleached topknot bobbing. "Enough cash to set all my people and their kids up. Enough to fix this neighborhood."

"It does sound tempting," Kevin replied quietly. "Why are you turning down the offer?"

The gang leader leaned over the side of the table and spat on the warehouse floor. "I'm nobody's drone. And my people's better'n that." Blue laser eyes pinned Kevin in place. "Yours too, maybe." Blucifer remarked eventually. "Thought you should know, anyway. There's some hungrier than me. There's some smarter too."

"I'll bear it in mind. And I appreciate the heads' up." Kevin acknowledged.

Blucifer grunted. "Last thing. Watch your back. Eagle's renting drone swarms to private contractors. Just the low-fly kind. Short range. But still. Eyes up."

Kevin blinked, and forced down any sign of reaction.

"Eyes up." he repeated, agreeing. Turning, he walked from the warehouse, pulling his long brown coolant-coat tight about his body. Behind him, the warehouse door buzzed to life.

"I about pulled the trigger when he said that about bounty."

Lazarus remarked as he melted out of the brickwork and fell into step with Kevin eight blocks later. The munitions officer tugged off his slick poncho, folding it neatly and tucking it in a battered backpack as he walked. A few seconds later, he was just a down-on-his-luck guy in a battered jacket with a pack on his back. He ran a hand through his hood-mussed hair, tousling it horribly. Kevin pulled a comb from the inner pocket of his coat and passed it over without comment. The munitions officer took it and ran it through his pale thatch for a moment.

"How's that?"

"Passable. Did you catch the line about rented swarms?"

"Yeah. Fuck."

"You can say that again."

"Fuck."

Kevin sighed. "Well, at least we can get the intel recorded. And the maps will be a lot of use."

"Think they'll be good?" Lazarus asked, his eyes scanning their surroundings.

Kevin nodded. "The Kings shoot you in the chest, not the back. They have the classic honor of thieves."

Lazarus shot him an impatient look. "Real poetic, dude. Time we got to the next job?"

Kevin inclined his head, agreeing.

Together, they crossed into the better, louder part of the city and found the cafe Kevin had been using for his contact meetings with the foreign agent. Lazarus casually split with him for a bar across the street. Stepping inside, Kevin looked around for the pretty shock of blue hair and the books. This job was the perfect antidote to the last one.

The young woman was sitting at a table, her usual stack of tomes at hand. The analog books caught the eye of everyone who passed. Kevin really admired the cover ploy. People would remember the strangeness of a stack of analog books, not the face of the girl who'd had them.

She glanced up as Kevin took a seat, a quick smile flashing across her fine-boned face. He was going to miss meeting with her when this six-month mission was complete.

"Good afternoon, Mr. Smythe!" His companion exclaimed in that lovely French accent of hers, holding her hand out. Kevin shook it warmly.

"Joliet, it's great to see you again. Sorry I'm a bit late, an earlier errand ran long."

"Oh it's fine, I had a fat morning." the young lady remarked in French. Fat morning. Kevin took a moment to place the idiom. *Sleeping in and eating breakfast late, right.*

"It's great you got some rest." he agreed in the same language. "By the way, my grandmother says my accent is getting better on this lesson. I'd love to dive right in. See what you think."

The code phrase of his grandmother commenting on his accent lit a spark in Joliet's eyes. The apparent French tutor opened a book, pushing paper and a pen of all things across to Kevin. Joliet's cover of unorthodox French tutor and analog advocate who thought reading with artificial light harmed language acquisition in the brain had been so useful. It had started a minor fad among her many fashionable students in town.

"But of course!" she agreed in French. "I am glad to see you, by the way. For a moment I thought you'd put a rabbit on me!"

It took Kevin what he considered an embarrassing amount of time to remember the idiom was French for standing someone up. His French had gotten shamefully rusty in the last few years, and the program he'd used to keep sharp hadn't been getting the attention he should have been investing in it. Maybe Joliet's cover for the paper and pens had some truth: he did remember the language better when he wrote and spoke words in conjunction.

He shrugged. "I know, it's a shame the way time runs on. Is all well?"

"We're secure," the clandestine agent agreed with a smile, "and we've officially gotten the money turned into dollars and channeled into a secure account. Once we have the proper account number from you we will make the transfer, and all will be well. Oh, and to jump from the rooster to the donkey, I have something a little bit special for you."

"Oh?" Kevin asked, jotting down the French idiom for changing to an unrelated topic. Joliet gave him a genuine grin. She pulled an analog book from the bottom of the pile, and Kevin's jaw nearly hit the floor as she pushed it into his hands.

"It is for you, a gift."

The lush decorations of a book of French folk tales blossomed across the cover, inlaid with gilding.

Joliet beamed. "I remembered what you said about books. This is a thank you from Pierre and all our team. He's quite sure you saved his life, and our superiors gave us permission to show our appreciation."

"I was doing my part of the job, really that's all it was, but…wow…" With gentle fingers, Kevin turned the pages. The book was stunning.

He picked a slip of paper from the binding. On it, a series of numbers was written.

"That's my number here in the city, until I leave next week." Joliet added in English. Kevin glanced at her, and caught a wink. He smiled.

"Well then, I'll be a gentleman and return the favor."

Ripping a strip from his note-taking paper, he carefully printed the account number he had memorized. In a digital world, the most disruptive thing you could do was memorize your information and write it on paper. Pen and ink couldn't be hacked.

"I'll treasure this," he added in French as he passed the paper over. "And it's been wonderful knowing you."

"Perhaps when this war is over you can visit France, yes?" Joliet asked, carefully tucking the paper in her pocket.

Kevin shrugged. "Perhaps. We can hope. Please give the gratitude and regards of the Democratic State Force to your superiors. And please give my personal thanks to your team. Without your country I don't think we'd be anywhere near as well off as we are. We owe you a great deal."

Joliet gave him an impish grin. "Many of us remember your old

Republic fondly. And we did help you win your last revolution, in the eighteenth century. So what if we have to do it again in the twenty second? And if you need to know what to do with your aristocrats, you can always ask us."

"To the lampposts, hmm?" Kevin asked, chuckling.

Joliet's face lit up. "You know your history, very good!" She raised her latte. "To the lampposts, my friend."

Kevin clinked his mug with hers. Joliet sipped her drink, and made a face. "Ugh, you Americans have the worst coffee."

"Yes, Argentina won't trade with us any longer, Kenya's not speaking to us and everybody else lost their crop to roya. Our own breeding attempts haven't been good. Trust me, we hate it too," Kevin agreed gravely. "Bad enough we lost our liberty, but losing coffee was just too much to bear." He sipped it anyway. "Oh, and Joliet?" He added, carefully casual. "Keep an eye on the news. I can't say much, but all this may come sooner than you'd think."

"Oh?" Joliet asked, tipping her head.

Kevin smiled carefully. "Let your superiors know, would you? We have things in motion. Enormous things."

The Frenchwoman nodded, her smile small and full of secrets. "I'll do that."

Event File 6
File Tag: Code Injection
Timestamp: 11:00-4-20-2156/16:00-4-20-2156

Sweat trickled into Tweak's eyes as she set the last tiny nano-clamp into the wires strung along the wall, teeth locked in a grin of satisfaction. So far, so good, and this batshit crazy plan was actually working. She could almost forget she was under fucking EagleCorp, which was good: shaking fingers would screw her up.

Only problem now was the busted light overhead. It was really beginning to bug her. The TC interlock must've gotten shorted in it, and the LED was flickering like summer lightning. Yeah, it was really beginning to piss her off. She could deal with the smell, the hot concrete, the hot air that sent sweat skittering down her body under her tanktop and made her cargo pants and boots into ovens. She could deal with the sound of a couple rats screwing somewhere in the shadows. It was pissing her off, but she could deal. She could deal with the fear. But that light...

Finally, the sewer maintenance nanoids did their damn job, and the light stabilized. Somewhere, some nano-programmer was getting told off for slow, sloppy code. Or maybe not. After all, they hadn't noticed her slip in and remotely reroute every sub-basement camera to looped footage. From their end, everything was looking just fine. Besides, who double checked the code for a maintenance tunnel nobody used? Nobody at all, if she was lucky.

Luck. That was the biggest problem with this plan. Too much hoping for luck. Luck was a bitch. Somebody could always show up. But Kevin had scored the work rosters with the maps, and based on those she had at least six hours before she needed to worry about getting out of here. 'Only six hours', that was how the guys had talked about it. Tweak snorted as she worked. 'Only' six hours. Were alphas really that slow? Gammas weren't slow. Six hours was a luxury. Down here in the maintenance tunnel beneath EagleCorp's main Sector hub, she had everything she needed; a solid physical door into the system using the fiberoptic nano-clamps she'd hooked into a minor optic bundle just here, time to work, silence, and the worm she'd written ready to wiggle in there and start scouting for building specs. Once they had specs on the physical backup sites, they could really get to work. And then they could take these fuckers down.

No more Citizen Standing Reports, no more secret files. No more blacklists. No more hit lists on Gammas like her.

But not if she didn't focus and get to work.

Focus.

If only it didn't *stink* down here.

As her tab made the physical connection through the tap she'd just attached, Tweak ran a small hand irritably over the bandages wrapping her forearms. They were stained now with God knew what. Damn, she'd have to change them when she got back to the base. But at least they'd kept this place from touching her skin.

Well, okay. Not her skin. Her scales. But still. She'd *hate* to brush bare scales over anything in this place. It'd feel bad enough to make her barf.

She *wished* she could do this work from home, but hacking EagleCorp remotely had left her banging her head against the wall. Their entire system hopped frequencies in the Wi-fi so fast that it shook off any attempt to keep up with it. Tweak had already wasted three weeks trying to write codes that'd stabilize her connection. This was her second option, and she'd really been hoping she wouldn't have to use it. She puffed a breath out, her black bangs swinging with the movement. The light sheened them in dark rainbows. She'd hated getting down here, but Kevin's map had been perfect. And for this? For this, it was worth it.

The EagleCorp authorization page popped up, and Tweak punched the air. "Yes! In!"

Then she got to work. Firewalls were ducked, maze algorithms were jumped. One protection at a time, she got that much closer to the encrypted file storage system that held her prize.

She'd been working for less than half an hour when her pad's screen flashed a blood-red warning.

Device Detected. Device Detected, 2000 yards.

"Fuck!" Tweak hissed, on her feet in the blink of an eye. Device detected. Her tab had picked up on the signaling of another tab. That meant somebody else down here. Damn it! She hadn't been more than half way in!

She darted to the wall and, much as she hated to, disconnected her nano-clamps and stuffed everything back in her pockets, cursing in her head as she yanked her long-sleeved shirt and her jacket back on.

"—down here anyway?" someone whined, their voice echoing off the concrete.

"Just do your job." someone else scolded. "Jesus Harry, you keep whining and I'll write you up I swear!"

"I was only—"

"Shut the fuck up. We fix the goddamned light and we go, can you quit whining for that long?"

Too close. They were too close. Tweak's eyes skittered around the maintenance tunnel. Quietly as she could, she took off running.

"That was fast." Kevin remarked, watching her as he passed over a duffle full of clean clothes in the safe house he'd chosen for this mission. The tiny apartment was cold after the tunnels. Tweak snatched the bag, fighting down the snap of rage and the words that wanted to spit from her mouth. Why did the guy have to say everything like he thought it wasn't good enough?

She stood for a moment, staring at her scuffed boots and getting her head on straight. Take a second and think about your feelings, Psych had said. The psychological coaching program Aidan gave her had been fun to work on. She'd gotten in to fix the appearance and speech patterns first, and it was easier to talk to now. The base code had already been kickass. And it had some good ideas. She liked talking to it. The world made more sense after she talked to Psych.

Her brain was just fancy code, it said. When everything feels wrong, it's letting you know there's a bug in your code. Find the bug.

Okay, she could find the bug. She was angry because she felt guilty, because she'd fucked up. Not because of the way Kevin was talking.

"Fucked up." Raising her eyes, she glared at Kevin, hating his all relaxed I'm-better-than-you looks. She knew this wasn't really on him, but the way he looked at her some days made her want to punch him on principal. Or bring him down a peg, anyway.

"You gave me bad intel. Crew showed up!"

"What kind of crew?" Kevin asked, tensing. Tweak sighed. Okay, so she wasn't angry at Kevin. She was angry at fucking up. And her head still wasn't on straight. She was shivering with the fear and the anger. Fucking brain, overreacting again

She shoved her hands in her pockets, balling them into fists. What had Psych said to do?

Breathe really deep. Count as you breathe in and breathe out.

One, two, three, four. One, two, three, four.

She let out the breath. "Maintenance. Was a b-broken light where I set up. Wasn't on s-s-schedule. F-freaked me out. Guess s'not your fault."

Kevin smiled, looking tired. "Well, we'll try again another day.

Let's call this a dress rehearsal and chalk it up to experience."

"Whatever." Tweak muttered, staring at her boots again. She had no clue what a dress rehearsal was. She hated it when he said things she didn't understand. He didn't need to make her feel any more clueless than she knew she was, did he?

Kevin reached out to pat her shoulder, and panic ran through her body. The touch would burn. It always burned.

But he caught himself, and tucked his hands in his pockets. "You did a fine job, Tweak."

Tweak snorted, but she didn't answer. They both knew that was bullshit. She hated people slinging bull. But calling it out was a waste of words.

After a moment, Kevin drew a breath. "Let's go home. Topher's meeting us at the fence."

The bullet train's seats smelled of sweat and disinfectant, the metal of the rails scuffed. Tweak stared at the speeding city grimly, counting white buildings as the skyline unraveled. High rise gave way to low rise, to sprawl, and finally to industry and factory before petering out all together. She switched to counting the scratches on the metal rail. She needed to keep her focus on something. Otherwise everything would come down around her: the ads, the guy breathing next to her. The texture of her clothes against her skin. The smell in here.

She needed to focus.

Her tab would be more fun to pay attention to, but she could get too deep into it and have trouble coming out ready to go when the train stopped. It was better to focus on stuff that she didn't care about, right now.

There was a hot wind blowing at their stop, and nanomesh fence surrounding the terminal. Tweak glanced at Kevin's face for the first time in the trip. She wished he'd yell at her and get it over with. She hated trying to figure out if other people were angry or not.

"Kev. Didn't do fine. F-fucked it up."

Kevin pressed a finger to his lips, and nodded to the side. They walked to the terminal's back, then ducked in through an 'employees only' door and down a staircase, passing through a slick tarp that hid a back door as part of the wall.

There was a long walk down a maintenance tunnel in the dark. When they came up, the terminal was out of sight.

There was the faintest shimmer of something like a heat mirage. Then a face appeared as Topher pulled down his slick-poncho's hood.

"Hey Kev!"

"Shhh," Kevin ordered quietly. "Where's the bikes?"

"Other side of the mesquite, with your riding gear." Topher replied, his voice lower. He was barely visible, except for the glitter of his eyes. "Only got two, though, 'til you get us the stuff to fix the other one. We're gonna have to double up."

Kevin nodded. "Probably best."

Maybe for you, Tweak thought, trudging after the two men. But she didn't want to talk; she wanted to get out of the danger zone.

Climbing on behind Topher once they'd reached the bikes and gotten into their gear, Tweak gripped his waist through the fabric. The bikes purred to life, nearly silent, and they took off. The bikes raced over the uneven ground as if it was road, though every jolt ran through her bones. She *hated* bike rides. There was too much to see. Too much to feel. Too much *everything.*

Tweak was almost dealing with it, when the first bullet pinged off the metal of the bike. She screamed before she could stop herself.

Topher twisted the steering controls hard to the right. The bike skidded across the dry ground as more bullets bounced off its metal casing. In the spinning world, Tweak could just see a black drone overhead. A gun drone, quiet and ugly, five gun turrets mounted in five different directions around the ion drives that kept it in the air. Somebody had wanted silent and nasty, and they'd got it when they built gun drones.

Out of the corner of her eye, she saw Kevin zig-zagging on his bike to the left.

"Fucker!" she hissed, and fumbled for her tab with one hand. "T-t-t-topher, IR. Now! Gonna c-code a c-c-c..." she gave up. Of course her fucking stutter had to kick in now, when she was scared of getting killed. And make it more likely that she'd get killed, because she couldn't talk to the people she was with. Fucking classic.

But right now she needed to focus and code.

"Roger!" Topher's voice snapped in her helmet's mic.

"Can you get a lock, Kev? Take a shot?"

"Trying!" Kevin's voice snapped over the mic.

Tweak ignored the world and pulled up her saved code cache with one hand, hanging on to Topher with the other. It took a lot of firepower to bring down a drone, but one simple command sent to the thing via an IR laser blast could destroy its directional programming and send it flying back to its hangar for repairs. She finally sent the code command to the bike's IR emitter, commanding the device on the front of the bike to fix on the nearest Corporation-registered device and beam it a signal broadcast. Their tabs all ran on non-corps systems, so that'd be fine.

She knew she'd got the beam locked onto the drone when it froze. She sighed in relief.

The drone shuddered in the air. Any second now, it'd fly away. Any second...

Then every gun turret began to fire at once.

"Shit!" Kevin's voice yelped in her ear, "They've reprogrammed! It's firing blind!"

Tweak's heart pounded in her ears, nearly drowning him out. The zig-zagging bike was starting to make her stomach turn over. She could *not* throw up in the helmet.

Burning hornet stings snarled into her leg, and she forgot about her stomach. She cried out, arms instinctively tightening as the wave of heat raced up her leg.

"I'm s-shot! Shot. Fucking shot!" She panted into the mic.

"Oh bloody hell, this day just gets better!" Kevin hissed. "Topher, step on it, once we're out of range we should be safe. Head for the poplars, we can get under cover."

"Roger Kev. Tweak! Don't squeeze! I gotta drive!" Topher's voice replied.

Tweak screwed her eyes closed. "F-f-fuck you, I'm s-s-s-shot!"

When she opened her eyes, a huge, half-dead stand of trees waved a handful of green leaves overhead. Under them, grasses grew in scrubby tufts.

Kevin climbed off his bike, yanking off his riding helmet. Looking down, he blinked at the long furrow cut into his poncho. Tweak could see blood dripping off his glove. Blood didn't look real in sunlight. It was so bright.

"Looks like I got lucky." Kevin muttered. Absently, he pulled his poncho off, staring at the sky between the knotted limbs.

Topher turned in his seat. "Tweak, can I touch you to help get you off the bike?"

"No. I got it," she snapped. She slid her good leg off the bike, but the other leg throbbed when she put weight on it, and she tumbled to the ground. Blood stained her ripped jeans and dripped into the grass. There was so much blood. The white bandages under her jeans were turning red.

Topher ripped off his helmet and knelt beside Tweak. Panic raced up her backbone. Her jeans and her bandages were ripped. He'd see what she looked like under her protections.

She scuttled back as best she could. "L-l-leave me al-l-lone or I'll b-break your n-n-nose again!" she snarled, clutching at her leg.

If she bled too much, she was dead. But if he saw her legs, she was definitely dead.

Blood smelled like pennies. The red looked unreal. The light was so *bright*.

Her heartbeat banged in her ears. Her leg was on fire. She curled into herself, trying to shut it all out.

Through the thrum of her heart, she could hear Topher's voice.

"She's bleeding bad, Kev. Round went right in; there's no exit wound."

"Run the check," Kevin murmured. She could feel his body heat as he leaned close. Too close. Their voices rumbled like thunder in the distance.

"Topher. Trackers?"

"Can't tell. It's in too deep, I can't get a lock...wait...shit yeah there's the signal."

"Bloody hell. Block it. Alright, Tweak? We'll have to do a bit of work before we head home."

A hand touched her leg. The shock of touch on her skin sent electricity spiking through her. She uncoiled, lashing out with her good leg. "T-t-touch me and you'll l-lose your fucking b-balls!"

Kevin grunted into the kick, doubling over. When he caught his breath, he glanced back with steel in his eyes. "You little beast, get ahold of yourself and let me see that leg."

Fuck that. She'd been through this before. She wasn't going through it again.

Kevin's hand started to lift Tweak's pant leg.

This time she took aim and got him a foot in the side of the jaw, sending him to the leaf-strewn earth. He took time to sit up, rubbing at his jaw.

"You know," he remarked coldly, working his jaw, "I could just wait until you passed out from blood loss. It won't take much longer."

She knew he was right. She was already seeing the world like she was looking at it down a tube. But they *couldn't* see what she was. They *couldn't*. If they did she'd *die*.

"Just g-g-give me the s-s-shit, I'll do it m-myself." Tweak hissed between her teeth, sweat beading her brow. "I g-got first aid."

"Not in this shape, you don't," Kevin replied sharply, staring her down. "Lie still and let us work."

"I'll fuck you up if—" Tweak snarled, but Kevin grabbed her by both shoulders before she could get the sentence out. The man's eyes looked like steel balls. His hands burned on her skin as he snapped out his words.

"*Tweak!* There is a *tracker* in that bullet lodged in your leg, if we don't get it out before we take you home the operator will be able to pinpoint our location, and *everyone at home will die!*" He shook her a little as he made his points, sending the terrible electrical tingle of his skin on hers up another notch. "Aside from that, note the fact that we're trying to *save your life*. Now let us *help*!"

His touch was unbearable. She shook her head.

"L-l-ll-let   g-g-go.   D-d-don't...l-l-let...s-s-skin...t-touch   h-h-hurts..."

The touch on her shoulders eased. Kevin's eyes studied her. Then he changed his grip, shifting his hands so that there was a layer of fabric between his hands and her skin.

When he spoke again, the words were quiet. "Tweak. I know you're frightened. I know you're hurting. And I'm sorry I lost my temper. But we swear we won't hurt you. We want to help. That's what families do. We act as a family. We talked about this, remember?"

Family. He kept saying that. He kept telling her they were a family. Everybody did.

A tracker in the bullet. That was why he was so angry. He was scared. The sons of bitches could track her, until she got the thing out.

They could track her to the base. Billie was on the base. Tommy was back on base. He was so much like Bao Li used to be. And Andrea and Alice were on base. People she *liked* were on base. She couldn't risk them.

But if they saw her leg, they'd know what she was.

Her head was spinning. There was a rope around her throat.

She wished Aidan was here. He'd fix it.

But Aidan did trust Kevin. Kevin knew all about Aidan. And Kevin still got all goofy and in love around him. If he could be cool with that, maybe he could be cool with this.

And maybe she didn't really have a choice.

Swallowing against the tension in her throat, she nodded.

Kevin held her eyes."Nod twice if you're going to relax and let us do this."

She did.

Kevin gently lowered Tweak to the ground, moving to roll up the leg of her pants. He cursed under his breath.

"Topher, the bag."

The light hurt her eyes. Tweak closed them. Something cold touched her leg. Air ran over her scales.

There was a gasp.

Tweak's eyes were hot. Tears prickled in the blackness behind the lids as she listened to the two men talk.

"Blessed Mary Mother of God…"

"What? How bad? Is she…holy fuck…"

"A Gamma…no wonder she didn't want us looking…Alright Topher, hold the viewer steady. Trackers, right? Tweak, I'm going to inject a numbing agent. Don't move your leg."

"Trackers." Topher agreed, sounding freaked.

By the time they pulled up under the compound's slick tarp, Tweak was barely able to climb off the bike for dizziness. Kevin gave her a dry look as she stood beside it. "Will you let us take you to Damian? You may dislike him, but he keeps secrets quite well."

Tweak tried to shake her head, and lost her balance. A puff of dust went up as she landed on her ass in the dirt. Her leg was sticky, the cloth of her jeans black with blood around the auto-pad. "F-fuck." she muttered. "Fine."

After all, she reasoned muzzily, she could always get Billie and run like hell, later. Good plan.

Kevin held out his arms, covered by his slick poncho. "I can carry you, if you'll let me."

Tweak sighed, hating everything about this situation. "I guess."

Damian looked up from his desk as they lumbered in. Tweak felt like a complete idiot, being seen like this.

"Bit of a problem." Kevin called, like it was all some big joke. "I think the young lady could use your services."

"On the table to your left." Damian ordered, and Kevin laid her carefully down.

"G-go g-g-get Aid-dan," Tweak muttered at him. "G-g-gotta tell him about the f-fucking d-drones. N-new f-f-fucking trick."

"I'll take care of that." Kevin assured quietly. He glanced up at Damian. "And shall I fetch Alice and switch the 'surgery in progress' sign on? By the way, try not to touch her skin-to-skin. I think it might be important."

"Noted." Damian agreed, grabbing a pair of scissors and snipping away her pants. *Damn,* Tweak thought distantly. *I liked these.*

Damian stood still for a moment. Then he snapped into motion. Grabbing a genome reader, he ran it over her leg. She tried to sit up. "D-don't—"

"I'm taking your blood type. You're going to need a transfusion. And I'm not recording your genome. You're holding still. Got it?" Damian intoned. He turned his cybernetic eyes on her. She got the message.

At some point she must have passed out. She was in a bed when she woke up, and her leg was wrapped in a new auto pad under the blanket. The bandages on one of her arms had been taken off. A little auto-pad covered a long scratch down the outside of her upper arm, right where the scales started to turn into normal skin. Her hand had tubes coming out of it.

She raised her eyes at the sound of someone moving, panic shooting through her.

Three sets of eyes fixed on her: commander, medic, and doctor.

Aidan gave her a smile where he sat beside her bed. "Hey. Heard you might wake up about now." He looked her over. A little bit of anger twinged through her head. What the hell gave him the right to stare at her while she was still asleep?

"How're you feeling?" Alice asked with a friendly smile, stepping over beside the bed. "Mind if I take a look at the leg?"

Reluctantly, Tweak flipped the blanket back. "Oughta charge for the freak show." she added irritably as the medical technician began her work. "I'd make bank." She turned her eyes on Aidan to ignore what Alice was doing. "Where's Billie? She freaking?"

Alice laughed down by her feet. "Yeah, she is, but it's okay. We'll let her in tomorrow, but we're keeping everybody out tonight."

Tweak nodded at Aidan. "Except you."

Aidan tipped his head, agreeing without saying it. "Sort of my job to check on the wounded." He was looking at her like she was a starving kid begging on the street corner. Like he *pitied* her. Fuck that.

"What're you staring at? Never seen no Gamma before?" Tweak snapped. She wanted to wipe that sad look off his face. She wasn't a baby, and she didn't want anybody's pity.

"Never seen a wound so easily fixed," Aidan replied evenly. He leaned back in the chair. "Get it straight, Tweak. I don't care what you are. I care that you can do your job. And given who else lives on this base, we'd be a really epic assholes if we treated you any different because of what you are."

Tweak shifted uneasily in the bed, eyeing the guy. She kind of hated it when he talked like this, all squishy and honest. Problem was, she kind of loved it too.

"And let's be clear. You're not a freak." Alice added, keeping her voice quiet as she inspected the wound through a viewing panel. "You're a genetic subspecies."

"Sub means less. Fuck that." Tweak hissed. She wasn't a complete idiot. She'd heard the word subpar before. And the word subhuman. Yeah, she'd heard that one a lot.

"Sub means a couple of things," Aidan countered quietly. "Right now it means different. Worse in some ways, sure. Better in other ways."

"In fact," Alice added, "these scales? Natural armor? Pretty cool. You didn't have these scales, this bullet would have completely destroyed your leg. We would have had to amputate it, most likely."

Tweak snorted. "Don't start with 'cool'. The 'special snowflake' talk is shit."

It had been shit when her parents told her she was special. And it was still shit. *Lucky dragon daughter, my ass,* she grumbled silently at a mom and dad who were long dead.

"I'm not saying it just to say it." Alice passed the wand-like electrometer over her injured leg. "I'm saying it because it's true. You're lucky this wasn't as bad as it could have been. Honestly. I'm not even reading nerve damage."

Tweak grunted, shrugging. "How soon can I run again?"

"Depends on how you heal," Damian replied, reading Alice's holo-screen as she took notes. "There are rumors of Gammas healing faster than normal folk, but I've never seen it first-hand, so I'm not sure. I'd say a week. Maybe two."

Tweak's eyes widened, her gut clenching "You s-shitting me, man? Two weeks g-gimpy, I'll be d-d-dead!"

Alice shook her head and gently replaced Tweak's blanket. "No, you won't. We'll do PT with you and see if we can't get you up faster, but…no promises."

Tweak sighed. "Should've known." After a moment, she glanced up at the people around her. She probably needed to say something. Psych kept bugging her about it. *Alphas do things that are hard to notice to tell each other everything's cool, and it's even hard for them sometimes,* the psychological wellness program had said, *so if you want them to know you're not mad, you need to tell them. You want them to know how you feel; it helps them feel better about things and about you. If you don't know what to say, just thank them for something they helped you with.*

Aidan was being nice. And Alice was being sweet. She should say something to let them know she appreciated it.

She cleared her tight throat. "Alphas. N-not 'normal'. You guys, you're alpha. That's how w-we say it... T-thanks for the leg. And for keeping people out."

Aidan shrugged, smiling a little. Alice gave her a smile like the sun rising over farmland, so bright on her dark face. "Hey, alpha. Sounds good. And it's cool. We like having you here. We couldn't get such cool stuff before we got your codes."

The words brought a wave of something that wasn't nasty through her head. Something warm. She was worth something in a coding chair. Hell, she was fucking *good* in a coding chair. "Yeah. You couldn't." she agreed. Aidan and Alice chuckled. Even Damian cracked a bit of a smile.

"Well, while you're here," the bony man added, "anything we can do to make you more comfortable?"

Tweak glanced between the three of them. Finally, she let her eyes settle on Aidan. He was the safest person.

"We got problems. Stealth drones. Somebody's p-personal things. T-trackers in the bullet that w-went into my l-l-leg. And we didn't g-get the m-mission done."

Aidan nodded. "I heard. Shitty day, hunh?"

Tweak snorted. "Shittiest. Gimme a tab and I'll get started on new c-code for the drones tonight."

Aidan nodded. "Need anything else?"

Tweak glanced away. Meeting everyone's eyes took too much work. "No r-r-records?"

Damian shifted his weight."How about I make you a deal. I'll keep records, for my sanity. And you'll put them behind a firewall that you and I have passwords to. For your sanity. How's that?"

Tweak raised her eyes at that. The black plastic orbs the doctor used for eyes stared right back at her. But the face around them was smiling a little.

She was actually talking to a doctor who wanted to make a deal with her. *Her.* Docs always saw her as a thing. A test subject. An interesting case.

But this one wanted to make her a deal.

"No l-lie?" she asked, hating the way her voice came out. She sounded like a goddamned *kid*.

Damian's little smile fell off. "Do I look like a liar?"

Tweak gave the doctor her best bitchy once over. "You look like a b-bastard."

"I am a bastard," Damian agreed, "and that's the only reason I'm listened to around here. But I don't break client confidentiality. So. That record?"

Tweak stared at him for what felt like forever. He was actually asking. No doctor had ever asked before. They'd just taken.

She stuck out her hand. "Shake."

His hand was huge. Her skin zinged with the touch.

She swallowed hard. "I'll w-write the f-firewall for my stuff n-now. B-bored an-nyway."

"All worked out?" Kevin asked, looking up from where he leaned against a wall as Aidan stepped out of the medical bay. He stepped over, slipping his fingers between Aidan's as they walked.

"No," Aidan sighed. "But she's okay, and she's not fighting us. It's getting better, I think. We'll see."

"Que será, será." Kevin murmured, squeezing Aidan's hand. "I think—"

"How is she?"

Kevin spun on reflex. Billie could have been a ghost, the way she materialized in the corridor behind them. The girl cringed back. It was then that Kevin realized he'd fallen into something of a combative stance.

Good God I'm getting jumpy these days. I have got to relax.

He forced himself into an easier stance, smiling at the gawky girl. "Sorry about that, Billie."

"You checking up on Tweak?" Aidan asked the youngster. Billie nodded, her hands nervously clasping in front of her. Aidan gave her one of his gentle, crooked smiles. "She's in great shape. Damian's still not letting anyone in yet, but I had a talk with her and she's asking for her tab. You can go in and see her in the morning, okay?"

Billie dropped her eyes to the floor, her fingers fidgeting. "And is she...I mean did people see...is she scared?"

Stepping in, Aidan laid a hand on her shoulder. "She's kind of freaked. But you know it's not a big deal, right? I mean, have you seen this base? We're all weirdos."

Like an animal in the hands of a skilled trainer, the young lady relaxed. Aidan was so good at doing that with people. Billie gave a bashful little smile, glancing away. "I guess. Just...she is okay, right?"

"She's great," Aidan repeated soothingly. "And she's got a tab. Go ahead and message her tonight. She'll like that."

Billie nodded, stealing glances at both of them. "Um...did she fuck up out there? Is that why she got hurt?"

"She did beautifully." Kevin reassured, trying for the same soothing tone that seemed to come naturally to his love. "The mission simply went a bit off-kilter. But I was impressed today...well, until she kicked me, at least." He rubbed at his jaw ruefully. It really did ache.

"Go get some sleep, Billie." Aidan added quietly. "We got this."

The blonde man held his confident pose until she was out of sight. Only when they were alone did Aidan let his shoulders slump.

"I take it Billie knew she was Gamma?" Kevin asked in an undertone. "That was what she meant by 'seeing', I assume?"

Aidan ran a hand over his face."Ugh. Talk to me about it tomorrow, okay?"

"I second the motion. It's been a hell of a day," Kevin agreed quietly. He put an arm around Aidan's waist, pulling him close.

Hand in hand, they flopped onto their bed. Kevin closed his eyes. Adrenaline was really calling in its debts after the day he'd had. He'd be lucky if he had the energy to take off his boots.

"How's your arm?" Aidan's quiet voice asked. "I should have got some antibiotics from Damian for you..."

"I had some in our kit. It'll heal. It's my jaw that aches." Kevin murmured. One hand touched the side of his jaw gingerly, feeling the swelling. "Tweak can really kick...."

"Maybe I can kiss it better," Aidan muttered, the barest hint of laughter in the words. He rolled over and planted several soft kisses along Kevin's throat, headed in the direction of his jawline.

"Or you can make it sting." Kevin grumbled, feeling the twinges as his muscles relaxed. His jaw really was painful. "Kiss something else please."

Aidan chuckled and kissed Kevin's lips instead. "I'd kiss something lower, but sleep sounds really good right now. Especially with how much recon we're going to have to do when we can think straight."

Kevin groaned and rolled over to hide his head under a pillow. "I don't even want to think about it, after this debacle..."

"It's not that bad." Aidan replied, gentle amusement in his voice. He lay back down, putting an arm around Kevin and snuggling in. It was such a comfort when he did that.

Kevin sighed, feeling the rock of guilt shift in his chest. "It is, actually...I never should have let her go down there on her own, love. That's when things started to hit the proverbial fan. And that gun drone wasn't standard issue. I've been hearing rumors that EagleCorp is renting drone swarms out to what they charmingly call 'private contractors.' If there are bounty-hunters with their own drone swarms around now... I've got to think of less risky tactics."

Aidan kissed his throat. "And you will. In the morning. Right now, get some sleep, okay?"

Aidan's hands massaged his tense shoulders. Peace began to seep into his soul.

"Okay," he agreed quietly.

The night was far advanced when a fist banged on the door. Kevin sat bolt upright in bed, scrambling in the dark for his glasses and his gun as Alice's voice shouted. "Guys! Aidan, Kevin! Damian wants you right now! Wants Kevin anyway, says hurry!"

Aidan was out of bed nearly as soon as he was, fumbling with pants and yanking on his shirt. Kevin didn't bother with the formality of finding his own shirt. He yanked his pants on and bolted out the door.

"What's up, Alice?" Kevin asked as they all but bolted down the corridor. The woman's dark eyes were wide. "Tweak's having a blood reaction."

Aidan cursed behind them as Kevin skidded around the corner and pushed his way into the med bay. "What can we do?"

"You can sit down and give some blood; we need a universally accepted blood and there's no time to print enough," Damian rapped out. "Girl's got a delayed reaction to the blood transfusion she got, we went through routine crossmatch procedure but she's too different."

On the bed, Tweak was slick with sweat, her chest moving in rapid puffs. Kevin handed his gun belt to Aidan and dropped into the nearest white plastic chair. "Will she be all right?"

"Hell if I know. " Damian growled. "I trained on normal humans."

"Fucking...bastard." the words were a whispered rasp from Tweak's lips. Her body was shaking hard enough to make the wheels of the bed rattle.

Damian whipped around. "Damn it Alice, get her stable!"

"I'm trying!" Alice snapped in exasperation, her tied-back braids swinging behind her. "She's already gotten everything, Damian. Nanoids are keeping the clots from forming but she's losing blood volume!"

Damian checked the stats, brushing past Alice. "Take Kevin, I'll deal with this." he added brusquely.

Alice nodded and handed over her duties, rounding the bed to swiftly prepare Kevin for the blood draw. "Sorry," she muttered as she pricked him a bit more forcefully than necessary, her hands shaking. Kevin gave her a reassuring smile. He'd certainly had worse.

Over the table, Damian worked furiously as Tweak's breathing grew faster. Then he spat a curse word.

"What?" Aidan called over, as Damian scrambled and a long, low bleep filled the room. Kevin's gut tightened. He knew that sound. The long whine of a flatlined heart.

Death.

"Cardiac arrest!" Damian snarled, grabbing for a heavy-gauged needle. "I need more epinephrine! Damn, the blood must have—"

Blip.

Kevin sat up, electricity shooting along his spine. Damian hadn't so much has touched the injector, much less applied it to the girl. But her heart was actually…

Blip.

The raw-boned doctor froze as the bleep steadied into a rhythm. Damian stood stock still, staring. "Holy shit…"

"What?" Aidan asked for the second time, and Damian turned to him like a man who'd seen a ghost. "Her heart just started back up on its own."

For a moment, the room was silent. Then Damian got a grip on himself and got back to work.

Half an hour later, the two medical staff stood back, the officers looking on.

"Will she be all right?" Kevin asked, watching them hover over their tiny patient. Tweak's body was swathed in the glow of a full-body scan, the workings of her circulatory system superimposed over her prone body under its blanket. She looked like a sick child, tiny and vulnerable.

But she was alive. Her heart was beating.

Her heart had started again. *On its own.*

Kevin's reverie was broken when Damian spoke. "We'll know in the morning. The printer's running new clotting proteins for her. So far, no signs of major clots causing problems, but we're monitoring. There's a chance of kidney damage, but I think we caught it. I'll keep modified blood in the fridge for her going forward." He sighed, glancing at the time. "I'll keep an eye on her for the rest of the night. You two go to bed, there's nothing you can do here. Kevin, drink some electrolytes before you go."

With a moue of distaste, Kevin downed the cup of over-sugared stuff Alice passed him. "Damn, stiff upper lip and all that, but I'll admit it: I miss orange juice at the doctor's..."

"Poor CES baby," Aidan teased tiredly.

Alice laid a hand on Damian's shoulder. "You get some rest, too. I'll stay with her and get some knitting done. I can call you if anything else happens."

Wearily, the big man shook his head. "Case this weird, I better be on hand. Besides," he glanced at the bed as he spoke, "I've got some research to do on Gamma biology."

"You aren't the only one," Kevin agreed ruefully.

To his bleary surprise, he watched Damian turn to pin Aidan with a stare, crossing his arms. "This would have gone a hell of a lot better if I'd had warning. This is why I didn't get any more information on her from you, I assume?"

Aidan returned the medical man's stare impassively. His eyes were heavy-lidded. "Wasn't my secret to tell, Damian."

"Your courtesy could've killed her, you know," the doctor rapped out.

"Yeah? And telling on her could have made her shut down on us." Aidan shrugged. "I didn't have great choices here. I did what I could."

Kevin blinked at his boyfriend. "Wait...when did you find out?"

Aidan shrugged. "Last time she had a rough panic attack. Before Christmas."

Kevin sighed, running a hand through his hair. So much for Aidan refraining from keeping secrets from him, then. Granted, it wasn't really his secret to tell, and Kevin understood the importance of that. But still. He *needed* details like this to work effectively. Nobody ever seemed to understand that.

"And she swore you secrecy," he suggested wearily.

"Nah," Aidan demurred, "I promised her I'd keep it to myself."

"This is people's lives, not a middle-school note-passing thing." Damian snapped. Aidan turned, regarding him for a long, slow moment.

The core of resolve he usually kept under diffident wraps was laid bare now, and Aidan looked like the implacable warrior he was as he stared the doctor down.

"Yeah. It is lives. You're right," he agreed, and Kevin heard the note of warning in his boyfriend's voice. "And TechoCo kills gammas when they get found. It's her life. I waited 'till she trusted us a little before I asked her to put it in our hands. That a problem?"

Damian's black cybernetic implants couldn't blink. He gave the same effect with a quiet grunt.

"I suppose we'll find out in the morning. Either way, she'll be in bed for a while."

Kevin watched as Aidan let the weariness weigh his shoulders down. "I'll tell the other bases and rework the mission timetable. In the morning."

Reaching out, Kevin took his hand. "I'll help you out with that."

Event File 8
File Tag: Health Assessment
Timestamp: 04:00-4-21-2156

It was four in the morning when Kevin woke, slid from bed and slipped from the room to get to work. He started the 3D printer working on the tools they'd use the next time they tried the run. While it worked, he turned on his tab, slipped on his 'buds and started to dig.

He found much of what he expected. Tweak had been right when she bragged that there was a bounty out on the heads of the group responsible for the Folder. If you knew where to look, the chatter was loud and the price was impressively high. That explained yesterday's damned drone. Somebody had gotten lucky. They must have thought they'd hit pay day.

Somebody was going to pay for that.

Tracking through several sites with the rough beauty of Social Distortion in his ears, Kevin scoured the bounty-hunting notice boards under the alias of an 'independent contractor' whose tab had been scavenged after he'd died in the Dust several months back. Four groups and an alliance composed of three small bounty-hunting firms had all officially taken on the contract, paid on delivery.

Kevin smiled coldly in the blue light of his screens. Now that he knew who he was working against, he could run rings around these plebes.

"I'll do it my way, I'll always win," he hummed under his breath as he tracked the ID number Tweak had locked onto. Five minutes later, he found a buyer for the gun drone. A registered private contractor for EagleCorp. He read up on the man for an hour, trawling through his social media and getting into his laughably encrypted system. You'd think a professional would have something better for cyber-security.

Once he was in, Kevin smirked and planted a folder of gay porn on the man's hard-drive, adding his number to several very disreputable call lists for rent boys in town. It wouldn't be long before EagleCorp went after the bastard in accordance with the same goddamn Morality Laws he'd signed up to help them enforce. Karma, performed in real time. See how he liked it.

Of course, it still left Kevin asking how the hell a bounty hunter had known exactly where to look for them and when. But even bounty hunters got lucky sometimes. And the man might have simply put a drone on every outlying train depot. It would be efficient. Expensive, of course, but efficient.

Still, the question nagged in the back of his mind. Even O'Brien slamming away on the drums in his ears couldn't drown it out.

It was seven-thirty in the morning when he arrived at the medical bay door. Billie was already there, and he gave her a nod and a smile. A smile flicked across her face in turn, quick and shy as a sparrow.

He wished he could do something for the poor mouse. He settled for a quiet question. "Damian not letting anyone in yet?"

Billie shrugged. "Didn't knock yet," she whispered at the floor.

"Want me to?" Kevin asked. The mute appeal in her eyes was answer enough.

Damian's classic deadpan was firmly in place when he opened the door. "You're early. She's asleep," he remarked, arching a brow at Kevin. Holding the doctor's unblinking eyes, he put a hand on Billie's shoulder. "There's no harm in having a friendly face by her bedside when she wakes up, is there?"

Damian sighed, exasperated. "Don't get in the way," he warned Billie, opening the door a little more widely to allow the girl in. Kevin stepped away to fetch a few plates of breakfast.

It was nine in the morning when Tweak opened her eyes, staring at the ceiling. When she spoke, it was a hoarse rasp. "What got fucked up?"

"Your body tried to reject the first blood transfusion we gave you," Alice replied over the breakfast Kevin had brought her. "Everything's all right now, though."

Tweak rolled over in the bed, and groaned. "I feel like shit...and I'm starving..."

The holos around her bed began to fizzle and bleep. Alice bent down and turned them off.

"Kevin brought you a plate a little while ago, for when you woke up," Billie whispered. The gawky teen jumped up from her seat and grabbed the plate of breakfast from the counter. She shot a glance at Damian where he sat in his small office, updating his paperwork on several screens.

"Sir? Can I?"

Damian glanced up at the girl, frowned, but nodded. "Don't stain the blankets."

Despite the admonishment, Tweak wolfed down the food and spangled the blankets with crumbs. She glanced at Alice as her fingers picked them from the fabric. Her bright eyes flicked to Damian's hunched form at his desk, and back again. "I guess you two got me straight." she remarked, fixing those oil-slick eyes on Alice. "Hard work?"

"Definitely a surprise," Alice agreed. "But you did a lot of it on your own. I still don't know how, but...you went into cardiac arrest for a minute there and your heart restarted on its own. So we can't take all the credit."

Tweak's thin shoulders hunched, and she focused again on her plate. "Yeah." But she glanced up again, and this time, she managed a faint tug of the lips that was nearly a smile. Then she glanced at

Kevin."Um… guess you helped too. Out there."

"I suppose I did something useful," he agreed patiently.

Tweak dropped her eyes to the plate in her hands. "S-something. Thanks. And sorry. I was kind of a b-bitch."

Kevin parried with a thin smile of his own. "Actually, I think you were a bit of a mule." He pointedly ran his hand over his bruised jaw.

Tweak flicked her eyes up, and smiled tightly. "Yeah, well, you're an ass, CES. We're square."

Kevin gave the girl a smile. "I suppose we are. And I'm sorry we had to put you through that. If I'd known what I was asking...well." He shrugged.

Tweak gave him a quick, crooked smile. "Eh. We lived."

Billie sat carefully on the edge of the bed. "Good?" she asked, holding Tweak's eyes. For an odd moment Kevin thought they were discussing the food. It didn't merit anything like the gravitas they were giving it. Other possible connotations eventually occurred, but the girls didn't exactly give context when they talked to one another. Their one-word conversational style was practically code.

Tweak nodded. "Yeah. Good. Watch."

Kevin didn't realize what the little woman was going to do until Tweak was already in motion. Flipping her blankets back as if she were swirling a matador's cape, Tweak swung her legs out of bed, and tried to stand. The brave gesture ended with her flat on her back in the bed again, blinking dazedly at the ceiling. The holographic warnings around the bed went mad.

"Shit..." she muttered weakly. "What the hell..."

"You won't be good if you try that again," Alice remarked in the tones of a patient older sister as she turned the bed alarms off. "If you want to help, Billie, don't encourage her. Tweak, we're going to lift the sheets around you and put you back in bed. We won't touch your skin."

Kevin instinctively reached for the blankets, placing himself to help, but Damian's bony hands pushed his out of the way. With a handful of economical gestures, the medical professionals had the tiny girl lying in the center of the bed again.

"This time, stay there." Damian stated, voice flat and hard as marble. "You don't just bounce back from cardiac arrest and a blood transfusion gone wrong. Either you let your body rest or you end up in here for a month. Got it?"

Tweak sighed, staring at the ceiling. "At least gimme my t-tab, and I'll get some work done."

Kevin smirked. Now that sounded like Tweak. He leaned nonchalantly against the wall. "I suppose I could bring along something to occupy the poor invalid." That said, he turned away with exaggerated ease.

"Fuck you," Tweak called when he turned his back. To his own surprise, he found himself smiling as he gave her the middle finger over his shoulder.

Three hours later, he was back in the medical bay, dropping a small white hemisphere on the bed beside Tweak's hand. She blinked at it, then at him.

"Hunh?"

"This should help the next time we go out to run that mission. Motion sensors," Kevin explained as he dropped into a chair. "I'm planning to make a solo trip down into the tunnels and plant these in all directions for a quarter of a mile. Along with these," he added, dropping a slightly less graceful device beside his first toy. "The range on these small signal interruption devices isn't much, but they're remotely controlled. I imagine anyone would leave the tunnel if the routing program on their tab began to fritz out. Or if the tab itself ceased its proper function, for that matter. You'll be able to cause that, with these little lads planted about the place." He tipped his head to one side, noticing Billie curled up napping in the chair on the other side of the bed. Tweak glanced her way, then shot Kevin a wary look.

"Don't w-wake her."

"Didn't intend to," he agreed, watching the girl sleep. "Er...are you two..."

"Fuck buddies?" Tweak snapped. Kevin gave her a dry look. "I was going to say 'a couple', but yes."

Tweak narrowed her eyes. "What's it to you?"

"An idle curiosity," Kevin replied with care. "I'll drop it if you like."

Tweak seemed to consider the words. Then she shrugged. "Nah. No big. We don't fuck. Buddies." She glanced away, picking at the blankets. "S-sisters," she added quietly.

Kevin smiled slightly. "I see. Lazarus and I are like that."

Turning his gaze away from her, he took in the room. "I see your fearsome guard dogs have wandered off?"

"D-damian and Alice went to l-lunch." Tweak agreed quietly. Kevin nodded. Tapping his tab, he brought up his list of tasks, moving the screen so they could both easily view it where it hung in the air.

"I assume you've already gotten started on code in regards to that new drone issue, so I'll mark that as noted and addressed. I've taken care of the bounty hunter whose drones got to us. I want to run over details for our next crack at EagleCorp. I've got software to connect to your new little friends there, but you'll want to customize it, I'm sure. With this setup you'll have ample warning the next time you're approached. Lazarus is going to give you shooting lessons as soon as you're sufficiently recovered, and you'll be armed with a tranquilizer gun on your next foray, just in case. Now, I need a rundown of physiological issues that will affect your mission performance. Let's start with your skin issue. I need details."

Tweak sat up a little straighter. "Say what?"

"Tell me what bothers you and what helps." Kevin explained, keeping his tone brisk and bringing up a note-taking screen. "Once I know that, I can plan missions accordingly. Hiding your arms and legs is a given, but I gathered that there's a tactile element...excuse me, I mean touch is difficult for you?"

Tweak stared at him. Slowly, she nodded.

"Docs said I have too many n-n-nerves in my s-skin. I make too m-much stuff in my brain too. Keeps me sharp. Makes me freaked."

"Adrenaline, I'm guessing." Kevin murmured, typing his notes in. Well, that did explain a great deal. A girl with hyper-innervated skin and a system flooded with adrenaline couldn't help but react to stimuli.

Damn, he wished he'd known this before. He'd assumed she was acting the way she did because of her background, and maybe that should have been enough for him to make some allowances. But he'd never realized how much she was coping with.

He'd been such a bastard to her.

"And I'm guessing that skin makes you hypersensitive to pain as well?" He asked carefully. Tweak picked at her blanket.

"Y-yeah," she admitted finally. Kevin repressed a wince.

"I see. Well, we'll get you something with reinforced weave to go under your pants, and...yes I do believe we can get flesh colored sleeves that will do a better job than your bandages on Grid. A poly-weave jacket will help minimize the touch issue. We can probably manage some reinforced shirts as well, something with a layer of coolant for preference."

Tweak eyed him, her eyes unblinking. He sat quietly, waiting for something that resembled a response.

"Don't need you to baby me," she stated eventually.

He sighed. "Tweak, this isn't 'babying you'. The more comfortable you are, the better you can work. The faster we take down the bastards. I assure you, it's completely ulterior."

Tweak gave him a cockeyed, impatient stare. "English, CES."

"I want us to win, and you're helping us do that. So I'm helping you," Kevin clarified patiently. He kept his eyes on the screen as he spoke. He needed her to hear this, but it was an awful lot to swallow. She'd just about broken his jaw the last time he tried to help her. Hell, she'd just about lost him his rank with her stunts. But now that he knew the reason, he had to say something.

"Aside from that… someone like me has a duty to do what they can, for somebody like you."

"Hunh?"

Kevin sighed. Looking down, he pulled off his glasses and got to work polishing them.

"It wasn't your choice and it wasn't mine," he murmured as his fingers worked, "but I know my history. I know you have to deal with genetic burdens because of people like me. You are the way you are because people wanted to make me the way I am. You've had to deal with things I can't imagine, and you've still managed to become an incredibly good coder—and an incredibly valuable member of this team—in spite of the garbage they gave you to work with." He did his best to keep his vocabulary in check as he spoke, choosing words that would be easy for Tweak to understand. "You were given an egregious...excuse me, a hell of a handicap from day one, and you've managed to do so much in spite of it. So if I can help—aside from refraining from acting like a horse's ass, which I'm going to do—let me know. If you can do this much by yourself, coping on your own, what you can do with a little help when you ask for it is going to be absolutely fantastic." Replacing his glasses, he gave her the most genuine smile he could manage. "I look forward to seeing you do it. And the Corporations ought to be bloody terrified."

Tweak stared at him for a long, long time, the screens reflecting blue in her black eyes. She cocked her head to one side, then the other.

"Kevin," she stated finally, "you're an asshat."

Kevin sighed, tamping down the flare of annoyance the words sent racing through his mind, and the pain it sprang from. She was right, after all. "Yes, Tweak. I'm an asshat. You keep reminding me."

She reminded him in more ways than one. He had been an ass. He hadn't understood her, but he'd passed judgment. Hadn't he sworn never to do that again?

Tweak stared at him for entirely too long, her face blank. He held her eyes, a corner of his mind wondering what animal had provided the

DNA that made blinking barely necessary for her. Then, of all things, she flashed him a grin.

"Cool asshat, though. Sometimes." That said, she turned to the screen, moving elements. "C'mon. Work. Stuff to do."

Forcing himself to smile, Kevin followed her lead.

"Hey."

Aidan glanced up from his work screen. Leaning against the doorway, his boyfriend gave him a tired smile.

Aidan pushed his chair back. "Hey. What's up?"

"Just checking in to see if you're near the finish line," Kevin replied quietly, stepping in and picking up the flimsy plastic chair in the corner. Setting it beside Aidan, he dropped into it. He looked wrecked, even as he smiled.

"We missed our movie night last week. Any chance you're in the mood tonight?"

Aidan gave his boyfriend a smile. "Definitely. I'm just dealing with the disciplinary roster at this point. Check this out, you'll get a laugh."

He pointed at his screen, where a note of complaint was lodged.

Complaint Filed: Physical Assault

Complaint issued by: Daniel O'Rouke, Personnel Officer Base 1491

Note From Individual Issuing Complaint:

Commander Headly, I request a formal reprimand of your munitions officer. He punched one of the men he was supposed to be training in small arms. Your base needs discipline.

Note From Individual Accused:

Commander, there's a vid on our truck's dashcam, Sarah turned it on remotely. The guy started chatting her up, then he tried groping her. Either I punched him or Sarah shot him, those were my choices here.

Kevin could practically see the shrug Lazarus would have made with the statement. He snorted. "Vintage Lazarus. Though I have to say, any man in this Sector who hasn't figured out that he should leave Sarah alone is probably overdue for a psychological evaluation. What are you going to do?"

Aidan shrugged. "I watched the dash-cam, and our guys were right. I'm going to send it to the Personnel officer over there, with a note saying that we'll just skip writing anybody on his base or mine up. And I'll tell Laz and Sarah that they're supposed to turn incidents with assholes in to me for reporting; when they beat jerks up we can't write them up formally. And a write-ups lasts longer than bruises."

Kevin nodded, amusement turning up the corners of his lips. "I do believe that might actually get through to them."

Aidan typed out the last notes, sent them, and shut down his system. Turning, he laid his hand on Kevin's knee.

"Vids?"

Kevin was still a little down when they curled up on the couch, so Aidan chose a series they both liked based out of New Zealand about the history of ancient cities. The international content was always interesting. And it was cool to be reminded that things were better than this, in other countries.

The film panned across the international goodwill excavation being done in the sunken city of New York, displaying vid clips from history beside the submerged excavations of the buildings as they were in the present. Halfway through the film, Kevin grimaced, closing his eyes. "Turn it off."

"Something wrong?" Aidan asked, stroking Kevin's hair back. Kevin's nose scrunched as he grimaced. "Take a good look at the man on the podium."

Aidan studied the vid. "Fat guy, sort of...orangey? What's up with him?"

"He was the President who took us on the first steps down the road to the Dissolution," Kevin grumbled. "So do me a favor and turn it off. I don't want to watch that bombastic poltroon rant tonight."

Aidan flicked the vid away. Kevin curled against him in silence. Aidan wrapped his arms around the other man, offering the comfort it looked like he needed.

"You want to put on something else?" He asked.

Kevin glanced up at him with a soft, sad smile. "If I say '*Hook*', what will you say?"

Aidan smirked. "I'll say 'oh please no, not again'."

"*RENT*, then?" Kevin asked wistfully. Aidan gave in, kissing his throat.

"*RENT* I can live with."

By the end of the film Kevin was smiling again, but there was still something in his body language that worried Aidan. He kissed his boyfriend's throat, the line of his jaw.

"You want something else, or...bed?"

Kevin turned his head, returning the kisses softly. "Bed sounds good," the redhead murmured against his skin.

Once they'd shut the door of their room, Aidan turned, brushing his hand over Kevin's cheek.

"Hey. You're kind of down. Can I help?"

Kevin sighed, looking away. "It's nothing. It's only...I'm just feeling a bit of an ass, and a little defeated. Nothing to worry about."

Aidan cupped his cheek, gently turning Kevin's face back to his.

"You don't let me drop things. You don't get to either," he murmured, brushing his lips over Kevin's. "Why're you feeling down?"

Kevin shrugged. "This mess with Tweak, mostly. I should have been more careful, sending her down there. I should have gone with her myself."

"Then who would've watched the security feeds and the area to make sure she didn't get nabbed?" Aidan asked quietly. Kevin dropped his eyes. His words came out haltingly.

"It isn't just that, it's...this is going to sound ridiculous, but...I didn't just get her shot, Aidan. I wrote her off. I put her down as a hassle, as a street kid with useful skills. I wrote her off in my mind as...as low class and unmanageable."

Aidan blinked. "And...that's bad?"

Kevin sighed. He pulled away, walking to sit on the bed. "Like I said, it sounds ridiculous," he remarked, the words stiff.

Aidan crossed the small room, the plastic floor creaking under his feet. Sitting beside his boyfriend, he put a hand on the other man's back. "So why does it hurt you?"

Kevin didn't look at him. His fingers tugged and pleated the hem of his jacket.

"Kev?" Aidan prompted quietly, unnerved by the silence.

When Kevin spoke, it was in a whisper. "I thought I'd overcome that trait. Every time I think I've gotten past this eugenic garbage in my head, it creeps back into my actions." He signed. "I... I'd thought I wasn't like that any longer. Classicist. Eugenicist. The type to write someone else off and categorize them as something less than fully... human." He drew a breath. "But I did act that way, with Tweak. I wrote her off as a gutter rat in my mind. I had no idea what she was dealing with, and I wrote her off." He swallowed. "How many other people have I treated that way, without realizing what I've done? How many others are out there with bodies ruined because my Corporation tried to perfect humanity?"

"Cavanaugh fucked up that last bit. Not you," Aidan suggested quietly.

Kevin shook his head, eyes squeezed closed. "My great great grandfather designed the beta project, Aidan. My great grandfather helped him make the international deals to implement it. Their ideas are the reason people like Tweak suffer and newborn babies are *thrown away* for being *aberrant.* I have a debt to pay. I *can't* act like them."

Aidan's heart flopped over at the pain in his boyfriend's voice. Gently, he leaned in, wrapping his arms around Kevin.

"You've probably acted like that to a couple people. And it'll probably happen again," he murmured. "But you care that you've done it. You try to fix it. And that's why your great-grandfather was an asshole and you're a good guy."

"Will I ever be good enough?" Kevin whispered. His words seemed to snag in his throat. "I've everything the Cavanaugh and Craydon families have done—generations of sins— on my shoulders. My hands are covered in blood... will I ever be able to atone for it?"

Aidan held him close, his head resting on Kevin's shoulder, giving his boyfriend an anchor in the storm. He knew how this stuff went. Telling Kevin he wasn't responsible for shit his ancestors did wouldn't sound true while he was feeling like this. But maybe something could get through.

Softly, he kissed Kevin's cheek, "Maybe you will. Work on it a little bit every day. That's what you do with the big problems, right? A little bit every day. And maybe just the trying's already making you better."

Kevin was still for a long time. Finally, he nodded.

"Maybe so." Turning his head, he kissed Aidan softly.

Aidan stroked his hair. "Can I do anything to help?"

"Hold me tonight?" Kevin asked, and his voice nearly broke Aidan's heart. "Help me feel like I'm...worth something?"

Aidan squeezed him tight. "Yeah. I can do that." he agreed. Kevin finally relaxed, leaning against him.

Aidan stroked his hair softly. "Question for you," he murmured, tracing the ridge of Kevin's ear. "When you said hold you, you want to snuggle, or do you want more tonight? I'm good with both."

Kevin chuckled, his voice still a little ragged. "Yes, yes you are," he murmured. Shifting, he shucked his jacket and set his glasses in their case, then leaned in to pull at Aidan's jacket collar while his lips found Aidan's again.

"I want your arms around me, and your body inside me. Help me let it all go tonight. Please."

"I can definitely do that," Aidan murmured. He tugged off his own jacket and dropped it, leaned in for another kiss. He stroked his hands down Kevin's sides.

Kevin's fingers tugged at the hem of his shirt, and Aidan let his boyfriend pull it off. He returned the favor. Skin to skin, they kissed for what felt like ages, Aidan making sure he had every bit of his boyfriend's attention. He wove his fingers between Kevin's as they kissed, the other hand rubbing the man's back in slow circles.

"Could we dispense with the pants?" Kevin asked softly. Aidan was happy to agree. Standing, he got out of his boots and pants, his boxers and packer. When he turned, Kevin was bare already, the covers pulled back. Aidan reached under the bed for his strap-on. He lifted it out of its box and got ready to put it in place, but Kevin's hands caught his.

"Let me put it on for you?" The other man asked softly. Looking at the sweet yearning in his face, Aidan couldn't help but smile. "Yeah, sure."

The prosthetic attached with a moment of pain and a sweet tingle of electricity as its thousands of tiny suction cups set against his skin and its sensors made a connection with the nerves in what Aidan had for a dick. Kevin's hands stroked over it, hot and gentle; a teasing invitation.

Aidan joined Kevin in the bed, stroking his hands over Kevin's gorgeous body.

"How about we spoon?" he whispered in Kevin's ear. Kevin smiled blissfully, and rolled to press his back to Aidan's chest. Aidan twined the fingers of one hand with Kevin's and used the other to trace

Kevin's long, lean body. His guy loved doing it like this; it'd be the perfect thing to get his mind off what was getting to him. Aidan followed the lines of Kevin's flanks up to his shoulders, brushing his collarbones with fingertips. Then he ran his hand downwards. He drew a spiral around Kevin's navel, traced his hipbones. Sliding his hand down, he ran his hand over Kevin's dick. The man was already hard.

Kissing his throat, Aidan teased the head of Kevin's erection, earning himself a gasp and a whimper. He left that alone and traced lower, sliding his hand down to cup Kevin's balls.

"You are worth something." he whispered in Kevin's ear, licking the ridge gently. "You're good already. And wanting to be better? I love you for that. But right now, just be good."

Kevin chuckled breathlessly. "Given where we are, there's quite the double-entendre in there."

Teasing was good. Teasing made the dark days easier. And if Kevin was up for teasing, Aidan wasn't going to drop the ball. "You want to talk about 'in there', hunh?" he murmured, kissing Kevin's throat as he traced his hand down the line of his spine. "We can do that."

Reaching down, he found that the strap-on had automatically lubed itself up as his excitement grew. He loved the features on this thing.

Slicking his fingers in lube with a stroke that sent a quick jolt through him, he laid his lips against the pulse point in Kevin's throat and slid a finger inside his boyfriend. Kevin gave a happy little whimper, leaning back against him.

"Aidan? Take me?"

Aidan's heart jumped. He would never get over the way Kevin wanted him, or how hot it was to be begged to top. But he was going to make this last tonight. If he could keep Kevin's body right on the edge, he could keep the man's heart out of the shadows.

"In a minute." Aidan whispered in his boyfriend's ear. "Not done with this yet."

The words made Kevin moan a little. Aidan slid a second finger into his entrance: teasing, soothing. Kevin panted, his pulse hot against

Aidan's lips. Crooking his fingers, Aidan stroked Kevin's prostate.

Kevin gave a little moan."Aidan… please?"

"Pretty soon," Aidan murmured, kissing Kevin's brow as he stroked. Kevin's fingers tightened in his. He'd gotten to know Kevin's body so well now. He loved knowing exactly what made Kevin go crazy.

Slowly, he slid the head of his dick inside his boyfriend. Kevin whimpered again. Aidan urged his long white leg back a bit, giving him better access and deepening the sensation for them both. Heat radiated through him, but the sight of Kevin was the real thrill. The man was utterly abandoned, head thrown back, eyes closed. Damn he was gorgeous.

Aidan lowered his hand between Kevin's legs, pressing the skin behind his balls with two fingers, and made his first thrust as slowly as he could.

Kevin groaned in his arms. Aidan held himself in the heat for a heartbeat. Then he withdrew, sliding back. He teased Kevin's balls. His boyfriend's white back arched against him. Aidan slid in again as slowly as he could bear, fingers back on the soft, hot skin above Kevin's prostate.

"Aidan… Aidan please..." Kevin begged in a whisper. Aidan quieted him with a kiss as he thrust.

"You said remind you that you're worth something? All night, Kev. I'll do this all night."

"You do this all night and I'll lose my mind," Kevin panted. Aidan chuckled. "Good."

He kept his thrusts as slow as humanly possible, moving inch by inch. The heat was wonderful. The throb of a first, slow orgasm blossomed in him, and he nearly closed his eyes. But he wanted to see this.

Kevin was right on the edge. Aidan watched the gorgeous man's body as he made another slow thrust, watched the way he'd started to shiver. His dick was bright pink and twitching, the tip leaking.

Perfect.

Kevin's free hand reached out, grabbed Aidan's and pressed it to his dick.

"Please!" he gasped out. Aidan loved it when he sounded like that; absolutely honest and completely out of control.

Leaning in, he stole a last kiss. "Now?"

"Now!" Kevin begged. Aidan's own body was on fire.

"Okay. Now."

He stroked Kevin and thrust himself inside the man, hard and sure. Kevin clutched at the pillow with one hand, burying his face in the fabric as he cried out. Aidan grinned as Kevin's body clenched around him, and his own second orgasm hit hard and fast. Kevin's dick throbbed in his hand as it emptied.

Aidan milked every last drop of pleasure out of himself and Kevin both, going until they were both exhausted. Finally, he rested his head against Kevin's and they lay, breathing together.

"My God..." Kevin whispered.

Aidan chuckled. "Glad you had fun. Let's get cleaned up before you fall asleep."

"Mm..." Kevin agreed weakly.

They cleaned themselves and one another up quietly, crawling into bed together. Aidan snuggled up close to his gorgeous guy, holding him close.

"Kev?" Aidan asked softly.

Kevin turned his head a little, though he didn't open his eyes. "Mm?"

"You're worth it to me." Aidan whispered, kissing his throat.

Kevin let out a satisfied little murmur, smiling as he fell asleep.

Event File 10
File Tag: Fit For Duty
Timestamp: 21:30-5-9-2156

"You're sure you're okay?" Billie asked warily.

In the privacy of their room, Tweak rolled her eyes, dropped her packed bag and jumped up and down a few times. "Leg's fine! I'm fine. Sat too long. Been three weeks. Wanna go!"

Billie glanced away, biting her lip. Tweak cocked her head. Billie did that when she was upset.

"Billie. What?"

Billie stole a glance at her, then flicked her eyes away. She sat on her bed, hugging herself.

Tweak hopped onto the edge of the bed. "What?" she repeated. "You okay? You look freaked. How come?"

Billie lowered her head. "Tweak. You didn't see yourself in that bed. If you get shot again, I...I don't think you'll make it."

Tweak blinked. She'd been so busy being scared herself, then getting work done, that she hadn't noticed Billie getting scared. She let out a sharp sigh.

"Shit. Sorry. Missed that you were freaked."

Billie glanced at her, smiling a little 'S'okay. But I am scared. Aren't you?"

Tweak shook her head, slapping her hair back when it got in her face. "Nope. Was before. Not now."

Billie raised her head. Her pretty chocolate eyes were one of the only pairs that didn't make Tweak's stomach turn over when she held them. She gave her buddy a smile. "I'm gonna type. Kay?"

"Kay." Billie agreed with a quivery little smile.

Pulling out her personal tab, Tweak typed her thoughts out for her friend.

> "I'm not scared, because last time shit did hit the fan. And the guys totally had my back. They said they would, and they did. I mean yeah, I got shot, and that fucking HURTS, and I don't want it to happen again, for sure. They fucked up the blood thing, but I thought about it. I didn't tell them a lot, so I guess that's on me. Basically the guys got me covered, got me fixed up, and the most shit I got was for hiding it from Damian. Nobody gave a shit that I'm gamma."

She glanced at Billie and grinned as she typed.

> "They kept their promise, B. They really did. Nobody's ever done that but you, before."

Billie read the message carefully, before raising her eyes to Tweak's again. "Okay but...if I...I'm scared for you." She was, too. She was shaking.

Tweak bit her lip. "Yeah. You wanna run Psych with m-me?"

Billie nodded.

Tweak reached for her tab and ran her thumb over the surface, putting in two passwords. A rolling ball of colors flared up out of the tab.

The young anime punk gave them a wave when he appeared, long green hair flopping over one eye. "Hey girls. You want to talk as a group today, or one-on-one?"

"Group." Tweak replied easily. The hologram nodded. "So what's up? Billie, I'm getting some hot readings off you. You want to talk about it?"

Billie swallowed. "Tweak's going somewhere dangerous again, and I'm scared."

Tweak nodded, feeling a lump forming in her own throat. "Yeah. I'm a little s-scared too."

The holographic teen nodded. "I get that. Fact is, if you guys weren't scared I'd worry about you. You know why we've got fear?"

"Cause it tells us something's bad," Billie murmured, staring at her hands. The program nodded. "Got it. Fear preps you. It keeps you sharp, and that keeps you alive. It's kinda like a big dog on a leash though; it can protect you, but it can wreck your place too. I want you guys to keep the dog. Your fear isn't a bad thing. But we're going to work on training it so it doesn't piss all over the house, okay?"

Tweak grinned crookedly at the image. "Okay."

Psych smiled. "Let's try this." A four-spoked wheel appeared beside Psych's head. He gestured at it, and the top right quadrant glowed. "Think of this. In here're your five senses, right? All the stuff your outsides are telling your brain." He moved to the next quadrant. It lit up at his touch. "In here's everything the inside of your body is saying. All those gut things and muscle spasms and stuff." The third quadrant glowed. "Here's what your brain's telling itself; all your feelings and stuff." The last quadrant lit up. "And this is your relationships with other people. So, four sections and a hub. You guys have wheels inside, too. Thing is, wheels have hubs. If you close your eyes, I bet you can picture yourself sitting in the hub. None of the stuff in the wheel can mess with the hub. Picture yourself sitting there."

Tweak closed her eyes. Psych's voice eased into something neutral, calming. "Picture your five senses quadrant. Ask yourself what you're feeling. Put it in the wheel."

Time passed. Psych spoke. Tweak filled in her wheel, trying hard to keep her mind on it. Her brain wanted to go over the mission, to think through plans, to jump to a bunch of stuff. But she was going to learn to focus on what she wanted, and not what her crazy brain wanted, if it killed her.

"If there's a problem, that section's going to be kind of rough looking. You got a spot that's hot, Billie?"

"The people one?" Billie suggested quietly. "I'm scared about Tweak. And the inside-me one. My stomach hurts and I'm shaky."

"Yeah, and that's no fun. But those are things in the wheel. You're in the hub. Where it's safe." Psych's soothing voice continued. "Okay. Now, imagine one spoke in the wheel. It's pointing at the hot spot. But you're on the hub. You can move the spoke. So let's move it to breathing. Move the spoke off of what's hot and onto your breathing. Feel your breath going in. Going out. Slow. And easy. Breathing in. Breathing out. Let's do that for a couple minutes."

Tweak felt like she was floating by the time Psych said, "You guys can do this on your own, any time you need to get your heads straight. Picture the wheel, get into the hub, and look at what's going on from there. Move the spoke if you need to. We'll try it again next week, kay?"

"Kay." Tweak agreed, opening her eyes. The cute hologram smiled. "Kay. Billie? How you doing?"

Billie smiled. "Pretty good. Thanks Psych."

"No prob. You ladies done?" Psych asked. Tweak smiled. She'd done good on this thing, on top of the guy who'd done the base coding. "We're good. Seeya, Psych."

"Seeya."

The hologram fizzled into shards of light, fading away.

Billie turned to her on the bed. "See you by when?"

"Tomorrow. We think." Tweak replied, nodding at her tab. "Schedule. Lookit."

Billie glanced at the tab, her lips moving as she read.

"Kay. Send me a copy?"

"Yep."

Billie bit her lip. "If you're sure..."

Tweak nodded. "Sure."

Billie smiled. Putting her hands out at her sides, she spread her fingers. Tweak reached out and touched her fingertips to Billie's, the closest thing to a hug that was comfortable for her. Her fingertips fizzed.

"Not getting shot again," she reassured.

Billie smiled weakly. "Better not. Be safe, 'kay?"

"Kay." Tweak chirped with a quick, sharp grin. "Be great; kick ass!"

Billie gave a quiet laugh. "Yeah you will. Okay, go."

Half an hour later, she was climbing into the back of a truck. Topher and Kevin were already settled in, ready to go. Kevin glanced up, gave her a quick nod and a smile, then turned his eyes back to whatever he was reading. He sang something old and weird under his breath, but he didn't say anything. Tweak was cool with that. They'd done major talking in the last three weeks, working out planning and details. Quiet was okay right now.

In her mind, Tweak ran through their prep work. Two weeks with her leg up had been a perfect time to get a couple batches of the zombie accounts up and start their Wipeout virus spreading throughout the Net. She'd run a ton of stress tests on the systems and had used that information to query Regional. The big boys had sent a handful of bases on small missions to deliver the virus to all sorts of accessible ports. If it spread the way she wanted by next week, she'd test a small-scale DDOS attack and see how it worked. The week after that, she could export the trick to the other bases and have them try it out.

She fingered the gun in her pocket, the smooth plastic warm under her hand. The week she'd been cleared to move around again, Kevin and Lazarus had started drilling her like crazy on using hardware: guns and all kinds of stuff. It'd been kind of fun. She knew fighting with her fists, but guns were new.

Everything was working out. Everything made sense.

Everything but that drone.

"K-kevin?" she asked. The man glanced up from his tab. "Hm?"

"The drone," Tweak stated. "The one that s-shot me. How'd that hunter know where to l-look for us?"

Kevin met her eyes levelly. "You're wondering that too, are you?"

Tweak nodded. "L-luck, maybe. But still."

"Still," Kevin agreed quietly, staring out the window. "I've been checking up on my own contacts, wondering whether we were informed on. I don't have anything there so far. But I'll keep looking."

"I l-looked ar-round online. Just n-normal hunter chatter," Tweak replied, making every word she used count. She didn't have time for her throat to seize up right now. "'Cept, you know. It was right there. On top of us. And r-ready for our IR trick. Bad news."

At the wheel, Topher glanced back at them. "We're okay today, right?"

Kevin glanced his way, smiled and nodded. "For now, we're just fine. We're just keeping ourselves on our toes."

He was always trying to make Topher feel good. She'd noticed that.

"We need more intel," she repeated. "Need to know more."

Kevin glanced at her, and smirked. "And here I thought that was my line."

Tweak glared at him. "Ass."

That smirk from him, again. "Hee-haw."

She sighed, pulled out her tab and put in her headphones. The conversation was too much work.

Two hours later, they were standing in the maintenance room, studying the hatch that would let them down into the tunnels.

"I'll be watching your back and keeping an eye on all security from an empty apartment just down the block," Kevin murmured, repeating what they'd already agreed on. "This time you'll have ample warning if you're being approached. Instead of running, you—"

"Wrap myself in the s-slick poncho and hold s-still," Tweak repeated, bouncing on her toes. "C'mon! I know the stuff. I hacked the cams. You got my back. Let me get this d-done!"

Kevin eyed her long enough that she had to glance away. There was the sound of the hatch opening.

"Be careful, Tweak. We can't afford to lose you."

The words did something funny in her head, flopping around her thoughts like her favorite cozy sweatshirt. Glancing up, she shot Kevin a grin. "Damn right you c-can't."

Then she grabbed the first rung of the ladder and swung herself down.

The maintenance tunnel's air wrapped around her; a hot, stinking blanket. Quiet, she headed down the tunnels, double checking the map on her tab. She ignored the cameras over her head; she'd taken care of those before they'd gotten to the maintenance room.

She found the junction where she'd worked before. The fiber-op bundle was still right there, inviting as an open door. The fiberoptic nano-clamps snicked into place.

Tweak dropped cross-legged to the floor. She brought up one screen showing the reads on every device Kevin had put in throughout the tunnels, setting it on her right. She opened the slick-poncho and set it at her right hand. The gun, her water-bottle, snacks and the EMP device she set on her left.

Then she got to work.

Five minutes later, the EagleCorp authorization page popped up, and Tweak started working her way through the defenses. The tunnel, the smells, and the heat faded away. The world was made of code and puzzles.

Four hours later, a folder stuffed with files popped up on her screen. She did a silent dance of victory, punching the air with both hands. She'd landed the files. She'd actually landed the files. *Fuck* yes!

But she still had to get them out of here. Pulling her gear together and stowing it in her pockets, she pattered down the hall.

Kevin followed the plan when she knocked on the apartment door, opening it just a crack. She knew he'd have an EMP ready in his other hand, in case the answer she gave to whatever he used for a question wasn't right.

"Afternoon," the redhead quipped, "When was the first time we had a conversation in which you didn't insult me?"

She rolled her eyes. "The hailstorm. Asshat. Lemme in."

Kevin closed and locked the door before he turned to her, the question written all over his face. "So, how did it go?"

Tweak finally let the excitement that had been bubbling in her gut come rushing up. She bounced in the air, her whole body lit up with the feeling. "I did it I did it I did it I did it! I got the f-files! All k-kinds of b-buildings, all the l-locations, all the p-plans, everywhere in the c-country! I did it!"

Kevin grinned at her, watching her bounce. "Good Lord and all His Hosts, I see that you did! Bring the volume down just a notch, all right? I've got sound-boxes around, but still."

He was probably right, she was probably making a lot of noise. She stopped bouncing, but there was nothing on the planet that could make her stop grinning right now. "Kev. I did it. I hacked Eagle! I kicked their ass!"

Kevin nodded. "I know you did. In fact, I knew you would. We just had to get you the chance."

Again that funny, fuzzy feeling wrapped her insides up, making her glance down as Kevin talked.

"We'll have dinner and sleep here tonight. In the morning we'll head home and start playing with these lovely new toys. Anything you want to do to pass the time?"

Tweak scratched at her arms. "Get these sleeves off. They itch. Check my chat with the other c-coders on the other bases."

"That conversation will have to wait until we're home; it's too much of a risk on EagleCorp land," Kevin replied.

Tweak sighed. "I'm connecting with a VPN, I'm going through a tor and I can go past the Corps routing points and b-bounce off a couple international nodes, *genius*." Did the guy think she was an idiot?

Kevin blinked. "You can get around the routing nodes?"

Surprised, Tweak met his eyes for a second. "Wait, you don't do that? Are you *crazy*?"

"Apparently I'm ignorant," Kevin replied with a small, cockeyed smile. "Will you show me?"

Tweak studied his face for a moment. But she couldn't see a lie. Eventually, she shrugged.

"Sure. Come sit."

It took a little time, but she got the guy straight on his signaling methods while she was scrolling around. Finally, she opened her own secure messages.

Then she froze.

"Tweak? You look as if someone's walked over your grave," Kevin remarked quietly. "What's going on?"

"Something b-bad," Tweak stated. She pointed at her screen. "See this?"

She ran her finger over the screen, highlighting it. Kevin leaned in to read.

Instead of text, somebody with the screen handle of 'Sednaschild' had sent over a screenshot of a packet. Most of it was coded coordinates and instructions for what the computer should do with it, but at the very bottom, in plain script, were the words 'package en route'.

"See these d-dates?" Tweak asked, her mouth a little dry.

"I can't read code that well. When was this?" Kevin asked. She could feel his eyes on her. She kept her focus on the screen.

"This's l-like half an hour before we left the g-grid last time. When I got s-shot. S-Somebody took time and coordinate data, and encoded it, s-s-sent it out to a hunter with a d-drone. S-s-somebody was t-telling a b-b-bounty hunter to d-do stuff, on our n-networks. Right before shit got r-real."

Kevin was silent for a long time. Too long. Long enough that she turned and looked at him. He was sitting still as a statue.

When he finally spoke, his voice was quiet, and it made Tweak's scales shiver under her shirt.

"So. We might have a traitor on our hands. Lovely."

Sitting back in his chair, Aidan glanced between the two genetically tailored people in front of him. Both incredibly smart—a lot smarter than him, that was for sure—and both looking freaked.

And both of them sure that the other was wrong. Again. They'd been at this since they got home two days ago, and it was really, really getting old.

"Don't d-do it!" Tweak repeated for the fifth time. She stamped her little foot. "Don't fucking d-do it!"

Kevin crossed his arms. Watching his body language made Aidan tense. Kevin was hanging onto his temper by his fingernails. It wasn't that easy to see, but he knew the signs by now.

"Tweak, you are being insufferably histrionic," Kevin stated coldly. "We can't refuse to send mission pertinent information to base commanders because you have a bad feeling about a packet of code. People are waiting on us!"

Aidan had to fight down the nervous urge to glance at the clock. He took a slow breath.

Tweak's boot slammed against the grey plastic floor. "People! People gonna die! You w-want them to d-die?!"

Aidan could feel his chest tightening. They both had good points. Neither of them were completely wrong, which made deciding a hell of a lot harder.

He just wished they would quit arguing. The noise made it hard to think.

"Of course I don't want anyone to die," Kevin snapped, "but we have to share information when we're engaged in a collaborative mission, and—"

"And if it's one of them?" Tweak demanded.

Kevin's mouth set in a thin line. "You're talking about base Commanders, if we can't trust our Commanders then—"

"Then we're n-not fucking s-stupid, or d-d-dead!"

"Guys!"

Finally, silence. Tweak and Kevin both turned to stare at him, startled. He sat back in his chair, holding their eyes.

"Tweak. You're worried in case this intel is leaked and used against us. Right?"

Tweak bobbed her head, glaring at Kevin. He pointedly didn't look in her direction.

Aidan turned to him. "Kev, you're thinking that we already wasted a lot of time and that the other bases are waiting on us, right? You feel like waiting is going to lose us our opportunity to pull this off?"

"Precisely," Kevin agreed, biting off the end of the word.

Aidan drew two long, slow breaths. "Okay. Then this is what we're going to do. I'm going to tell the other Commanders that we've got the intel and it's in the process of being vetted by Regional." He turned in his chair. "Tweak, make me something fake about where our people are going to be, twelve days from now. I'm going to get ahold of Commander Hall privately and tell her what I'm worried about. And we're going to sit on this for two weeks. We'll focus on getting the zombie accounts raised and making sure the virus is spreading. If nothing else weird happens and our fake intel doesn't turn up anywhere in those two weeks, we'll assume that what we saw was just coincidence and go on with the next steps. How does that sound to you guys?"

There was a heartbeat when nobody moved. Then Kevin's shoulders relaxed.

"Could you bring up a calendar, Aidan?" The other man asked.

Aidan tapped his work station, and a new screen with a calendar came into being. His system's fan whirred a complaint.

Kevin added a red dot to the date, and another red dot fourteen days out. "Right. If we all track suspicious information for this period, we'll not be too far behind the times, and we'll be comfortable in our assumption of security going forward." He glanced over his shoulder at Tweak. "I'm amenable if you are."

Tweak shrugged, crossing her arms. After a moment, she nodded. "I'm cool with it, I guess. I'll make some trawling b-bots to track the b-bait. We'll see where it comes up."

Aidan nodded. "Okay, that's our plan. I'll pass it on."

Nobody was thrilled with a two-week wait. Hall's reply message could be boiled down to 'thanks for being careful, but the clock's ticking.' When Aidan gave the other Commanders the news, Anderson took his hat off and slapped it against his chair.

"Shit! Vetting for two weeks? What the fuck for?"

Aidan shrugged. "Security," he stated simply. "Better safe than dead."

"He has a point," Seattle agreed quietly, though their face was blank. "Why the sudden security worries? You seen something down there?"

Anxiety crackled through Aidan's mind. What if Tweak was right and one of these three was the leak? Was he showing their hand to the enemy?

Or was he leaving valuable allies in the dark?

He wet his dry mouth. "You're not the only one who's had some mimic scares," he remarked, nodding at Hagge. "And our hacker's the really fixated type. Either I let her vet intel all the way and check it with Regional, or she makes my life hell around the base."

"Your hacker and her time off's the reason we put things off this long." Anderson grumbled.

Aidan fixed the older commander with a look. "My hacker was on bed rest recovering from a life threatening injury. I told her to stay in bed that long. She wanted to work sooner."

The little man grunted, looking away. Aidan glanced at the other Commanders. "My team sat down with the calendar and really looked at things; we're still in good shape. We'll have our area tested with a small virus attack by the week of the third. My people will use that as a distraction to go plant the EMPs in our nearest station; it's close to us. After that, I guess we'll just have to see."

"Wait and see," Anderson sneered irritably. He sighed. Then, finally, he put his hat back on. "Well all right, then I guess we 'wait and see.'"

His image flicked out.

Aidan didn't have the stomach for lunch. He headed to his room instead, typing in five passwords, and watched as the multicolored ball of holographic light spun while his psychological wellness coaching program loaded.

"Good afternoon, Aidan." the program stated quietly. "You seem emotionally depleted. Have you been dealing with something difficult?"

"Yeah," Aidan agreed, "trying to make everybody happy and remembering it's impossible. Again."

The hologram that looked like his baby sister pretended to sit on the edge of the bed, bringing one leg up in a half-cross-legged position. "That sounds exhausting. Tell me about it?"

Aidan sighed. Closing his eyes, he laid out the situation piece by piece for his AI program.

"So if Tweak's right, I probably just handed information over that could get somebody killed. If Kevin and Commander Hall are right, I'm wasting time. And I don't know who the hell is right anymore."

"You are in a complicated situation," the psychological health program stated quietly. "It's better to think of things in other terms than 'right' and 'wrong.' What would be a better way to frame the situation?"

"Cost-benefit analysis, I guess," Aidan muttered. Omi had told him this before. Don't think about right and wrong, it never went to good places. Think about costs and benefits.

"So the cost is time," he continued, doing his best to stick with the exercise. "And time could mean more danger down the road, when the Corps aren't as distracted with protests and stuff brought out by the Folder and they'll notice what we're doing more easily. The benefit's making sure that we're secure, and everyone is about as safe as we're going to be when we do this."

"That sounds like a worthwhile trade." Omi murmured, the program's blonde hair swinging down in a nearly-real way as she tipped her head. Aidan tried for a smile. "I guess. But we're losing cover, and that's...not...wait." He sat up, the idea fizzing in his head. "Wait, we don't have to lose cover! Sorry Omi, go to standby, I'll catch up with you in a second okay?"

"Of course." The hologram smiled, and fizzed out. Aidan jumped off his bed and hurried down to his office. Getting on his work machine again, he typed in his passwords and let the system read his retina. Then he sent his message to Commander Hall.

Message Handle: AceOfSpades

Message Authenticated

Message: Commander, I know what to do to balance the time we've lost. Can we reach out to our contacts in the Grapevine? If we can get a big protest organized in two months to work with everything else we're doing, we'll still have that element of distraction we need to keep us covered. If you think the Grapevine will go for it, we'll definitely be ready for our stuff in two months.

He stared at the message for a moment. Fingers shaking, he typed the last words. If they can pull together the manpower, I can guarantee that we'll get our project to work in time with theirs.

He was shivering with nerves by the time he got back to his quarters, his hands shoved deep in his pockets to hide the shakes.

"Okay Omi," he said aloud, and the program's hologram faded back to visible. Omi smiled.

"I take it that you found a solution?"

"Either I did, or I just made a promise I can't deliver on." He sighed, resting his head against the wall. "Either way, I guess we'll find out. I started it, but right now I've got to see where the pieces fall. For now I guess it's out of my hands."

"That is a very realistic way to see the situation. I'm glad to hear you taking it so calmly."

Aidan chuckled. "I don't know if this's 'calm', Omi. It's just…it's this or go crazy thinking about all the things that could go wrong."

"And knowing that fact is sanity," Omi stated. Aidan couldn't argue with that.

<u>Event File 12</u>
<u>File Tag: Catastrophic Damage</u>
<u>Timestamp: 9:00-5-27-2156</u>

Aidan glanced between the two munitions people, the technical specialist and the logistics people. After two long weeks, everything was in place. Tweak's virus was everywhere it needed to be. The Grapevine was organizing a massive rally, and the Corps were busy sniffing after them. Now all they had to do was get the EMP bombs in place and they were good to go in the West. Pretty soon they could mark this off as a verified technique, send it out, sit back and relax. Aidan was really looking forward to that.

"Okay, so you guys are set?"

Lazarus kicked the packed bag by his foot. "All good to go!"

"Said the Charge of the Light Brigade," Kevin added sardonically. Aidan shot him a sidelong, half-warning smile. His weird little jokes out of history were fun when they had time to relax and Kevin explained what he meant, but there was no time today.

"Let's get serious, guys. Run through your mission plan one more time with me before you head out, okay? Tweak's setting off a small-scale DDOS attack at nineteen-hundred."

"Yep," Tweak agreed. "M-most people gone h-home. Traffic's l-lower. Easier for it to get m-missed for a couple hours by m-most people, but it'll freak the people on call and pull them away from their dinners. Keep them messing with that, they won't n-notice me re-routing the security cameras at the b-backup facility. I got into their internal work shift c-calendar and m-messed with it, made it look like somebody else was on shift for all the guards and the n-night cleaning crew at the b-backup center." she splayed her hands in a 'nothing to see here' gesture. "No guards. Some patrol drones, but you guys g-got c-copies of the cleaning crew's pass cards. They w-won't fire on those."

"Sarah and Lazarus enter at twenty-one-hundred and get to work setting and concealing the EMP bombs," Kevin continued, "while I act as external eyes. Yve stays here and runs routine requisitions, acting as my locum and designated survivor."

"I hate it when you say designated survivor. You don't get to get yourselves killed and leave me with the paperwork," Yvonne put in. She glanced between officer and commander, giving them a smile that took most of the bite out of the words.

"Anyway, we ought to be done by the witching hour," Kevin continued, "and after that we're home free and ready to watch the fireworks in another few weeks."

"What the hell's the witching hour?" Sarah laughed.

Kevin gave her one of his haughty looks. "It's midnight, Sarah. Come on, I know you've read at least one book in your life."

"Yeah, and it wasn't written by somebody who's been dead three hundred years."

"Your loss, I'm sure."

Aidan chuckled. "Okay guys. Just be careful out there. Don't get to razzing each other and end up coming home full of holes. You'll piss Damian off." *Or you won't come home at all,* his mind whispered. He did his best to step on that thought.

Lazarus lifted his bag with one hand and flipped a lazy salute with the other. "Sounds good, can we head out?"

Aidan nodded. "Go for it. Keep your heads down."

Kevin stood, smiled, and leaned in to brush his lips across

Aidan's. "For luck," he murmured.

The easy beauty of the gesture made Aidan's heart turn over. "Luck." he whispered.

"Awwww!" Yvonne, Lazarus and Sarah chorused from the doorway. Lazarus mimed fluttering eyelashes and a swoon into Sarah's arms. Yvonne grinned like a loon, as if she hadn't just been kissing Sarah.

Kevin turned his eyes to the ceiling. "Don't worry about the Corps, love. *I* may be the one who kills these two chuckleheads before we're done."

"Dream on, geek-boy," Sarah retorted from the door. Kevin sighed. "Once more into the breach we go, we band of blockheads. See you."

"See you guys." Aidan murmured, smiling.

Tweak watched the team troop out with raised brows.

"Why do they do that?" she asked, staring at the doorway they'd left through. "Get w-weird and say they're gonna k-kill each other before all the m-missions?"

Aidan shrugged, his lips still tipped in a smile and tingling with Kevin's touch. "It's how they handle nerves before missions. All that goofing around and teasing lets them stay relaxed, so they don't tense up and get so scared that it messes with them. It's a good trick, I do it too sometimes. I'm just not as loud." He shrugged. "It gets your mind off stuff."

Tweak studied him for a moment. Then she shrugged. "Whatevs. If it works. Can I go?"

"Sure," Aidan agreed, "message me if anything comes up."

Tweak almost managed a salute as she headed out the door.

Aidan had plenty to do while he waited: there might be a big mission on their plate, but the world didn't stop turning because of it. He ran over and approved Blake's financial statements for the base, checked Janice's maintenance report for the month and her expenditures. Feeding the plants and getting soil for them to go into the mobile beds was costing less than he'd expected. He checked off the motor pool's reports, sending everything to the right Regional officers who kept everyone straight on the supplies each base got and what they needed to requisition as a whole.

He ran through other base's mission reports, noting with interest a pretty cool idea from up north that let their people get ahold of the designs to print their own pain-killing nanoids and a couple of anti-inflammatory medications. Grinning, he filed the plans they'd been sent into the accessible part of Damian's database. Being able to make some of their own medical stuff out of easy-to-get chemicals was going to make life easier.

Other reports slid through his screens: this base getting refugees to safety here, that one stealing files to out a corrupt plant operator there. The Maple Leaf Trail was doing great, people in danger of death under their Corporation being handed off from team to team as they made their way to Canada and a claim of humanitarian asylum. The Grapevine was at work getting people moved South, across that awful expanse of the Mex desert and down into the lush green lands of the Republic SudAmerica where they valued farmers and free speech.

Days like this were the good days, when he felt like a part of something meaningful: it seemed like everywhere something was being done to make somebody's life that little bit better.

He barely noticed time passing, until feet clattered in the hall and a high voice called his name. Turning in his chair, he blinked at Tommy, standing flanked by Dilly and Donny. Dilly was giving her classic disapproving look, and he wondered for a moment what kick she was on this time.

"Um...hey guys," he remarked after a second.

"Mom wants to know, should she put a plate together for you or are you coming to dinner." Tommy stated. He was way too old for his years, solemn and polite. The twins apparently thought the same thing: the two thirteen-year-olds rolled their eyes behind their younger buddy's back.

"You're not supposed to skip meals," Donny stated, fixing Aidan with one of his disapproving stares. Dilly nodded emphatically, backing her brother up.

"Damian says," she added pointedly.

Aidan couldn't help but smile at the kids, so insistent on taking care of their elders.

He glanced at the clock on his screen as he stood. 19:20.

"If Tweak isn't at dinner, how about you bring two plates to the code room, okay? Tweak and me are working on a lot of stuff, and it's—"

Behind him, his system blared with a drone proximity alarm. There was a high shout down the hall. Heart hammering, Aidan looked out. Tweak was barreling down the hallway, her voice high and panicked.

"Fuck! Fuck! D-d-drones! C-coming! Get down, get—"

The first explosion knocked Aidan to his knees. Donny gave the high yelp of a scared kid. Grabbing the twins and reaching out to yank Tommy close, Aidan pulled them down and did his best to cover them as the ceiling overhead groaned. Another blast rattled the world. Darkness came raining down, lanced through with pain.

<u>Event File 13</u>
<u>File Tag: Mission Failure</u>
<u>Timestamp:1:00-5-28-2156</u>

"How's it looking? Kevin asked, watching his friends through one holographic screen as the others showed him the surroundings and the halls of the Broomfield facility through hacked cameras.

"Looks great!" Sarah chirped in reply, swaggering down the hall beside Lazarus. The two munitions people were cocky with ease: they'd already run their check on the building, and they knew they had the place to themselves. Kevin wasn't exactly thrilled with that attitude.

He shifted his seat in the chair of the vacant office down the block.

"We may not see anything particularly concerning yet, but let's not get slapdash, shall we?"

He watched Sarah roll her eyes in the camera, listening to her dismissive laugh. "Jeez Kev, chill. This's no big deal."

"That's what Marie Antoinette said, right before the revolution."

"Will you quit?"

Kevin smirked. "You first?"

"Geek," Sarah snorted as they passed a security drone, both she and Lazarus pointing their weapons at it until it had passed. It was a good thing the security drones were simple things, designed only to look for heat signatures and credentials. Shoot if one was present without the other, that was their guiding principal. All the same, the fact that they'd blocked the drones' ability to set off the building's alarms or call human security forces days ahead of time let Kevin breathe a little easier.

Then his family was into the main server room. Kevin allowed himself a cautious sense of pleasure. So far, so good.

He checked over the exterior cameras and his own visual through the office window. Yes, they were in good shape.

In his feed, Lazarus unslung his pack full of EMP bombs and passed three to Sarah. Kevin watched as they set to work placing the hemispheres, opening small maintenance hatches and pressing the devices to the innards. Around them, drones floated like jellyfish, placid and deadly.

Kevin watched as Lazarus bumped his head on the underside of one server, chuckling quietly.

"Careful there, champ."

"Bite me, dude."

"Oh my, and here I thought you didn't bat for my team."

"Ooh, look who finally figured out sexy snark! Aidan's good for you, Kev." Sarah chuckled. Lazarus glanced at the camera with his famous cocky grin, flipping him off. Kevin laughed, watching him.

Watching the drone behind him stop moving. And pivot.

"Lazarus! Drone!" Kevin shouted into his mic. "Get—"

The impact of the bullet knocked Lazarus to his belly. Four more shots zinged over his head.

"Shit!" Kevin yelped, every muscle in his body tensed into whipcord. "Sarah! Set off the EMPs manually!"

Sarah slapped feverishly at the EMP in her hand, setting off its ten minute standing wave. The drone that fired crashed to the floor in a lifeless heap. The nearest server's lights burned themselves out. Thank God their own tech had lead foil lining for times like this, Kevin thought as he frantically checked camera feeds.

"More on the way! Sarah! There's six more headed for you!" He snapped into the mic, watching the drones speed down hallways in the camera feed.

Feverishly, Sarah activated EMPs and lobbed them towards the doors, until a barrier of dead drones lined each one. Dead servers stood like tombstones around the room.

"Scatter more behind you as you go, I'll set them off remotely," Kevin added. He watched Sarah nod as she bent over Lazarus.

"Laz!" He called into his microphone. "Lazarus! LAZARUS!"

"Fuck...man, don't yell," his best friend's voice groaned in his ear.

Kevin's body sagged in relief. "Oh thank you Lord. Sarah, how is it? You've got ten minutes. Laz? Laz, can you move?"

"Stupid question, dude." Lazarus's voice husked in his ear, the hint of a laugh hidden somewhere in it.

"It's not great," Sarah added. "Bullet went through his back, under his ribs. There's a lot of blood."

"Shit," Kevin hissed. "You have the nanoid foam, right?"

Sarah glanced up at the camera with helpless eyes. "Kev, it was in our fanny packs. The EMPs probably hit it."

Kevin ran both hands through his hair in frustration, his thoughts racing. "Do it anyway. The chemical component will still expand, fill the wound and stop the bleeding. We'll do the rest later. Move!"

"Roger," Sarah agreed, moving quick and sure now she had her orders. She pulled out and shook the pink tube, sliding it into the wound. Lazarus spat a long series of curses.

"Fuuuck!"

"Curse later, move now." Kevin snapped. "I'll stay here and watch your backs until you're out, set off the EMPs remotely. Right now, get to the doors. You need to get up and *move*! Now!"

"I'm moving, I'm moving." Lazarus sounded as if he wanted to joke, but his voice was tight with pain.

He pushed himself to his hands and knees with a cry, then to his feet, Sarah under his arm.

Together, they stumbled down the hall, Sarah dropping EMPs behind her. Kevin set them off in sequence. Drones crashed down behind his family.

Twenty feet to the door.

Fifteen.

"Come on guys. Come *on,*" he gritted between his teeth.

There. They were out. They were in the street.

Slapping the power button on his tab and shoving it into his pocket, he bolted from the room.

Lazarus gave him a pained smile when he pushed his shoulder under the man's other side. "Okay, little...little harder than we thought?"

"Just a touch." Kevin agreed with a bleak smile of his own. "Let's get you in our ride, before..."

The high whine in the air made him look up, and his stomach fell down into his boots.

Kevin had seen a locust storm once, eating away at a field of engineered corn that killed them as they chewed. The rising drones looked like those locusts.

Dropping to the pavement, he yanked out a slick poncho, spread it over them, and prayed.

Eventually, the whir of whining rotors passed. Kevin breathed again.

Slowly, he brought out his tab and pulled up his tracking program. The drones hadn't stayed in the area. That was a relief, though where they'd gone was another fear. He set it aside in favor of the more immediate worry.

"Right, up we get," he whispered. "Count of three. One...two..."

Lazarus cried out when they stood, and the sound froze Kevin's blood. The man needed help, and he needed it now. But they were far out of reach of any safe contact, and Denver proper would be crawling with people and tech that wouldn't miss a wounded man being shuffled along.

"We're going to have to make a run for home," Kevin muttered. "It won't be too hard. We'll take the car back to the garage, tie you onto one of the bikes and...no that'll never work. Right. We'll grab a bottle of booze. Laz, you'll need to be drunk for this charade to work. The other passengers can't see obvious signs of pain. We'll take the bus out to the outskirts of town, one of the cheap spots. We're using credentials that'll allow it. We'll call Topher, he'll pick us up from there. It's a risk but we'll have to take it this time. Yes, that'll do. Won't take long."

Lazarus nodded weakly. "Just don't make it rye, okay?"

Kevin made the buy in a small liquor store. Sitting behind it, they helped Lazarus into his denim jacket and street clothes, doctoring the wound as best they could with an auto-pad over the wound-filling foam. "Well, at least we don't have to worry about you bleeding out!" Sarah quipped, trying to sound cheerful.

"Externally," Kevin muttered. "Without working nanoids, we don't know what's going on inside." When he saw Sarah's face, he could have kicked himself for a damn fool. "But I'm sure he's fine," he amended lamely.

"Dude, that right there was a sucky save." Lazarus chuckled, already halfway down a bottle of the best rum Kevin had been able to find.

They buttoned the blonde man's coat up tight to hide the wound. The rum didn't completely ease the pain, but it certainly helped.

The bus's autonomous system allowed them on without issue, though the other riders had more reservations. Lazarus was well and truly drunk, half awake and half grinning.

"Hey, hey Sarah. Hey Kev. If this shit...this shit goes bad, you take care of my little cousin, 'kay? You take care of Eevie."

"We'll take care of her," Kevin promised, since there was absolutely no point arguing with a drunk.

Lazarus lolled his head over, grinning at Kevin. "You...you take care of you too, 'kay? You don't put this shit on you, 'kay? Sarah, don't...don't let him bury himself in bullshit, you got me?"

Sarah shook her head, biting her lip halfway between a laugh and a sob. "We are going to give you so much shit for this later."

Lazarus grinned, glassy eyed. "Yeah well...I give you shit 'cause I love you guys. You know that right? I love you guys. You and Yve. You and Yve and everybody. But you guys 'special. You guys're...yeah. That. What's that...family! That thing. Love you."

Kevin's heart was hammering, but his best friend's drunken ramblings were somewhat adorable. He could only hope that drunken was all that they were.

Kevin tapped out a message when they were halfway to the stop. They sat on a bench at the ZonCom stop, cheap and unfenced. They waited.

And waited.

Kevin paced, snarling at his blank messaging app. He tripped over a cleaning bot, turned and kicked it savagely. It emitted a kicked-puppy sound and a holo message that read 'damage fee deducted from your card. One Citizen Standing point deducted.'

Like he gave a damn about his falsified credentials.

"Where the *hell* is that truck?!" he hissed between his teeth.

"Kev," Sarah murmured. "C'mere and sit. Let's keep him warm."

Kevin glanced back, biting his lip. Quickly, he shucked his own jacket and laid it over his friend. Lazarus gave him a drunken smile.

"Relax man. Wors' that happens is I kick it. I c'n live wi' that."

"You can't actually, but I take the point." Kevin murmured, trying for a smile. The blonde man snorted. Kevin really didn't like the color of his face. Too pale.

"Dude," Lazarus muttered eventually, "I'm...drunk as hell, and I'm havin' trouble stayin' awake. If this goes down sideways...you need to know. Wasn't your fault. You hear that? This one's on me. I signed up for this. We signed up for this. Remember?"

Lazarus flopped a hand in Kevin's general direction. Kevin caught it. He had to fight past a lump in his throat to speak.

"We signed up together. I remember."

Lazarus closed his eyes, a blissfully drunken smile on his lips. "Yeah..."

His hand was cold.

Three hours crept by. Four. Lazarus fell into a fitful doze, his breathing too fast.

At four in the morning, the transport finally rumbled up. Topher climbed out.

Kevin strode off the platform and grabbed the boy by his jacket, fury burning through his nerves. "Where the *hell* have you...been...Topher?"

The boy's face was incredibly pale, his eyes staring.

"We got hit." he murmured, his lips barely moving. "We got bombed."

Ice chased the fire out of Kevin's blood.

"Did we lose anyone?" He demanded. Topher swallowed hard. "We had people in surgery when I left. Don't know..."

"Right." Kevin agreed, his words sounding strange in his own ears. "Right. Well, we've got one more for surgery. Help us; Laz's wounded."

In the morning light Lazarus looked dreadful. The bags under his eyes were purple. His lips had a bluish tinge.

Internal bleeding. Kevin did his best to force the thought away.

"Drive as fast as you can, Toph," Kevin murmured, laying his hand on the young man's shoulder. "And I'm sorry. I'm sorry I shouted. And that you had to come get us."

The look on Topher's face was frightening in its emptiness. The boy set the truck into gear without a word, and the speed knocked Kevin back in his seat.

The base was a disaster. It had been moved to their site by the Hogback Reservoir, and moved in too much haste. Two of the modules were gutted shells. The intact modules huddled under what was left of the slick tarp. Dozer and Janice were working with someone from another base to spread a new tarp over the shredded remains of theirs. In the background, the base IR emitter hummed.

"Right. Let's—" Kevin began. But Sarah's choked cry cut off his thoughts.

"Kev! He's not...shit!"

Whipping around, Kevin watched as Sarah began chest compression on their friend, slamming her brittle bird-bone body into the moves. He turned to Topher and pointed out the window. "Run and get the medical team up here *now!*"

Topher was out of the truck in a breath, taking off fast enough to kick up dust. "Help! Guys! Help!" He shouted, his black hair streaming like a banner in the morning light.

Kevin wriggled into the back seat and shouldered Sarah aside. "Let me, I'm heavier."

He'd made it through four rounds of chest compression when Yvonne and Alice came up to the truck, Liza hot on their heels.

"I need to get him bagged,"Alice rapped out as they worked, her braids hidden under a white scrub cap and her front daubed in blood. Yvonne choked back a sob, working with Liza to get her cousin onto a backboard and lift him out of the truck. Kevin helped as best he could, replacing Liza at the head of the board. Alice kept with them, laying an imaging screen on Lazarus's chest and squeezing a manual ventilation bag over his mouth and nose.

The black blot around the liver in the image looked like a sea of ink.

"Damian's already operating, we're going to have to stabilize Laz!" Alice called as they raced into the medical bay. It was like a scene out of a nightmare for Kevin: all his family in one place, all suffering. Dilly with a patch over one eye, her gorgeous hair shaved away. Jim sitting beside her, arm in a sling. Henrietta bawling in a cradle. Was she wounded too?

Yvonne was openly crying now.

There was blood on the back of Topher's shirt. Had he been bleeding all this time?

Blake was in a bed, eyes closed. His face was peppered with small burns. Kevin couldn't see anything more under the white sheets. Billie was in the bed beside his, wild-eyed and covered in auto-pads down the left side of her face, her neck, her arm.

The black and white cut-out of Damian performing an operation flicked into the corner of his eye. The whine of a flatlining heart monitor filled the room. Damian snarled, grabbing for tools. Kevin watched him with the numb dissociation he recognized as shock, as the doctor frantically scrambled. Andrea's chestnut hair fanned out against the pillow under Damian's hands, nearly matching the blood around her head.

Tommy stood watching in the corner, still as a mannequin. He was watching his mother die. Kevin's instinct was to go to the boy, but he seemed to be frozen in place.

And there was Lazarus on the table. So much blood had pooled inside him.

They'd sat there on that fucking bench while all that blood leaked out inside him.

They'd walked right into a setup.

He'd let his best friend walk into a trap.

"Pump this every time you count to five!" Alice ordered, grabbing Kevin's hands and placing them over the manual bag. He did as he was told. Turning, Alice yanked her gloves off, tossed them off the floor and pulled on a fresh pair.

"Yve! Sarah! Get his clothes off!"

Sarah used scissors to cut away his shirt.

Positioning the long needle, Alice sank it into his chest. Snatching her viewing pad, she moved it up, slapping it down over Lazarus's heart.

The heart was still.

Alice grabbed up another needle and injected it.

A reading came up on the screen.

Nanoids Attempting Stimulation of Brain Activity

Attempting

Attempting

Attempt: Failed

Patient: Deceased.

Yvonne let out a groan that tore Kevin's heart into confetti. Dropping her head onto her cousin's silent chest, she sobbed. Sarah rubbed her back gently, staring at Kevin. She shook her head helplessly.

He was frozen in time. Frozen in place. He knew he needed to do something. But he had no idea which way to turn.

He wished desperately that arms would comfort him as Sarah comforted Yvonne. But his sensible mind knew that Aidan would be busy. He would be organizing. He would be seeing to everyone.

Kevin glanced around the room. But Aidan wasn't there.

Outside then. He needed to report. He needed to find Aidan.

Numbly, he turned.

The new slick tarp was in place, the team who'd done the work rolling with sweat. Kevin stared around him, lost.

Tipping his head up, he met Janice's eyes.

"Jan? I can't..." he had to swallow to get the words out. Something was wrong with his throat. "I can't find Aidan."

Janice's face folded into worry lines. That look completed the ruination of Kevin's world.

Slowly, the older woman glanced at her comrades. "You guys got this?"

Silent, Dozer nodded.

Climbing down the ladder, Janice stepped over to Kevin and enfolded him in a hug.

"C'mere *mis chico zorrito*. It's gonna be okay. Just hang onto me for a second. That's it. Just hang out here for a second."

Janice's long hands rubbed his back. Kevin didn't know why, but he nearly melted in her embrace, breathing in sweat and the smell of rain. He assumed he was in shock. He had to be in shock.

"Where's Aidan?" His voice belonged to a boy, not a man.

Janice kissed the top of his head softly. "C'mon lil' red. We'll go see your boy."

Janice's gentle hands steered him back down the hall, back into the medical bay.

"But why—" he started to ask, but Janice squeezed his shoulder. "Over here."

She walked him past the bed where Andrea lay, covered in a white sheet. A different bed had been wheeled into Damian's operating area in her place.

"Stay behind the blue line on the floor." Damian snapped. "Any closer and it isn't sterile."

"We're stayin' here." Janice agreed quietly. That response was enough to make Kevin sure that the world had gone wrong. So wrong. Janice ought to be taking the doctor apart for a snap like that. She shouldn't be obedient.

On the table, Aidan lay on his belly. His back was a hellscape of sliced skin and wounds filled with things that did not belong in a living body.

The beeping of machines and Tommy's quiet sobs filled Kevin's ears. He raised his eyes to Damian's. "Will he live?" he asked, his voice absolutely uninflected.

Damian's black plastic eyes held his. "If I have anything to say about it, he will. But I need to work."

Kevin nodded. Turning, he crossed the room. Finding Liza, he held out his hands. "Give me something to do. *Please.*"

Burnt plastic. The world smelled like burnt plastic. Antiseptic. There was antiseptic in there too.

His eyes were so heavy.

Burnt plastic meant something. Something bad. Burnt plastic meant...a bombing. They'd gotten bombed. Naomi had been beside him, before the bomb came down.

Aidan's eyes snapped open. "Naomi?"

He tried to roll over, and alarms went off around his bed.

"Please do not move," a mechanical voice warbled, "Please do not move. You are injured. Please do not move."

He sighed, dropping back onto his belly. His body was numb and the bed alarms were set to keep him from moving. That wasn't good.

Fingers gently touched his shoulders, one of the places that wasn't numb. Words whispered fervently in his ear, rising to a shout over his head.

"Aidan, don't try to move, please, love. Your back's a mess. Damian! He's awake!"

That was a voice he knew. Kevin.

This wasn't Dad's base. This was *his* base. His base had gotten bombed.

He forced his eyes open again. "Am I on...pain blockers? I feel kind of...numb." His throat was dry.

"I'll say you're on pain blockers. Your back got filleted when you shielded the kids," Damian's granite voice dropped the words into the air.

Aidan turned his head to look at the doctor. Damian's eyes were focused somewhere over his shoulder.

The whine of a drone. The ceiling groaning. The kids.

So that's what happened.

"Can I move?" Aidan asked, though he should have known the answer.

"You wish." Damian stated flatly. Aidan tried to nod.

"The kids okay?" He asked, trying to wet his lips.

"Dilly's face and the side of her head got a slice," the doctor stated. "Otherwise she's fine. Tommy and Donny don't have a scratch on them."

"Tweak? She was running down the hall..." Aidan squeezed his eyes closed. "She was a ways off...I think?"

"Tweak wasn't wounded," Damian stated. "In fact, she got you in here."

Aidan gave a grunt of agreement. "Okay. And everything else? I need a situation report."

"The situation is you're lying here and letting the auto-pads work." Damian stated sharply. "Your back's cut open in twenty places, you've got a catheter in and you may not feel it yet, but you are ripped up. If you think you're getting out of this bed you're wrong."

Aidan swallowed. "I'm not getting out of this bed. I'd be less likely to want to get up and see for myself if I felt like I knew what was going on and what shape we're in."

Over his head, Damian gave him a slow, cockeyed stare. Then he turned his head.

"Liza. Take a break. Come give the Commander a situation report. If he tries to get out of this bed I'll make you both regret it."

Liza's face was pale when he saw it over his bed, but she smiled. "Thank god you're awake."

"That bad?" he asked. He felt Kevin's long fingers stroke his hair.

"You were being operated on when I arrived. It looked as if every splinter in the roof had ended up in your back," his boyfriend's voice murmured.

Aidan sighed. Talking to people without being able to see them was going to get irritating fast. "Okay. I know the office module got bombed. Security report?"

"We're secure." Liza replied quickly. "We're in our planned bug-out location by the Hogback. Our neighbors at Base 1412 brought us their spare slick tarp."

The numbness starting to ease in his mind, Aidan nodded. "Okay. Good. Structural report. What'd we lose?"

"Half the general-use computers and any live data on them." Kevin reported the details with his usual precision, his words mechanical. "The workspace module itself is scrap. The coding rig is salvageable; Tweak and Janice have it working again. It's in Tweak's quarters for now. The backup for the base survived. The canteen module will need to be scrapped, but we were able to salvage the refrigerators and one stove. Some pots and pans. We've hooked everything to the power system in the rec-room, for now. That survived. The dormitory wing is fine. Hydroelectrics maintenance is fine...but the blast knocked many of the seedlings off their shelves. We've lost about two thirds."

"Fuck." Aidan muttered. Weariness crept through his bones. The amount of work they'd have to do to get this place back in shape... "Okay. Personnel report?"

This was the part he'd been dreading.

"Six wounded-ambulatory," Liza stated quietly. "Damian's gotten a dose of propranolol into everybody who's awake. Three wounded non-ambulatory, including you. And two...dead."

A lead sheet folded down over Aidan. He took a moment to manage the word.

"Who?"

"Andrea and Lazarus."

Aidan tried to tug his fuzzy thoughts into line. "Wait...Laz...you guys weren't here then. You were gone on the mission..."

"Our mission was compromised," Kevin stated. He was so distant as he spoke. He sounded like a recording. "Lazarus sustained a slow-bleeding internal injury via an armed security drone. He bled out as we were trying to get him home."

A second lead blanket settled into place inside Aidan, the weight making it hard to breathe.

"We got exposed, didn't we?" He asked into the quiet.

"Apparently." Kevin agreed quietly. "Our team definitely walked into a trap. Whoever was pulling the strings waited until we were in the center of the building before ordering the security drones to read us as threats. Someone knew we were entering. Someone set us up." He looked away. "And it isn't only us. We must have sprung something big by walking into that building. Fifteen percent of the bases across the country were hit simultaneously. Several drones were observed dropping bombs in recently vacated areas. The drones seemed to drop bombs on the general area rather than aiming for the hydroelectrics rooms on the bases they hit. That little oddity gives us a clue. The general conclusion is that the drones were shooting blind, guided by a table of coordinates and nothing more. Casualties are...lower than they could have been, but it isn't good." He swallowed. "The Tearaways and the Riptides were both hit as well. The Riptides are reduced by half. The Tearaways are in fairly good shape."

Aidan closed his eyes. So many people wounded. So many people dead. So much damage.

He wished he could stay there, in the quiet dark.

Maybe he should.

But he wasn't the only one who was hurting right now. He forced his eyes open.

"Okay. Right now I need a timeline for when everybody who's in a bed can move. I need a setup that's going to let me sit up in bed. And I need a working tab. Until I get one, Kev, I need you to take some notes."

It was easy to stay focused in the medical ward on the first day, resting with an air-cushion produced by his bed keeping his body from touching anything solid as he worked out problems. It was easy to stay focused when there were problems to solve.

Kevin and Liza helped him file the damage reports with Sector. Sector sent back a formal note of condolence, and extended them a three-week rest and recovery period. Their only assignment for a while would be getting themselves put back together. Aidan focused on that. He didn't have the bandwidth to think about all the balls they would drop while they were down, though they were falling in the back of his mind.

They put in the emergency aid requests and the requisition requests that needed to be made, including the use of a structural printer to make new modules. Kevin drew up a schedule for runs that could land them enough plastic to recycle into building parts. Dozer and Janice moved Andrea and Lazarus's bodies to the garage, zipped up in coolant-lined body bags. Aidan and Kevin set a date for the burial in three days. They had to take care of the living first.

Liza spent a little time handing out black arm-bands. Finishing her round, she wandered back to Aidan's bedside and discreetly pointed at Tommy. Aidan would be surprised if the kid was noticing anything; he sat in the corner with his head down. His fingers played with his black arm band. Donny sat beside him, a hand on his back.

Liza nodded at their task list. She'd written 'figure out situation for Tommy.'

Aidan nodded. "Does he have any next of kin?" He asked quietly.

"Bobby—Barbara—and Sam Lawrence. Grandparents, up in the Foco Rest and Retirement base." Liza murmured, her face blank. "They're old Wildcards. They're in their mid-eighties. They waited a long time to have Andrea."

The words laid a little more weight down inside Aidan's chest. Tommy's relatives were elderly wards of a Rest base. When they passed, Tommy would end up a ward of a Rest base with all the other Force orphans. It wasn't the worst outcome, but something about sending the kid up to live with people he barely knew just in time to watch them decline and die sat wrong with him.

He glanced up at Liza. "How well does he know his grandparents?"

Liza shrugged, her mask of military perfection firmly in place. "Bobby and Sam retired before he was born sir, they've been up in the mountains for years. Vid-calls at his birthday and Christmas are how he knows them, sir. Not a lot more."

Aidan closed his eyes. "Okay. Ask Dozer to come over here when he has a second. Do we have any leads on the info leak?"

Kevin shook his head. "Nothing that anyone but Tweak understands. And Tweak's in bed. She passed out at her station."

Aidan blinked. "What?"

"The little idiot hasn't eaten, drunk anything save coffee or slept since the bombing. She's been on her station since she set it to rights, hunting our malefactor." Kevin stated dryly. "We asked Billie, and she suggested that we wait until Tweak collapsed and then put her to bed. Apparently this has been an issue before, and in the state she was in she's completely unreasonable."

Aidan sighed. "Fuck. Okay. When she comes around send her to me. She started yelling during a drone attack: this isn't on her, but we got to remind her to get quiet when there's a drone in the air. How's our food situation?"

"I've put Billie in as our new cook," Liza said, ticking off an item on the task list. "She's doing alright. And...Andrea was teaching her." Aidan heard the stumble in her voice.

"We're well-stocked for the moment," Kevin added.

Aidan nodded. "How are we on meds?"

"We're hurting." Kevin admitted without any attempt to sugar-coat it. "I've got Yvonne and Sarah out requisitioning. Yvonne's better when she has something to do."

"Most people are," Aidan agreed. He glanced up as Dozer came shambling over.

"How you doing?" The big man asked.

Aidan gave him a crooked smile. "Shitty. You?"

"My garage is a morgue, so yeah. Shitty." Dozer agreed.

Aidan nodded. "Grab a seat. I want to hear about the garage. How's your setup?"

Dozer waved a shovel-like hand. "Fine. No damage. Some stuff fell over was all."

"Nice to hear good news," Aidan acknowledged. "So, next thing: I need to know how you did with taking care of Topher when he first arrived. He was fourteen, right?"

Dozer nodded slowly, studying Aidan. He glanced across the room. "This's about Tommy?"

Aidan nodded. "He's a lot younger than fourteen. I need to decide if we're putting somebody up as a formal guardian for him, or sending him to his grandparents in the mountains."

Dozer sighed. "Bobby and Sam are gettin' up there. They were old when they left us to retire. Won't be around all that much longer."

Aidan nodded. "That's what I was thinking."

Slowly, the mechanic nodded. "Let me think about it today. I'll ask around, quiet. See what the word is."

Aidan nodded. "Thanks, Dozer."

By the end of the day, they'd done the urgent things. Damian came over to glare down at the team around Aidan's bed, ensconced in their cocoon of floating screens and overworked, fan-whirring tabs.

"In case you hadn't noticed, this man's wounded. I'm going to need to check his condition and add a new layer of muscular auto-pads with nutrient dressing for the cells," Damian stated flatly.

The word 'dressing' stuck in Aidan's ears as Kevin and Damian glared at one another. Dull fear climbed slowly up his gut.

He glanced from Liza to Damian. "About dressings. You said Tweak got me in here. Who got my clothes off? Who put in the catheter?"

Liza bit her lip. "Damian was working on Andrea when you got brought in. Alice said get your clothes off, and everybody kind of jumped in, and...and..."

Aidan closed his eyes as another tablet of lead sunk down over his heart.

Kevin's hand stroked his hair gently. Aidan knew he was trying to be comforting, but he had to fight down a flare of anger and panic at the touch.

Liza started to babble. "Commander...I mean, Aidan, I take full responsibility, but we didn't know. We never would have guessed that you're—that you—and we don't care, really we don't. Janice will tell you if it's hard for you to believe me, we don't..."

"Yeah Liza," he managed woodenly. "I get it. You didn't know. It's fine."

"And you're our Commander," Liza continued, panic in her voice, "we were so focused on making sure you pulled through, all we were paying attention to was the wounds, I swear. I swear, we didn't mean to...we didn't know that you..."

"I said I get it." Aidan was surprised at the way his words came out, far too loud. Conversations around the room fell silent.

Aidan tried to count his breaths. There was no time for this bullshit. They needed him to be steady.

"I'm not angry at anyone, Liza. I'm just messed up. I think we all are right now."

He opened his eyes. Damian was standing, impassive.

"I need to work on you, Aidan. I'm going to have to turn the pain-blocking nanoids off to allow new nervous tissue to grow in. I'm putting on a topical painkiller. We'll turn the nanoids back on in the morning. And I need everybody else to clear the bed and take a couple steps back." In spite of the dark man's expression, his words were gentle.

Aidan nodded. "Yeah. Go ahead."

It was easy to handle the day, when people needed him. It was the night that was hell.

In the dark, Blake snored in his bed. Billie tossed and turned in her sleep on the far end of the room. Their small night sounds didn't do enough to fill the silence.

Aidan stared at the ceiling. He should have kept his tab. He should have turned Omi on when everybody went to sleep. Kevin had taken the device with him when he'd gone to bed. Aidan hadn't even thought about it.

He should have been more careful. He should have paid attention to the threat that Tweak had seen in the data. Scenarios unspooled themselves in his head.

He tried to focus on his breathing. His brain was trying to figure out what he could have done better. It was just overdoing it. He needed…

He needed to be a decent Commander, or he needed to get out of Command. Laz and Andrea had died because he'd taken a risk. He'd given the go ahead on the mission. Because of him, two people were dead. Half of his unit was wounded.

He'd done that.

"Stop it," he whispered. "Fucking stop."

But the thoughts were relentless.

He had let the unit down. Every single one of them. There had to be something he could have done to keep them safe. He just hadn't found it. He was too inexperienced. He couldn't handle this.

Everything he had ever done had led up to this massive failure. Two people dead on his base. God knew how many more, on other bases. Their blood was on his hands.

His base had treated him like some sort of hero. Now they knew better. Now they knew he was a fuck-up.

Hell, they'd seen him naked. They knew *exactly* how fucked up he was.

He tried to bring his thoughts back to his breathing. But the storm inside his chest made counting breaths seem pathetically cowardly. He was a weak, badly made freak who made mistakes that killed people, and he was sitting here trying to count to ten like a kid and pretend he shouldn't hurt. He should.

He needed something to focus on. Something real. And he needed to pay those he'd hurt back.

Reaching down, he brought up the bed controls. He hit the 'Air Cushion Off' button.

A query window popped up, asking for his credentials. He typed in his Commander's code. The screen blipped, the background turning green in approval. 'Would you like the air cushion turned off?'

Aidan hit 'yes.'

The jets of air that had been keeping his back a quarter-inch off the bed shut off. Agony seared along his back. He bit down on his lip to keep from yelling out.

Everything came into focus: the pain in his back. The sheets in his fist. He could be here and now. He could hang onto this kind of pain.

The pain in his body, he knew what to do with.

They stood beside the grave site on the ninth, the portable slick tarp tent over their group rustling in the evening breeze. Everyone in the team was on their feet, for the ceremony at least; nanoids and decent auto-pad tech could work wonders.

But not miracles.

Kevin stared down into the two graves, the two white-shrouded shapes. He turned his eyes to Aidan, who was staring into the pits. He'd wanted to help Aidan walk to the grave site. His boyfriend was still unsteady on his feet. But Aidan had pushed his hands off.

The blonde man's eyes were miles away when he looked up. Aidan brought his speech up on a holographic screen and cleared his throat.

"Today, we stand here to commemorate our friends: Andrea Diane Lawrence and Steven Lazarus Smith." Aidan paused, the hint of a smile flickering on his lips. "I don't think more than five people knew that his parents named him Steven."

"He fucking hated it," Yvonne murmured, smiling weakly.

Watery laughter ran through their group. Aidan swallowed hard. "Our people are fallen on the field of battle," he continued, using the words of the Force ceremony based on a famous speech of the past. Kevin knew it by heart. "Forever more that is their legacy. Their names are now enshrined on the scroll of America's hallowed dead. And where they shed their blood is sacred ground to us."

"This is sacred ground," everyone repeated in unison. Kevin heard a muffled sob. He didn't turn to see who cried. He wouldn't shame them like that.

The desert breeze wound around Aidan's voice. "Per Force protocol, the wills of the dead have been read and will be honored to the best of our ability. Lazarus willed his clothes to anybody who could use them, with the specification that his 'kickass coat with too many pockets' goes to Kevin. His games go into the general base collection. All his guns go to Sarah, and any bottles of booze in his possession go to Yvonne, with an exception. There's a note." He read it from the screen. "To Janice: If the base is still in good shape, there's a loose panel in the wall behind my bed. I've got four two-hundred year old bottles of whiskey back there. One's for you. I owe you for all the booze I snagged off you. Pass the others around and have a party."

Weak laughter ran through their team. Kevin shook his head, feeling tears prickle behind his eyes. Trust Lazarus to do something like that.

"And there are two notes from Andrea. I'll start with the bigger ask," Aidan continued. "She wrote this: Guys, I know what I'm writing is a lot to ask for. I've got my folks in the mountains, and maybe Dan is still out there and would take his son. But you guys are...are Tommy's family. If I'm gone and we're not totally screwed, please. Somebody sign up as his guardian on paper. It's not right for him to lose me and all you guys at the same time."

Tommy, who had been standing like a little statue in his best clothes and his black arm band, broke down and started to sob. Dilly and Donny both dropped to their knees, engulfing their younger friend in a tight hug. Jim sank to one knee beside the kids, rubbing the boy's back.

There was silence. It seemed to stretch for ages. Kevin's feet were itching to step forward, but Jim had opened his mouth.

"We'll do it," Yvonne's words exploded on the morning air. "Put us down as his guardians. We'll take him." Holding tight to Sarah's hand, she shot Jim a smile. "You can be our backup, deal?"

"Deal," he agreed quietly. Stepping over, Yvonne knelt beside Tommy, gathering him into her arms. Sarah laid her hands on her wife's shoulders, watching Aidan.

Aidan nodded, his face empty. That expression was starting to worry Kevin.

"We'll do the paperwork at base," Aidan stated quietly. "The other request she left's pretty simple." He lowered his eyes to the screen. "To Kevin: if you can say the prayer you gave over Josie's grave when she passed, I'd appreciate it. Everybody else, try to sing along when he gets the song going."

Aidan's eyes met his, distant and blue as the sky at twilight. Kevin swallowed.

He glanced at Jim where he stood, holding his daughter tight with one hand and comforting his friend's son with the other. The tall man nodded, giving Kevin the permission he felt he needed to use the prayer he'd put together specifically for Jim's sweet wife. He acknowledged the nod. Drawing a breath, he stepped up, closed his eyes and began the prayer he'd created by combining two half-remembered canticles.

"Lord, we come before you today as children

weeping for friends lost.

lead us from death to life,

from falsehood to truth.

Lord, we entrust those who have died to your mercy:

welcome them into your presence.

You loved them greatly in this life,

now give them peace,

and let perpetual light shine upon them.

Lord, lead us from despair to hope,

from fear to trust.

May we remember them in peace.

Lord, teach us to smile

as we think on those who have died:

For they are in your home, and in joy.

Forever.

Amen."

"Amen," his family murmured around him. Kevin glanced around. "Andrea asked for the song. Is everyone up for it?"

Janice grabbed a shovel with one hand. "Sing, boy. We'll catch up."

Kevin nodded. His voice came out husky as he spoke. "For those of you who haven't had to do this with us before, I'm going to start a song that everyone's welcome to join in on. It's become a tradition at funerals, for us. This is a very old song, sung by people in dark times when they wanted to believe something better was possible."

He took a slow breath, relaxing his shoulders and straightening his spine as a singing tutor had shown him so many years ago. Closing his eyes, he raised his voice.

"We shall overcome, we shall overcome

We shall overcome some day

Oh, deep in my heart, I do believe

We shall overcome some day."

The others began to fall into harmony tentatively around him. The kids joined first, though Tommy's sparrow-like voice was choked.

"We'll walk hand in hand, we'll walk hand in hand

We'll walk hand in hand some day."

Sarah's high, sweet voice joined in, and Yvonne's laughably flat voice with it. Dozer's heavy baritone underpinned the song.

"We are not afraid, we are not afraid

We are not afraid today."

Topher was nearly a match for Kevin in timbre, though his voice wobbled dreadfully. Alice sang like an alto angel.

A new, breathy voice joined the melody. Billie, Kevin guessed.

Tweak probably wouldn't sing. And there were Blake's nasal tones, and Damian's surprisingly powerful baritone.

He didn't hear Aidan's voice.

"We shall live in peace, we shall live in peace

We shall live in peace some day

Oh, deep in my heart, I do believe

We shall live in peace some day."

Kevin choked on a sob, his voice petering out. His family finished the song without him. He listened with a bowed head, hearing the holes where a man's strident voice had always, always come in just a few beats too early, and where a woman's sweet coloratura had floated above all the others.

Oh, deep in my heart, I do believe

We shall overcome some day."

The last shovelful of dirt thumped into place.

That night, they opened the whiskey and toasted. The rec room was crowded now that it was doubling as kitchen, but everyone crammed in to sit at the salvaged tables and share drinks, to laugh, to cry and to play Andrea's godawful Country music and Lazarus's favorite Sunk City Rap. They sang along to the easier songs, Tommy sitting in Yvonne's lap and hanging onto her as if his life depended on it.

Kevin offered his beloved a drink twice, but Aidan turned him down with a small smile each time. Eventually, he let his boyfriend have his space in the corner. He'd join in when he was ready.

They did what they always did at a wake, telling stories about the people they'd loved. Their team had been lucky over the years. But they still knew how to throw a good retirement party, and a better wake. They'd thrown a party like this for Andrea's parents just a week after Kevin arrived, as the old cook and hydroelectric assistant retired to a safer base. They'd thrown three retirement parties and five wakes in the last nine years. Kevin took another sip of his drink, before his mind started to reel off the names of people they'd lost. That was why they held wakes: mourning alone was dangerous. They all knew how to keep one another out of the darkness at times like this.

"You remember the first time he pulled a Touchdown Party on you?" Yvonne asked deep in the night, grinning behind her glass. Kevin eyed her with a sidelong smile, tapping her on the black arm band encircling her bicep. "What do you mean 'he?' Lazarus most definitely had help from you ladies on that."

"You punched him out!" Sarah exclaimed, sloshing her glass in one hand and laughing. "First thing he said when he came round was—"

Kevin chorused the words with the girls, Janice joining them in wicked glee. "You don't get to be good at fucking *and* fighting!"

They dissolved in drunken hilarity.

If he was honest, Kevin was less inebriated than he was letting on, but his team needed to see him laugh. They needed the companionship. They needed to remember their joking buddy and their sweet unit mother, not a man dying on a bench in the dark and a bloodstained white bundle.

Kevin turned in his seat, calling over his shoulder. "You think that time with us was bad, Aidan, you know what he did to me when I was with Mark? Bloody hell, I was eighteen and the bastard..."

Kevin blinked. "Guys, where's Aidan?"

Dozer nodded in the direction of the door, pouring another glass. "Said he wasn't feeling so hot. Went to bed down."

Kevin nodded, sitting down and accepting another shot. But the idea of his boyfriend alone in the dark didn't sit well with him.

Once his drink was finished, he stood.

"It is getting late, and I've got a man who needs attention in my bed."

As he'd hoped, that got him all sorts of jeering catcalls. He gave an exaggerated bow before showily trotting out of the room, acting as if he were exiting a stage.

Nobody else needed to worry tonight.

Slipping into their room and setting his clothes on the dresser carefully to wear the next day, he slid into bed beside Aidan, careful of his back. Aidan's eyes were closed, though whether he was actually asleep or not Kevin wasn't sure.

"You did a beautiful job today, love," he whispered in the dark.

He got no reply.

"So, did Damian mix the right amount of piss and vinegar to put back into your bloodstream?" Kevin asked with a smirk, leaning against the wall beside Blake's bed.

The older man turned up his nose. "*Bite* me, you little brat."

"I see he got it just right," Kevin quipped.

Blake snorted, swatting at him. "*Terrible* boy, go torture someone else. I'm *trapped* in this bed by that *tyrant* in a white coat, and everyone else is back at work. I've been *humiliated* enough."

"You did have a fairly impressive gut wound to repair," Kevin remarked casually.

Blake made a 'pfft' sound. "I have *plenty* of gut these days, I can *afford* to lose some of it."

"You can't afford to lose your lower intestines, and quit whining." Damian rapped out, striding across his white-tiled kingdom. "You've only been in bed seven days, and I let you out for the funeral."

"I feel *so* blessed." Blake shot back tartly. Damian pointedly turned away, ignoring the older man. He pinned Kevin with a stare.

"I want you in my office. Now."

Kevin blinked. "Of course."

"What are we out of? Is it serious?" he asked once Damian had closed the door. The spare man took his seat behind the desk and steepled his fingers.

"Apparently, you and our commander are out of common sense, from what I've seen." The words could have been carved from lead.

Kevin's fingers tightened in his lap. "And you've seen what, exactly?" He asked carefully.

Damian couldn't blink, but he gave the impression that he wouldn't want to.

"How long have you two been jerry-rigging an antidepressant regimen for him?"

"Oh," Kevin murmured, blindsided for the moment.

Damian's ocular implants whirred as his brows rose. "Yeah, 'oh.' You've been abetting an unapproved medical regimen, and all you have to say is 'oh'?"

Kevin glanced down at his hands. "He...well, he didn't want it on his record. I thought it was better that he have something than nothing, so I did some research and—"

"And you thought your twenty-minute Net search was as good as my years of medical-school training? You thought coming from a medical Corporation made you a doctor, maybe?" Damian's tone was as sharp as one of his scalpels.

Kevin sighed. "Damian..."

Damian cut him off. "You think taking illicit drugs would look better on his record? Or yours? Because I'm this close to writing you both up and putting him on medical suspension."

Kevin's brows shot up. "What?"

Damian held his eyes. "What you've got him on isn't helping as much as you seem to think. His back's healing, but his back isn't what worries me now."

"Is the medication interfering with the treatment?" Kevin asked, gut tight.

Their surgeon shook his head. "No, but if you had any idea how bad things could have gone when I was prescribing without knowing what was in his bloodstream..." the raw-boned man sighed. This time, he looked away. That frightened Kevin far more than his anger.

Damian's fingers tapped the table. "Fact is, Kevin...I think our commander may be unfit for duty. He's cutting himself."

Kevin blinked, electricity dancing up his spine. "What did you see?"

"Parallel slices on his legs, overlaying all that old scar tissue. Saw them yesterday. So that's twice he's lied to me, because I'll eat this desk if I buy his 'these scars are from barbed wire' story anymore." Damian stated quietly. "He wouldn't take off his clothes at first for a full body exam. Kept saying his back was fine. I had to work with him just to get that far. The auto-pads did their thing; his back's nearly perfect, he was right about that. But once I talked him into a full check, I got a look at the legs. If that kind of cutting is a battle injury, I'm a trash compactor." He raised his eyes. "Did you know he cuts himself?"

Slowly, Kevin nodded. "I found out back in December, when I got the seeds. I started getting him medication around then."

Damian's cybernetic eyes bored into his. "You should've reported this."

"I thought we had it handled," Kevin replied, feeling his gut twisting.

"Well, you thought wrong," the doctor snapped, "And that could have cost you both a hell of a lot."

"So I see," Kevin agreed quietly. Inside, guilt rose like an oily wave. He slept every night beside the man. How had he missed this old demon rearing its head inside Aidan again?

Because Aidan had been avoiding touch since the bombing. He spent each evening on his tab, doing paperwork until he fell asleep. He'd said he just needed to get through the backlog of work.

And Kevin had let him do it.

Damian's fingers resumed their tapping. The dark man sighed. "I don't want to put him on medical suspension, he's still giving good orders, but this behavior's unacceptable. His and yours. And if he's cutting, he needs *real* help. I need him in here. I need to work up a personalized regimen based off his genome, not whatever out-of-a-bottle shit you picked up."

"I'll talk to him." Kevin agreed quietly. "And if he doesn't make sense when I do...we'll talk about it."

Damian eyed him for entirely too long. "All right. You talk to him. And if he doesn't listen, I'll have to get involved. We're clear on that?"

"We're clear," Kevin agreed quietly.

That afternoon, he left a note on Aidan's desk. 'Let's get back to our vid nights. See you on the couch.'

That evening, he waited alone in the rec room for two hours, before heading for their bedroom.

Aidan was there, and he was working. Not much of a surprise. "Hi," Kevin murmured, standing in the doorway. "Work day's been over for a bit."

"Sorry. Kind of busy," Aidan muttered without looking up from the tab he was studying. He lay on his belly, the screen projected at an angle as he worked. The latest data on Corps movements marched like ants on the projection.

"Obviously." Closing the door behind him, Kevin pulled out his own tab and flopped down on the bed, starting in on the code for a new game. He could be patient.

After ten minutes of silence, Aidan glanced at him. "You didn't come in here to code while I worked."

"Keeping you company," Kevin replied easily, inputting color schemes. "Might as well."

Aidan humphed quietly and returned to his own work.

Very slowly, Kevin moved closer, until he was resting his tab across Aidan's shoulder blades, his chin on Aidan's arm. The sound of their room's quiet ventilators filled the silence.

"How's the back?" Kevin asked quietly.

"What are you doing?" Aidan asked in lieu of answering.

"Checking to see if I can get comfortable or not." Kevin replied calmly, fingers tapping on his tab, brushing Aidan's hair as they did. "If I'm going to be in here, I'm not going to lie on the other side of the bed as if I were some old Puritan housewife. Besides, most of you is rather comfortable...but not your shoulder blades."

"They're not a table, either," Aidan muttered, exasperation in the tone. "And you're heavy."

Ignoring that, Kevin turned over so that his head was resting on the small of Aidan's back, his tab on his chest as he typed in silence. He leaned against the other man companionably. Demanding answers rarely worked, especially not with someone as secretive as his Aidan. No, he'd sit here quietly, making his presence known, until his man started talking. If nothing else, he could be with Aidan. That was better than nothing.

He'd been missing the connection between them more than he'd realized, missed the closeness and the touch. He'd missed the sex too, but it was the companionship he'd really grown hungry for in the last week. And not only with Aidan. Everyone was so distant after the attack. They might banter, but they did it in the preoccupied manner of those going through the motions.

The unit needed to be pulled back together. But the man that needed to do that was pulling himself apart instead.

"Get off," Aidan said eventually, his body squirming under Kevin's head. "I need to pee, and my leg's going numb."

Kevin amused himself with a retro pinball facade for his current game, focusing on button design until Aidan was back in their room and on the bed again.

Very quietly, he moved until he was leaning against Aidan once more. Silence enfolded them.

He placed words into the quiet with care. "People are worried about you, myself not the least."

"I'm fine," Aidan replied distantly.

"No, you most certainly aren't." Kevin admonished, words quietly pointed. "'Fine' is practically synonymous with 'barely keeping it together'."

"Keeping it together well enough to do my job," Aidan muttered, his tone taking on a new, bitter note.

"Not if Damian has anything to say about it." Kevin replied quietly. He could feel Aidan stiffen against him, but he pressed on. "Aidan, he knows what he saw on your legs. You're cutting again. If you keep this up, he'll put you on medical suspension. It's in his purview. So instead of pushing yourself off the proverbial cliff, why don't you keep the promise you made and talk to me?"

Aidan's head dropped, his straight blonde hair curtaining his face. "What's there to talk about? We lost people. I have to figure out what went wrong. We have to rebuild. That's all there is."

"Bull. Shit." the words came out with all the honed precision of a knife blade, Kevin letting just a touch of anger harden his voice. "We've lost people before. We've never given up because of it. People die. That's why it's a war. You know this."

Aidan turned to face him, his face so frightfully blank. "Yeah, I noticed it's a war. So we need to get tough and deal," Aidan replied dryly.

Kevin shook his head. "You're not dealing, Aidan. You're suffering, and it's doing no good for anyone, least of all you." He held Aidan's eyes. "I'll miss them too, but we've got a job to do. People need us to do our jobs well."

Sudden as spring lightning, Aidan pushed himself away. "Then they better pick a different commander," he muttered under his breath. "One who isn't a fuck-up." He stood, walking towards the door. "I need some air. Don't come after me. Please."

Kevin could move faster than most people realized, and he used it to his advantage now. He rolled easily over the edge of the bed and was in front of the door before Aidan could reach it.

"Is that what this is all about?" he asked incredulously. "Aidan, it wasn't your fault. Somehow our mission details and a hell of a lot of base coordinates were leaked, that was what brought the drones in. They dropped bombs blindly, didn't they? They couldn't see us; they simply had coordinates. Otherwise they would have aimed for the hydroelectrics room, the way they always do. You know that. We did absolutely everything we could to prevent it." He stepped closer, softening his voice. "You did everything you could. You put all the safeguards you could in place. The leak wasn't on our base. It wasn't something you could have controlled." Reaching out, he put a hand on Aidan's cheek. "Nobody thinks this was your mistake."

"Yeah, well I do," Aidan replied sharply, tearing away from Kevin's hand. "I could have set up a better vetting process or had Tweak re-code the IR emitters to disable the drones. I could've been less wrapped up in my own head. I could have done *something,* and I didn't. Get out of the way, Kevin."

"So you can go off and try to get yourself shot?" Kevin snapped irritably. "If you want to do something, then you and Tweak and I will get together and work out new safety protocols. We'll learn from our mistakes. But if you destroy yourself with useless guilt any longer, you'll only hurt the people you serve." He stepped forward, kissing Aidan's throat. "Please. Come and sit with me, and we'll start working out solutions. And then I'll leave you alone, if you want."

Aidan froze in place for far too long. Then he shook his head emphatically. "Don't touch me right now. I don't deserve...I just need to walk. I won't leave the base, all right? Just...just let me clear my head. Please."

For a moment, Kevin hesitated. Then he forced himself to step back, leaving the door open and praying that he was doing the right thing. "I'll see you soon, shall I?" he asked, the words light as a paper mask.

"Half an hour," Aidan agreed quietly. He avoided Kevin's gaze as he slipped out the door.

For half an hour, Kevin sat alone in the room and tried to sort the problem out as if it were a puzzle.

Problem: Aidan felt unduly responsible for the deaths on his watch.

Solution?

Nothing presented itself.

After forty-five minutes, he growled under his breath and stood. If Aidan had broken his promise and gone outside, Kevin would have some choice words for him.

If a drone hadn't found him first.

He stalked down the hall, checking the rec room, Aidan's half-rebuilt office. Nothing.

Light spilled out of the hydroelectric maintenance room, and he ducked inside. It took him a moment to spot Janice amid the pipes running every which way and the cargo-nets full of parts lining the walls between the racks of tools. His eye eventually gravitated to the only spot of color in the mechanical jumble: the plants, and Janice framed against them.

He raised his voice over the gurgle of the hydraulics pumps. "Have you seen Aidan?" he asked, noting the irritation in his own voice.

Janice glanced up slowly from the plant she was culturing cells from, giving him a patient look.

"'Bout four times, goin' round and round the halls. Why're you chasin' after him?"

Kevin let out a breath, the tension he'd been allowing to masquerade as anger leaving his muscles. He breathed in the hydroelectrics room's scent of ozone and rain. "I thought he might have tried to go outside. I thought… well." He straightened. "I should get to bed, I suppose. Sorry to bother you."

"You should sit your lily-white ass down, now that you're in my space." Janice nodded at a battered chair positioned in front of one of the work benches, titrating the cells into a culture plate.

Kevin was too tired to argue. He dropped into the chair. A little foam fell out of its back, drifting to the floor. "An' now that you're set down," Janice added over her shoulder, "you gonna tell me what's wrong with your boy?"

Kevin ran his hands through his hair, frustration eating at his guts. "If I only knew, I'd tell you."

"Well? What d'you think it is then?" Janice drawled patiently. "You're the genius around here."

"Not at the moment," Kevin grumbled. He sighed, pulling off his glasses. Yanking his cleaning cloth from his breast pocket, he worked away on the smears that smudged the plastic. It was easier to get the words in line when the external world had gone fuzzy about the edges.

"He has...some problems."

Janice guffawed quietly, setting the plant she'd been working with back in its warm, nutrient rich tray and crossing the room. "I'll say."

Kevin scowled. "I'm not in the mood, Janice. He's hurting and…and I don't know what to do."

The words cut like shards of glass, coming off his tongue.

For a moment, the air and water filtration machinery's grumbling was the only sound in the room. Then Janice's calloused hand squeezed his shoulder gently. "How 'bout you talk to me?"

Kevin stared at the glasses in his hands, dropping the pretense of cleaning them.

"He said that if he'd done something differently, our people wouldn't be gone. He...he has some problems with depression. And everything that's happened has him feeling that he's no good as a Commander."

"Heh," Janice muttered. "He shoulda seen some of the ones we tried out before."

Kevin smiled bleakly, nodding. "Yes, well. He sees himself as...as a failure, I think. A fuck-up, to use his nomenclature." He handled the words with distaste. He hated it when Aidan called himself things like that.

Eventually, his fingers remembered their task. "I think getting outed during surgery was the last straw on this situation, to be honest," he added as the fabric squeaked against the glass. "It's the same way he talked when he told me about himself," he added softly.

"Oh for fuck's sake, he's worried about *that*? What the everloving fuck for?" Janice drawled impatiently.

Slipping his glasses on, Kevin eyed her. "His father ran their base and their family along conservative lines, Janice. He and Aidan's first boyfriend both hurt him for being trans, I think."

"Yeah well, my dad just about killed me for it, an' AgCo sure would have if they found me. Which is why I got the fuck out of there, didn't I?" Janice leaned against her work bench, dark eyes studying him. "We ain't back there no more. We're here, an' here nobody cares. Shit, he knows I'm here, an' nobody cares."

Kevin cleared his throat carefully. "The only record that would have mentioned that detail about you is medical, and Aidan's never asked for those."

Janice's eyes widened. "Wait, you...you did *tell* him 'bout me when you were gettin' to know him, didn't you?"

Kevin shrugged. "I assumed that was between you and him. It wasn't my confidence to divulge."

Janice raised her eyes to the parts-festooned ceiling. "You scrawny-assed *shithead*. You *dumbass*."

"What?" Kevin demanded, affronted. "I'm not exactly in the business of giving away other people's secrets, am I? I've had enough practice keeping my own."

Janice slapped the side of his head, just hard enough to sting. He recoiled as he always had, more in annoyance than pain. "Ow! What was that for?"

"For bein' a fuckin' twatwich gamma...fuck, not gamma, said I'd drop that...for bein' a fuckwit, anyway!" Janice spat. "For a smart kid you can be almighty fuckin' *brainless* when you want to!"

"But it wasn't—" Kevin began, but Janice talked right over him, her accent thick as corn syrup. "D'you think I'd care? If I thought it woulda *helped* I woulda brought it up myself! Only reason I didn't was cause it never came up. An' you knew he was fuckin' freakin' out this whole time 'cause of the same thing, an' you didn't give him no proof that nobody gave a shit? You didn't even send him to me an' say 'ask Janice about whether the base's cool'?!" She gesticulated as she talked, stomping from tool-lined wall to water pumps and back again like a belligerent pinball and cursing all the while. "You sorry scraggy shit for brains lil' *pendajo.* Dios, everybody around here's a fuckin' idiot! I swear!"

"Incessantly, it's true," Kevin added under his breath. The look Janice gave him could have melted lead.

She stamped around her workspace for a few more minutes, angrily arranging tools on the walls and workbenches. Finally, she leaned against a wall and sighed, looking back at him with weary black eyes.

"I'll talk to him the next time he comes 'round. You go to bed."

"I suppose I can try," Kevin agreed quietly. "Thank you?"

"Oh for fuck's sake, get out." Janice grumbled, pointing at the door.

"Hey Commander. I'm brewing a pot of shit and calling it coffee." The voice that came down the hall was half ironic, half amused. Aidan raised his head. He'd been staring at the grey corridor floors in dim night-cycle lights for so long that the light from Janice's lair made him squint. "Come and have a cup," the hydroelectrics specialist called.

He gave her the same smile he had used since the attack, tired but as honest as he could manage. "Thanks, Janice, but I should probably go to bed. How are things going in there?"

"Come on in an' see." the engineer called over her shoulder, returning to her mechanical den. A cup was banged down on the table as Aidan entered, but Janice focused on the work at hand, tapping away on the screen attached to the piping. "This fucking system sucks more than a five dollar hooker. Glad we had this big aquifer to fall back on. Don't like to think how long it woulda taken me to find another spot, the mess we're in." She sipped at her coffee. "The Corps started taking the groundwater back in the teens, that's part of why this place is a desert now. Y'know this used to be prairieland? Grass as far as you could see, real grass, not the scrubby shit out there now. That coffee tastes even worse when it's cold." she added over her shoulder. "Got this working though, pumping plenty good. We may be fucked for a dishwasher an' in trouble about meds, but we're good on water an' power."

Reluctantly, Aidan slid into the seat at the table and sipped at the bitter coffee. "Nice to get some good news," he murmured. It was good to hear something positive. His head and his life might be fucked, but at least there was water to drink his crazy-meds down with.

"How're the plants?" He asked. Janice nodded in their direction.

"Banged up pretty bad, but what ain't dead yet's gonna make it. Saved about a third, an' they'll go in the ground soon as I can find a minute. Some of 'em shoulda been out in the beds already, but shit hit the fan 'fore I could get them planted. I'll take some time an' do that tomorrow, prolly."

Aidan nodded, giving a quiet murmur of assent.

"Saw you got banged up pretty bad." Janice added, shoving her brown-black ponytail back over her shoulder. "Good to see you on your feet."

Aidan shrugged, staring into his mug. His voice sounded far away. "The whole compound saw, it sounds like."

Janice turned to eye him, and he knew he'd said the wrong thing. "Damian's better than we could ever have asked for. I'm fine," he added, hoping to paper over what he'd just said.

The older woman chuckled. "You've got guts, boy. At your age, everybody saw my dick, I would've shot myself."

The mug slipped in Aidan's hands, splashing his fingers in hot coffee. He looked up into a smirk and the glitter of dark eyes.

"Your mouth's open," Janice observed wryly.

Aidan snapped his mouth shut. "You….you're…?"

"Yeah, Commander, you got it. I'm trans." She tossed her head in a little 'so what' gesture. "Thought you were all alone, didn't you?"

Aidan swallowed. "Does...does anyone else know about you?"

Janice's smirk widened. "Does it matter, if you think about it? I'm a goddamn great hydraulics engineer, the best cussing artist in this region and the lady who can kick any ass that gets in her way. That's who I am."

She shrugged. "But yeah. Some people asked, some I told, Damian an' Kevin get me specialty stuff medicinewise. About half the unit knows." The older woman chuckled, the hints of crows' feet around her eyes deepening. "An' what's it matter for you either? You're a Commander. You pass just fine, if that's the kind of thing you worry about. Doesn't have to be, but that ball's in your court. Anyway. You got a unit that's pretty good when they ain't bein' fuckwits. You got a sweet boy— dumber than a box of donkey balls sometimes, but sweet—an' you got some people around here impressed. You even got people in the chain of command raisin' an eyebrow or two. An' not a fuckin' bit of that has anything to do with what's goin' on under your boxers." She sipped her coffee, smiling slyly. "Well okay, Kevin probably does have stuff to do with what's in your boxers, but I don't ask questions like that. I give answers though, if you want tips. Runnin' into those kind of problems, I got some books."

Aidan realized that his mouth was open again. He swallowed hard. "Um...I....I think we're good." he managed. "But... how did you... I didn't have a clue that you..."

Janice chuckled, gazing into the mug she swirled idly in one hand. "We all think we're alone. Freaks and dissidents, the artists and the dreamers and the shy kids and the angry kids. An' we all run so fast and push so hard and do so much, and look how far we get alone. Makes you wonder how far we'd get together, doesn't it?" she asked, toasting him as she took a slow sip of her brew.

Aidan felt a bleak smile turn his lips as he returned the toast. "If only the world wasn't so Goddamn set against us, maybe it'd be easier. Then again...maybe not. Maybe we'd be better off raising a real army and doing this head on, huh? At least then it'd be over."

Janice winced. "Over as in dead, sure. We tried that, remember? Dissolution time, it was about as useful as fucking a porcupine. Read your history."

"Yeah, but they wouldn't be expecting it this time." Aidan gave her a crooked smile, probably the strongest he had managed since the attack. "Element of surprise, maybe."

Janice stared into her mug. "Maybe. But we don't need more killings. What we need is to out-think the sons of bitches. They've got all the guns. We need somethin' else." Then she glanced up, and her bitter smile softened. "Look, I didn't call you in here to go through battle plans. I'm an engineer, for fuck's sake. I just wanted you to know that you aren't alone. And people around here do care. They can be fucking children sometimes, sticking their dicks in the power socket of life, but they care about you. And they need you. Include me in that group...well, 'cept for the first bit." Reaching out, she tapped Aidan's mug. "An' you got a problem? Talk about it. The General Patton thing you keep pullin's real grade-A bullshit. These guys are used to that old whoreson Taylor, he used to spit out what he was thinking like he didn't have no damn filter. You keep quiet, you'll get shit out of this compound. Goes for life, too," she added, sipping at her mug.

For a long moment, Aidan studied her, his chest aching. Janice wouldn't sugar-coat it. He'd get something he could believe, from her.

He wet his lips. "Janice… I've been here almost a year now…do you think I'm a bad leader?"

"Well let's see, we've had two deaths in a year, the average base has about ten a year. We got families here, we're hitting serious Corps targets, and we eat like fucking kings. An' look here." She pointed to slender green stalks. "We got actual fuckin' pea an' bean plants sproutin' in my office; I thought those things were im-fucking-possible to sprout outside AgCo. We're startin' a moving farm this year. An honest to god farm." Janice continued in a singsong, ticking off points on her fingers. "We eat good, we drink water, hell we even drink real booze once in a while. That sound bad to you?" she asked pointedly, one finger jabbing her commander in the chest.

"Kevin's the one who got the seeds," Aidan protested weakly. "And you were the one who found the water. And Laz was the one who smuggled most of the booze. You're giving me everyone else's credit."

"If you're gonna be a dumb little shithead, I can tell you where to shove it." Janice replied in a slow, scathing drawl. "They did their things. But you're the one behind them all, getting them to do their best. You stop that, we go back to eating cockroaches an' bickering like pre-schoolers. So are you gonna pull your head out of your ass, or do I need to look up that recipe for Prairie Dog Surprise again?"

"Good luck finding prairie dogs around here. I think the drones took them all out," Aidan managed with a crooked smile. He drew a deep breath and took Janice's free hand in his. "Thanks, Janice."

Janice snorted. "You been around Kevin too much, crazy little romantic bastard." All the same, her calloused fingers squeezed his. "No more freaky shit, got it? Cause I know where you are all day, and I got no problem kicking your little ass."

Aidan blinked at her. "Freaky shit?"

"Hiding in your office or your room, shithead. Acting like it's your ass dead." Janice retorted. "Knock that shit off."

"I wasn't hiding," Aidan protested weakly. Had he looked like he was hiding? "I got a boatload of new data from the other bases I need to comb through. We have a leak to plug. I have to find us a new munitions officer too, and—"

"You were hiding your whiny ass because you didn't like the shit life dumped on you. Too damn bad. None of us liked it," the older woman repeated with exaggerated patience. "Now, are you gonna go kiss that kid of yours and make him quit walking around like a dog that just got his nuts cut off, get some sleep, an' talk to folks when you get down like this? Or am I gonna hit you over the head with a wrench till your brain starts workin'? That's your choices."

The words, weirdly, made him smile. "I'll avoid a massive headache, thanks." He squeezed her hand once more and stood. With a mock salute, he slipped out and padded back to his own room.

Aidan half-expected a tirade as soon as the door opened. He was probably overdue for one. But there weren't any words: only Kevin sprawled across the bed, still dressed and dead asleep.

Aidan crossed to the bed, sitting carefully on the edge. He didn't want to wake Kevin; he knew his boyfriend was exhausted. Hell, he was probably the reason Kevin was passed out like this. He'd said he'd be back in half an hour. He'd lost track of time.

In the dim orange glow of the night-cycle lighting, Kevin looked unreal: a marble statue, not somebody that walked and breathed and played bad music.

He'd been so sure that Kevin would yell at him earlier, too. He'd been braced for a fight. But he'd been wrong again.

Kevin wasn't the yelling kind. He needed to remember that. There was no cursing or flying fists with him. There wasn't even real arguing, not compared to what Aidan expected.

There was anger, sure. But no cruelty.

He had to remember that. It was so hard to remember when his depression got going. So hard to remember he wasn't going to be punished. But he watched Kevin breathe softly, and reminded himself to keep trying.

Quietly as he could, Aidan undressed and slid into bed. He lay down beside Kevin, head pillowed on one arm, watching his boyfriend breathe until his eyes finally closed.

Kevin sat up with a start in the morning, waking Aidan with a strangled yelp.

Reaching up, Aidan pulled him back down. "Think you were having a nightmare," he suggested gently, nuzzling into Kevin's shoulder.

Kevin glanced over, eyes still a little wild. "What...what time is it?"

"Nine."

"Shit." Kevin threw back the covers. "I shouldn't have slept so much, there's stuff that I was supposed—" but Aidan sat up and pulled him close, running a finger over his lips.

"You were supposed to take care of yourself," Aidan replied quietly. "And I didn't make that easier on you. I'm sorry."

Kevin blinked. Slowly, the lightning left his grey eyes. A copper brow rose. "Oh, I see you've noticed then?"

"I got wrapped up in my own head again. I've been an ass," Aidan agreed with a weak smile. He kissed Kevin softly. "And I'm sorry."

Kevin drew back, studying Aidan's face very carefully for a moment. Aidan hoped he saw something true.

Then Kevin leaned in. This kiss was long and slow. "Yes, you have been an ass," the redhead murmured when they came up for air, "but at least you noticed. No more auto-flagellation?" he asked, stealing another small kiss. "That's a relief."

Aidan murmured his agreement against Kevin's lips. First the injuries across his back, then the thought of the dead had kept him away from this. But if he was honest with himself, this was what he had needed.

Kevin pulled away gently, kissing the tip of Aidan's nose. "We'll do more of this tonight," he whispered.

"Why not now?" Aidan asked softly. "I think we're too late for breakfast, anyway."

"We aren't too late to get some work done, sir." Kevin replied, rolling off the bed. Then he glanced over his shoulder, his teasing smirk making its first appearance in two weeks. "And if you decided to wait for this long, I'm sure you can wait a few more hours."

Aidan snorted, but he pulled himself out of bed. He couldn't argue with that, after all. Instead, he closed the distance between them and kissed Kevin once more. "I'm going to go talk to Damian. Get him off the idea of medical suspensions."

"Good idea. I already took my medicine; your turn." Kevin agreed, pulling deftly out of the kiss. He ran his hand down Aidan's belly. "Tonight."

"Tonight," Aidan agreed. For the first time since the bombing, his pulse jumped.

Kevin walked him down to the medical bay door before pecking him on the cheek. "Luck. I should have the module printer borrowed for us by the end of the day."

"Thanks," Aidan murmured as Kevin pulled away. Then he was alone in front of the medical bay door.

This was *so* not a conversation he wanted to have. Gathering what remained of his courage, he pushed the door open.

Damian glanced up from his paperwork at the tiny desk in his office, black plastic eyes studying his commander across the room. "Well?"

Aidan took a deep breath and crossed the medical bay, stepping into Damian's office and closing the door. "I have two requests. Have a minute?"

Damian flicked away his screens, leaving Aidan nothing to look at but his eyes. Those implants still creeped him out a bit.

"Something I can do for you?" The doctor asked blankly.

"Not put me on medical suspension?" Aidan suggested with the best smile he could pull off. Then he sighed and braced his hands against the chair in front of him. "After that, go ahead and call me a dumbass. Then help me get a workup for tailored antidepressants?"

The doctor's mechanical eyes studied him for way too long. "Got any good reasons why I shouldn't put a man who's lying to his medical adviser, isolating, and committing self-harm on medical suspension? Or write up a man who hid a medical condition?" Damian asked. "It isn't something I want to do, but I will."

"Because I'm not going to be isolating or cutting anymore," Aidan said, pulling up all the confidence he could scrape together. "I talked to Janice last night and…it helped. Kevin's after me about it too, and… basically, I need to get on top of this, and I'm going to need some help." He didn't allow himself to look away as he spoke. "This stuff isn't just screwing with me anymore. It's screwing with people who matter. Who matter to me, I mean."

There was another long pause. Then Damian sighed, and nodded. "All right. I've got a lot of psych training on top of the medical school. There are things we can do. But I'm warning you now; don't pull this 'suffer in silence' trick again. I lose enough people as it is without adding suicides."

"I'm not going to kill myself," Aidan stated quietly, holding the doctor's blank, black eyes. He'd thought about it before, plenty of times. He still wasn't sure if he'd been trying to die that time when he was seventeen. But that was then. "I'm hoping the meds will help with that."

Damian nodded. "I'm with you on that. When you manage to scare me more than my brother and sister, you know it's bad."

Aidan chuckled. "Yeah."

He spent the next eight hours running through possible munitions officer profiles. He'd tried asking Sarah if she wanted the spot, and that had gone over like a lead balloon. He'd thought she'd stopped breathing for a second there. That left Plan B: find somebody new.

What he was looking for was pretty specific: he needed somebody who was grid-savvy, good with covert munitions and also trained for Dust action and base security. There were plenty of folks good with Dust fighting and base protection, but he needed somebody who could do what Lazarus had done and run with Kevin to pull off Grid missions as well. On top of those considerations, he needed somebody who could work as a personality with his insane crew.

Tommy brought him a plate of lunch around one, and that broke him out of his thoughts for a second.

"Hey Tommy."

"Hey," the little boy replied, putting down the plate. Aidan watched him carefully. The boy never looked at him.

Getting out of his chair, Aidan knelt at Tommy's eye level. "Hey," he murmured. "How's your day going?"

Tommy shrugged, staring at his boots. "Okay, I guess."

"Yeah?"

Tommy raised his head, giving Aidan a tiny smile. "Yeah. Billie'n me are printing kitchen stuff today. I got to help put the old plastic stuff down the shredder."

Aidan smiled. "Sounds cool. And thanks for lunch. I appreciate it." He squeezed Tommy's shoulder.

The little boy's smile strengthened just a little. He bobbed his head. "Yeah. Bye."

"Bye." Aidan murmured.

Once Tommy had left, he got back down to work, wincing as he bit down on his meal. Billie still had some things to learn about cooking amaranth-based pasta. The stuff tasted like old shoes. But he chewed anyway, flipping through the profiles of people with munitions credentials who were interested in changing bases. He must have tried a dozen different keywords.

He flipped past another file of a guy whose record had way too many disciplinary notes regarding female peers. If nothing else, that'd mean Aidan would have to file a death report after one of his crew killed the guy.

A new profile flicked into place. Aidan was half-way down the page before he realized what profile picture he was looking at.

His heart lurched.

Naomi. It was Naomi's profile picture on the screen.

The information read 'currently deep cover Grid operative, 14-month tour. Scheduled for suitable base posting and/or duties exchange by 6-17.'

Aidan touched the date. His screen shivered and blipped under his finger. The seventeenth. That was tomorrow. And Naomi was an officer.

Pushing his chair back, he rested his back against it and stared at the screen.

Naomi. Kickass little Naomi. She'd already been on the fast track for her Officer rank the last time they were together, four years ago. She would be perfect. And her attitude would be the absolute best fit for this base.

And Naomi thought he was dead.

Aidan tapped his fingers against the chair. Standing, he paced the room.

Okay. She thought he was dead. He'd had a good reason. Well, okay. It had seemed like a good reason.

Would she think it was a good reason?

How could he explain it to her?

How did he explain it to himself?

He'd wanted her to stop suffering because of him. He'd wanted her to be free of the burden that watching his back had put on her.

They'd been separated by a base bombing. A week before that, Naomi had been written up trying to protect him. Again. The medical assistant who'd helped out with Aidan's checkup was a recent escapee from the Cavanaugh Corporation, and he apparently hadn't left the Cavanaugh Perfection Mandate behind. He and a couple like-minded buddies had jumped Aidan late one night on the way back to the quarters he had shared with Jackson. The three of them had done their damnedest to kill him for being a…

No, he wasn't going to think about what they'd said. This was about Naomi. She and Jackson had saved his ass. He remembered the way Naomi fought for him. She'd been a force of nature.

Everyone involved had gotten a disciplinary write-up. Didn't matter who'd been attacking and who'd been defending, not on that base. He'd been sure things wouldn't change. He hadn't wanted to see Naomi's record wrecked as she tried to protect him, over and over.

When the chance came up, he'd protected her instead. When the bombing of their second base had separated them, he'd had Jackson code Aidan Henderson-Adler onto the records of the deceased. Aidan Headly had gone into the record as a new profile.

Jackson had told him it was a shitty thing to do, but he'd done the code work.

Maybe it had been a shitty thing to do. But Aidan hadn't seen another good choice.

He was in a better place now. He could actually help Naomi's career instead of destroying it. He could offer her something he'd never had to give before: a good setup, security. A home.

But first he had to offer her an apology. And an explanation.

"Shit," he whispered. "Shit, shit, shit…"

"Rough day?"

The soft voice jerked his head up. Kevin leaned against the

doorjamb, smiling gently.

"Hey," Aidan replied, relief and something like happiness welling up in his chest. Turning, he glanced at the picture. "Give me a sec."

Before he had time to chicken out, he typed up the request for transfer and the scheduling of an intake interview, hit Encrypt, and sent it up to Sector Personnel. If it went through, he could schedule a meeting with Naomi, and pray that she'd let him apologize.

Taking a deep breath, he switched his work console off. The image of his sister dissolved.

"I was trying to find us a munitions officer, but I wasn't having any luck. Except..." He turned, unable to resist the hope that tipped his lips up at the corners. "Naomi turned up. She's looking to cycle off the Grid, wants a Dust posting."

Kevin's bland expression eased into a real smile. "Your sister? That's a piece of good news I wasn't expecting." Stepping in, he put his arms around Aidan, enfolding him in comfort. "It'll be good to have her about; I know you've missed her," he murmured. "I imagine she's feeling the same."

"Not exactly," Aidan murmured. "If I get approval I'll set an intake interview, but it could get kind of..." he froze for a moment. He hadn't told Kevin that he'd made sure Naomi thought he was dead. He really didn't want to deal with that right now. "Hairy. Kind of hairy. We have some old crap between us. I need to see if we can work it out. I'll meet with her in person. With any luck we can talk about it and she'll come around."

"Worth a try, I suppose," Kevin agreed quietly, resting his brow against the top of Aidan's head. "Will you need to go on Grid for this?"

"Yeah," Aidan agreed. "A vid-call won't be safe, not with her cover. And not with us leaking intel."

"We'll get a grid run scheduled, then." Kevin agreed. "It is late though, love. Come to bed?"

"Yeah," Aidan agreed quietly.

Behind their closed door, Kevin turned and kissed Aidan's brow, then his lips.

"How are you, tonight?"

Aidan leaned into his warmth, wrapping his arms around Kevin's waist. Kevin's hands stroked his back. The heat of Kevin's touch warmed him, but the aching weariness lay in his bones like lead.

He swallowed. "I'm not all the way there yet. I'm sorry, Kev, I know we said tonight we'd… I just…"

"Ssh," Kevin whispered, running his fingers over Aidan's lips. "Why do you think you should apologize, hm?" Kissing Aidan's knuckles, the redhead stepped away. He methodically got himself undressed, setting his folded clothes on their chest of drawers for the next day. Aidan followed his lead, pulling his clothes off and dropping them in the hamper.

"I found something I think you'd like," Kevin murmured, pulling the sheets aside.

"Yeah?" Aidan asked quietly. Kevin smiled softly, picking up his tab and sliding into bed. Aidan followed him, curling against the taller man's body. Kevin looped an arm around his shoulders, pulling him close. Kevin's fingers laced between his. Aidan allowed his head to rest on Kevin's shoulder.

Kevin pulled up something on his tab with his free hand, activating the holographic screen so the words floated in front of them. Aidan glanced through them. "Poetry?"

Kevin kissed his brow. "What else? Close your eyes, love. I'll read to you."

Aidan did, feeling his body relax in Kevin's embrace. "This is a poem by an amazing man named Rumi. I thought you'd like it," his boyfriend's cultured voice murmured.

Quietly, Kevin read.

"In my vertigo, in my dizziness

In my drunken haze

Whirling and dancing like a spinning wheel

I saw myself as the source of existence

I was there in the beginning
And I was the spirit of love

Now I am sober
There is only the hangover
And the memory of love
And only the sorrow."

Aidan sighed, feeling the ache in his chest, the ache in his bones. He didn't want to think about sorrow, let alone talk about it. If anything, the words underlined it. "Kind of dark for tonight," he murmured.

Kevin's lips brushed his brow. "Ssh. That's only the first part. Listen."

Aidan lay still as Kevin's voice picked up the cadence of the words again.

"I yearn for happiness
I ask for help
I want mercy
And my love says:
Look at me and hear me
Because I am here
Just for that."

Kevin's fingers squeezed his softly. His pulse beat against Aidan's skin. The words wove through the air.

"I am your moon and your moonlight too
I am your flower garden and your water as well
I have come all this way, eager for you
Without shoes on my feet

I want you to laugh
To kill all your worries
To love you
To nourish you."

Kevin's fingers stroked his, his cheek against the top of Aidan's head. The words were like painkilling cream on a wound, easing the aches. He could feel himself settling into this time and place: the warmth, the comfort, the tenderness and the poetry. He was grounded in his body, out of his own head for the first time in weeks. His body was tired, but this was the tiredness of a long day. The sick, debilitating weariness was easing out of him.

"Oh sweet bitterness," Kevin murmured,

"I will soothe you and heal you

I will bring you roses

I, too, have been covered with thorns."

His voice trailed away into silence. Kevin's lips rested against the top of his head.

"That's really gorgeous." Aidan murmured into the quiet. Kevin's arm squeezed him softly.

"It seemed eminently fitting; sweet bitterness. I knew I'd have to read this to you some time."

Aidan turned his head, resting his cheek against Kevin's skin. He nuzzled close.

"Kev?"

"Hm?"

"Thanks."

"Any time, Aidan my love."

Aidan listened to Kevin's heart, his breathing falling into sync with his boyfriend's.

"Got any more poems?" Aidan asked quietly. Kevin chuckled.

"Of course. This is me we're talking about."

Listening to Kevin read, Aidan found himself, finally, at peace.

Message Incoming. Sector Commander. Message Incoming

Aidan glanced down at his tab, and felt his heart jump into his throat. Carefully, he hit 'accept'

Message Handle: Sector40COM

Message: Headly, I want a vid-call with you concerning this requested personnel assignment. I'm available until 1100, and after 1800.

Call.

Quickly, Aidan typed out a reply.

Message Handle: AceOfSpades

Message: Will call in 5 minutes, sir.

He booked it down to his office, closed the door, and got the call placed on his work console.

Magnum's wide face appeared in the screen. He did not look happy.

"Headly. I want a word with you."

"Sir?" Inside his head, Aidan could feel his thoughts scrambling like frantic specialists in training, trying to find an act in the past that the sector commander might have problems with.

Magnum sat like a monolith. "Do you remember that I asked you about the discrepancies in your files during our first interview?"

Aidan's stomach lurched. He forced his hands to relax in his lap. "Yes, sir. I explained the falsified records."

"And I wasn't happy about them. Or about the state you'd left your family affairs in. Your sister has been a valuable asset. I don't want her morale ruined because you changed your mind about something that was a stupid idea in the first place." The big man's lips twitched. "Noble, sure. But stupid. And if she doesn't accept your apology, then I have two good personnel under emotional duress. During a very important time for the Force. I don't like it, Headly."

He sat back in his chair, crossing his arms. Aidan heard the chair creak through the link.

"Tell me why I should approve this," the big man asked. Aidan's voice scraped in a bone-dry throat.

"Sir. Naomi Henderson-Adler is exactly what my base needs. Grid-savvy, operationally trained, with a specialty in covert munitions. Versed in security on and off the Grid. She's quick, focused, and her temperament is a good fit for my team." He drew a breath. "And on the personal side, sir, you're right. I made an error in judgment. I take responsibility for my mistakes. And I'm going to try to repair this one."

Magnum's eyes held his for too long. Then the big man sighed. "Your base has been on recuperative downtime for the past two and a half weeks. It was sanctioned, but the clock's ticking, Headly."

"I hear it, sir," Aidan agreed. It was the reason for the tightness in the pit of his gut. He knew they were tight on time. He'd set things in motion that he couldn't hit the pause button on now: the Grapevine's organizing of a protest large enough to keep AgCo and EagleCorp distracted in—shit—five weeks now. The other three bases on the operation, waiting on him.

And the leaked information they still needed to find a source for.

He straightened his spine. "I still think she's the best person for the position."

Magnum seemed to be reading something off the back of his skull, the way he stared. Then, slowly, he nodded. "All right, Headly. Have your interview with her. And you better have a damn good speech ready to give."

Aidan nodded. "Think I do, sir."

Once he had the approval, Aidan gathered his operational team: this time it was only Kevin and Yvonne, Sarah and Tweak. Everyone else had too much to do.

Aidan took a breath. "I wanted to get us together and have a state-of-events discussion, now that everybody's out of the med bay. This mission's screwed us over so far, and I'm pretty done with that. We have to find another way to do this."

"And not die." Tweak interjected, every word as precise and punishing as a bullet.

"What are you thinking?" Yvonne asked, shooting Tweak a warning look that the Gamma ignored.

"We need to bring in someone else to head Munitions," Aidan muttered, his voice as tight as the fists on his lap. He took another deep breath. "Someone with a bit more Grid-savvy. And some savvy for explosives wouldn't hurt, either."

Sarah frowned. "You got someone in mind?"

"I do. I'm going to interview her this week. Naomi Headly. Naomi Henderson-Adler, on paper." Aidan's voice cracked on her name. "My little sister."

"Sister?" Yvonne asked in surprise.

Tweak snorted. "After they had you, your 'rents still wanted more?"

"Tweak," Kevin remarked with a level look, "you're rather badly in need of a lesson in social decorum."

Tweak rolled her eyes. "English, CES."

"That was English, in fact it's the original version of whatever you're speaking."

Tweak sighed. "Freak."

Kevin smiled thinly. "Pot and kettle much?" Yvonne raised a hand to cover a grin.

Tweak turned her attention back to Aidan. "So she's your sis. What's she good for?"

"She's been on-Grid for years, in several different sectors and cities, so she knows the layout better than any of us and isn't prone to getting 'buzzed," Aidan explained. "She can handle anything we need for this mission, operations-wise. And if we need anything blown up…well, she's even better than Laz was at that." Aidan shrugged weakly.

Kevin crossed himself. "God rest his soul." Yvonne closed her eyes, resting her head on Sarah's shoulder. Sarah rubbed her back gently.

Tweak nodded. "Okay, sounds good. So when's she get here?"

"I need to go on-grid and meet with her," Aidan sighed. He leaned back in his chair, running a hand uncomfortably over the back of his neck. "She may not be all that excited to see me, so I'll meet with her on my own. Logistics, I'll go in with you guys on the next run, and you can drop me off at her place while you get us the meds we need."

Tweak stiffened. She stood, pacing the room. The rest of the team watched her warily. After three circuits, she came to a sharp halt in front of his chair. "Don't d-die." He couldn't tell if it was an order or a plea.

Aidan managed to give the girl a smile. "I'm going to do my best not to. Liza and I have already talked about contingency plans, what to do if I don't come back. But we don't think it'll come to that."

"I take it this meeting is going to be awkward?" Kevin asked carefully.

"That might be an understatement," Aidan admitted sheepishly. "She's probably going to be pissed that I let us get out of touch."

Made sure they got out of touch, really. But with any luck Kevin wouldn't need to hear about that for a while.

Kevin smiled ruefully. "Well, forewarned is forearmed so they say. I'd hate to be in the middle of something I don't have the details on."

The words turned a knife in Aidan's guts.

The sun beat down the next morning as they set out. They took bikes rather than a truck; bikes were easier to hide.

"One of the near bases dug an entry right into the maintenance tunnel system under the Sweetwater Platform." Kevin remarked conversationally as they covered the bikes in electrified slick tarps and covered that with windblown rabbit bush and tumbleweeds. "Should be right over there and-ow! I hate the thorns on these things."

Sucking the blood off a finger, he poked around and found a dirt-covered trap door. Heaving it open, he bowed elegantly in Yvonne's direction. "After you."

Yvonne snorted, but she shouldered her gun and climbed down into the hole.

Aidan took a breath and followed her. It was dark in the tunnels, lit only by the dim blue glow of their tabs.

As they walked, Kevin passed Yvonne and Aidan Citizen Cards with small blue chips in the shapes of eagles in the corners that identified them as Citizen Secure Standing.

"Your transit tickets are recorded as being purchased." Kevin added in an undertone. "Just let them scan your ID's and we'll be shipshape."

Aidan accepted his credentials with care. The layer of epithelial Synth cells printed to match the genome on his card and plastered over his hands to disguise his own DNA always made him feel a little fumble-fingered. Considering the alternative if his actual genome got recorded, it was a small price to pay.

The alternative. Ending up as the subject of a public morality execution, if he was outed in a Cavanaugh, EagleCorp or AgCo neighborhood. Removed, detained and killed as a terrorist anywhere else.

Aidan focused on his breathing.

Breathe in for seven. Breathe out for seven.

His chest was tight. His mouth was dry. But they were using fake IDs coded by Tweak, with nothing to trace. There was no reason for the Peacekeepers to look twice. He just had to act natural.

The tunnel ended in a maintenance shaft leading upward. Yvonne climbed up first, cautiously looking around, then motioned for Aidan and Kevin to follow.

The station was slick and clean, quieter than most out here in the 'burbs. People scurried to and fro, chattering among themselves or engrossed in their tabs. Ad holos followed them like technicolor ghosts.

They found the CSS trains without much trouble. Kevin nodded down the platform. "Your ride's here, ours over there. We'll...bloody hell." He swiped 'decline' on an ad asking him if he'd like to upgrade his tab that had just appeared in front of his nose, grimacing. The ad dissolved. "We'll meet you back here in an hour, unless circumstances change. Have fun with the sister."

Aidan tried for a smile, feeling fake as a holo-ad for happiness. "Sure. See you guys. Come get me if trouble comes up."

"Roger," Kevin agreed with a quick, dry smile.

Aidan had a hard time relaxing on the ride. He sat fiddling with his tab, going back and forth between playing games and watching short vids with his 'buds in.

By the time he was two thirds of the way there, he'd started to sweat.

His tab shook in his hands.

The train shushed up to the station, and Aidan forced his knees to hold him. His feet felt like blocks of wood.

It was always the noise that hit Aidan hard: a mess of competing music and adverts from every store, all shouting for his attention. The neon signs flashed and strobed, info signs and adverts on everything. Road signs flashed 'Brought to You by CrescaCo, Road Safety For All. A Subsidiary Of ArgusCo' at drivers, along with images of cars for sale.

Heat haze sizzled off the sidewalk. He walked through a holo trying to direct him to a local food stand with his eyes half-closed. He moved as casually as he could, his hands in his pockets and his shoulders slumped, his billed hat pulled low over his eyes. It made him look like a teen playing hooky, but at least it kept him from worrying about making eye contact with the wrong person.

His tab led him down and off the main thoroughfare, into a nice mid-class district of family apartments and flats. "$320 dollars/sq.ft!" several discrete ads scrolled around the frames of entry doors. 'Great value! Beautiful living space!'

Further down the row, the ads petered out and the buildings got a little less fancy, though the neighborhood was still decent. Perfect cover, Aidan realized. The neighborhood was good enough that the Peacekeepers wouldn't be too pushy, not good enough to make people wonder how you afforded it. Their kind of neighborhood.

Aidan walked up to the next building and stepped into the foyer. It was clean, but nothing special. The elevator was smaller than Aidan expected, but still a nice break from the noise. The air-conditioning made him shiver after the heat outside.

Aidan hesitated a moment too long in front of the apartment door. What would he find when Naomi answered it? Would she be thrilled or furious? Would she even hear him out? Finally, he raised his hand, forcing himself to knock and swallowing down bile.

He stood in the hallway for what felt like years before the indicator light beside the door flickered into blue life.

"Yes?" His sister's voice asked. His heart leaped. It was so damn good to hear her.

"It's kind of a hot day." he murmured. "And there's a storm coming in."

There was a pause. "You want to come in out of the dust?"

"Yeah," he agreed.

The blue camera light glowed, unwavering.

Naomi's voice crackled in the speaker. "Can you take off your hat? Let me see your face."

Aidan's breath caught in his throat. With trembling fingers, he pulled the hat he wore off and did his best to smile.

"Hey Omi. Don't freak. It's...it's me."

There was a gasp on the other side of the door.

Aidan stared at the camera light, trying to smile. His heart hammered in his ears. "You probably want to ask me a couple things, make sure I'm not a mim—"

The door swung open, and Naomi stood there in jeans and a black t-shirt, a knife in left hand and...

And a cybernetic arm on her right side, the fist bunched.

A cybernetic arm.

There was scarring on the right side of her throat too, and she'd grown her ash-blonde hair out into swept bangs that hid the right side of her face. The eye he could see, blue green and brilliant, looked like ice. She was beyond furious.

Aidan swallowed.

When Naomi spoke, the words were high and tight. "I don't know who you are, but using my brother is just sick. Get out of my building, or I swear I'll gut you."

"No one's using me," Aidan replied as calmly as he could. He held his hands out carefully, showing his harmlessness. "It's me, Omi. Really. I'm here."

Naomi's eye narrowed again. "I warned you. Get out of my building."

"When you were twelve, you started experimenting with cherry bombs and one of them got caught in my shirt. Still have the scar, see?" Aidan desperately rolled up his sleeve and turned to show her the faint scar on his upper arm, a spatter of pale skin. "We both kept it a secret because Dad would have beat the crap out of you, so it scarred. Remember?"

Naomi's face went slack. Her eye flicked to his face. She gulped. Slowly, she stepped aside, giving him access to the small, classy apartment. Moving with care, he stepped inside.

Naomi stood in the open doorway, staring at him. The knife clattered to the ground.

"Aidan?" Naomi asked, her voice barely more than a breath. Aidan did his best to smile. He wished he had the guts to hug her, but you didn't grab Naomi when she didn't want it, if you liked your nose where it was.

"Hey Omi." he managed. "I've got a lot to explain, but we better shut the door." "Aidan?" Naomi repeated, staring at him. He didn't let his eyes drop to that terrible, mechanical arm. He could ask what had happened to his amazing little sister later.

He nodded. "It's me, Omi. Really."

Naomi stood stock still, her body tense as a wire. She looked as if she were fighting something inside her. Aidan tensed. When Naomi got like that, it meant somebody was about to get—

Naomi's voice came out sharp. "If it's you...then...then fuck you!"

She snapped into motion, faster than Aidan could follow, her left fist swinging. It slammed into Aidan's cheek. He dropped, rolling with the blow. Naomi straddled him, her fists flying, tears sparkling across her scarred face. "Fuck you for leaving me! Fuck you for letting me think you were *dead*! Fuck you, Aidan!"

Aidan covered his face with his arms, blocking the blows to his face as his sister flailed. "Ow! Damn it Omi! Ow! Not the jaw!"

Somewhere behind them, a man's voice snapped in the hot air. "What the...hell? Stop that! Yve, get the door."

Then Kevin was over him, down on one knee and blocking Naomi's fists on crossed forearms. "Stop!" he snapped, pushing forwards and up into the younger woman's chest; at her angle, it sent her toppling back on her rear.

A breath later, Kevin was kneeling with one knee and all his weight in the center of the girl's chest and the other resting very gently on her throat. "I don't know what the hell that was for, and I don't want to hurt you," he stated with quiet venom, 'but your shenanigans could kill us all right now and you just ripped into my base mate. With that in mind, are you done playing sociopathic bitch?" he emphasized the question with the barest shift of weight to put pressure on her throat, face impassive. "Well?"

Naomi glared up at him, tears wet on her cheeks, chest heaving. Her hair had been thrown back by the move, and he could see her properly now: the right side of her face was scarred, the skin looking burnt.

"Kev," Aidan groaned as he sat up, "Let her go."

His head banged as he moved. There was blood inside his mouth. He swallowed, tasting copper.

Kevin stood warily. Still watching Naomi, he stepped over and knelt beside Aidan, looking down. The steel in his eyes was gone in a breath.

"Oh dear... Aidan, let me see..." gently, he took Aidan's chin in his hand and carefully turned his head, studying the injuries as he pulled a small med kit from a zipped inner pocket of his jacket. "All right, not too bad, just hold still..."

Yvonne blinked at the tableau, looking from Naomi to them. "Um...Aidan? I mean sir? Not to be rude, but...what the hell?"

"I thought he was dead," Naomi growled as she massaged her throat. "Four years, I thought he was dead. Our base got hit. Couldn't find him. Thought he…fucking idiot, I thought he died saving my life. The base casualty report said you were *dead*, you dickweed. Why did it say you were dead?"

"Jackson," Aidan muttered. His jaw clicked as he talked. Ow. "He coded me out. Wrote me a new profile."

Naomi hissed between her teeth. "Of course. He would. And you would. You fuckheads."

Kevin's fingers froze. He stared down into Aidan's face as Naomi spoke. Aidan watched his rain cloud eyes ice over.

"Ah." he stated, his voice brittle. "That explains the fisticuffs, then. Excuse me for interrupting, sir; if I'd known I would have let you two sort it out without interference." His hands worked deftly to staunch bleeding and place blunt-trauma auto-pads, but the tenderness was gone from the motions. His vocabulary had gone through the roof. And he was using 'sir' again. It was usually a joke, but now the word could have been used to cool nuclear reactors.

Aidan closed his eyes, feeling pain begin to tie knots inside his chest. Goddamn, he was never going to catch a break. He hadn't wanted Kevin to know!

Kevin wasn't even supposed to be here. What was he doing here?!

Naomi's plastic hand clicked as it curled into a fist against her thigh. "Damn right, you should have. This whole time, I thought he was dead, and instead he was off running around."

"A little more than that, actually." Kevin carefully folded his jacket into a square and shoved it under Aidan's head. "Seems like there's a lot of details I wasn't informed of on this mission, sir." he remarked coolly. "I would have appreciated a little advance warning."

"Sorry." Aidan croaked. "What're you doing here?"

Kevin glanced at Naomi. "Are we secure?"

"Phage nanoids for DNA in the walls, sound boxes wired to every corner. Seals on the windows." Naomi stated shortly. Kevin glanced at Yvonne, nodding.

"Our medical contact got taken in by the Corps." Yvonne murmured. "You said come and get you if there was trouble. Well, yeah. Trouble."

Aidan nodded, touching his lip with his tongue and wincing. Split. That had to be where the blood was from.

He wish it hurt enough to distract him from the shithole he'd landed himself in, for a second. He was fucked, and it really was his own damn fault. How many times had he thought he should tell Kevin about what he'd done to protect Naomi? How many times had he swallowed the words for fear of sabotaging the mission, or getting in a bad spot with his guy about it? And now he'd done both.

"Sir?" Naomi asked, her voice quieter now. Aidan watched her turn to study Yvonne. "You called him 'sir'. You're telling me this idiot's in charge of something?"

"An entire base," Yvonne replied carefully. "He's our commander."

Naomi stared. "And you gamma dumbasses brought your commander *on the fucking Grid*?"

"We didn't bring him anywhere. He decided to come. He isn't a child." Kevin stated in clipped tones as he stood. "Though why he thought seeing someone whose death had apparently been rather exaggerated would make you amenable, I really have no clue. I'd had the understanding that you two had fallen out of touch for a few years. Not that you believed he was dead. Excuse my misunderstanding." Meeting her eyes, he gave a lazy salute. "Kevin, logistics. No hard feelings about the tackle I hope."

Naomi looked him up and down for a long moment. "You his new squeeze?"

Kevin's face remained politely blank. "Not a good question to ask a stranger, is that?"

Naomi's expression was just as unreadable as Kevin's. Aidan watched as she carefully twisted something in her mechanical wrist with her good hand. Maybe punching him a few times had loosened the mechanism.

"Whatever," his sister stated flatly, "I'm getting a drink."

For a moment, Kevin knelt again, studying the injuries on Aidan's face with cold eyes. Three curt sentences made it past his lips. "Say something if you need a pain pill. I'll start talking to her about the situation. Stay still until the bruising's down."

Aidan swallowed hard and nodded against Kevin's jacket. "Kev, I'm s—"

Kevin stood before he got the words out.

Lying still, he cursed in his head.

Event File 20
File Tag: Recruitment Interview
Timestamp:13:00-6-19-2156

"You want one, smooth talker?" Naomi called from her little kitchen as glass clinked.

"What brand?" Kevin asked. "If it's something decent, Yvonne and I would both love one."

"By the way, don't let his snob attitude put you off." Yvonne added dryly. "His parents never taught him how to act human."

Kevin gave her a look. "Yvonne. Not the time."

Naomi snorted, pulling three bottles of beer from the fridge unit. She popped the top on her bottle, setting the other two on the counter with a bottle opener beside them. Leaning against the wall, she took a sip of her own. "That's what I've got."

Yvonne snatched up one of the bottles and pried the cap off. "This is great."

"Better be. I pay enough." Naomi took another sip of her own beer, studying them both. "So. Why'd he drag you two all the way out here?"

Kevin sipped his beer, glad to have something to give him time to choose his words. The liquid was pleasantly cool in the apartment's heat. He chose his words, studying the label. "We've got quite an involved mission, and it...hasn't been going well so far. We're hoping that the inclusion of your expertise will make us a bit more successful."

Naomi looked at him, then gave an incredulous little laugh. "What, you need an explosives expert? Sorry, flame-o, I'm laying low for a while."

Kevin nodded blankly, ice thickening in his chest. "Yes, I was afraid we'd blown it." Aidan had, at any rate. He set his bottle down. "Excuse us. We'll get going. Thanks for the beer."

He heard Naomi snort. "No wonder you idiots are getting your asses handed to you."

Kevin glanced up at her, meeting one cold topaz eye. "Does that mean you're going to listen to a proposition? Or are you just working out the last of your aggression verbally?"

Naomi took another swig of her beer. "Depends. Are you going to be a coward and walk away, or are you going help me stick the dumbass on the floor over there on a couch and actually explain shit?" She spun the bottle between her hands, the glass clicking against her mechanical fingers. "You gonna be as gutless as my brother or you gonna face the music?"

Kevin gave the woman a grim smile. "I've always liked a tune myself. One of my greater passions actually." He leaned against the opposite wall, imitating the woman's casual pose. "And I won't disagree about the 'dumbass' comment." he added, taking another sip of his beer. In fact, he'd been snarling his own commentary about his boyfriend's intelligence and behavior in his head since the situation had been clarified. The idiot. The brainless lout! "But this isn't about familial arguments, is it?" He asked pointedly, "This is about a war we're fighting." He watched Naomi over the bottle. "How would you like to help deal the Corps a sucker punch?"

Naomi watched him a moment, toying with the label on her bottle. "Wasn't kidding about the explosives thing. I got a bit too hot last time. They're on the lookout for my best stuff, so I can't use it. What're you trying to do?"

"Take out the Citizen Standing System," Kevin stated casually, leaning back in case she spat her drink.

Naomi's cybernetic fingers loosened on the bottle. It shattered on the kitchen floor, the remains of her beer spilling everywhere. She barely seemed to notice; her wide eye was fixed on him. "The hell you are."

Kevin shrugged. "We've recruited a hacker who can take down a drone in under forty seconds and reroute a base's entire slick tech in under three minutes. We have myself on the logistical and requisitions front, and I'm fairly talented. We've got Aidan, who's quite good professionally if you can believe it. I don't suppose you've heard of the Wildcards base? That's us."

"Seriously?!" Naomi breathed the word as beer ran off her boots. Stepping out of the kitchen, she crossed to stand over Aidan. He sat up, meeting her eyes.

"You seriously run the Wildcards? The fucking Wildcards?" The young woman asked. Aidan nodded once, slowly. "Surprise?" he mumbled.

For a tense moment, Kevin thought Naomi was going to kick Aidan. His body tightened, ready to break up another fight.

Naomi looked away in disgust, meeting his eyes again. "So, what d'you need with an explosives chick, if you're so set?"

"It was Aidan's suggestion actually." Kevin glanced down at Aidan. "Can you move your jaw yet?" he asked, hearing the ice in his own voice. Ice was good. Ice kept the seething anger at bay.

Aidan carefully pushed himself to his feet. He sighed. "Yeah."

Naomi stepped away, grabbing a pad from the kitchen to clean up the spilled beer. "Doesn't answer the question," she muttered at the floor.

"The Commander can answer it." Kevin stated simply. He noted the slight wince on Aidan's face, and felt at once guilty and supremely satisfied. How did he manage to date a man who could *be* such a bastard to his own sister? How could Aidan, his sweet, thoughtful Aidan, do such a callous thing?

"We need your help, Naomi," Aidan stated, careful with each

word. "You've been on-Grid more than any of us, and we can't do this without someone who knows the territory. Our hacker can't wipe the Citizen Standing info without access to on-Grid structures, which means we need someone to help her get in and out. Someone who can fight, who knows her way around, and who…well, if worst comes to worst, can blow the hell out of the people trying to kill her." Aidan smiled crookedly. "Our munitions officer's dead too. We need somebody at least as good as he was to keep my base in shape. So we need somebody good at base work and Grid work. I did a search, and you came up as my best candidate."

Tucking his hands in his pockets, he shrugged helplessly.

Any other day, Kevin would have gone to his side. He was so woebegone: hair mussed, shoulders slumped, the bruise on his jaw slowly dissipating under the auto-pad. Lip split.

But a man who could break his own sister's heart in such a way and then call her up when it was convenient didn't deserve comfort.

Later, he promised himself, he'd get the story out of Aidan. And it would have to be a good one.

Naomi mopped at spilled beer and shattered glass on her kitchen floor, silent.

"While I can understand the inclination to refuse our commander anything he asks at the moment," Kevin added, "you'll do everyone a favor if you don't think of it as a personal consideration. People are going to die if we don't get help on this from someone like you. A number of people have already died. Good people." He drew a breath, steeling himself. "We need help, frankly. And something has to change. You know it as well as I, if you've got as much sense as your brother. Preferably more," he added, shooting Aidan a cold glance. Aidan wouldn't meet his eyes.

Naomi finished cleaning the spill and tossed the pad in a bin. She straightened, rolling her mechanical shoulder. It squealed. "So I'm coming on as a munitions officer, and playing babysitter to get the hacker in and out?"

"Generally speaking," Kevin agreed. "You'll have as much

support as we can afford, of course, but that's partially contingent on your skillset, of which I wasn't fully informed. Among other things. Once I know the particulars, I can work with them and we can start making a firm operational plan...that is, of course, if you're interested?" he added as politely as he could manage. He tried to ignore the blood on her plastic knuckles. Focus. Personal is not the same as important. What writer had that been from? Of course, Pratchett. And it was true. He was here to work, not to let his emotions run away with him. Focus. That was what he needed.

Naomi considered a moment, frowning at her flexing mechanical fingers. Finally, she looked back up, staring at Aidan. "Two conditions. One: I'm on a contractual assignment to your base. Not a permanent one. Set a time frame, and I'll opt out at the end, if I want. Two: I don't deal with you until this is over."

"Rather a contradiction in requirements there." Kevin suggested, allowing a hint of caution in his words. "Personal issues and the battle field shouldn't mix, and he is our commander..."

"I've been getting short, written assignments and carrying them out for three years now. I'm a grid operative. I don't like micromanagement," Naomi explained with another squealing shrug. "And he isn't running this gig, unless there's something you haven't told me. Seems like the hacker is."

Yvonne snorted. "The day they let Tweak run something you can put me to bed with a shovel."

"It's complicated," Kevin interjected before either his foster-sister or his boyfriend could dig the hole any deeper, "but I think we can meet your requirements. Our best munitions man is gone; you'll make a stellar Munitions Officer...if Aidan approves." he added, remembering himself at the last moment. "I don't give the orders."

Aidan leaned against the wall and met his sister's gaze. He smiled weakly. "It'd be good to have you, Omi."

"Don't call me that." She turned away, looking back at Kevin. "Sounds like a deal."

"I'll let our personnel officer get to work on your assignment orders." Kevin agreed. With a lopsided cynic's smile, he stuck out his hand. "Shake on it."

Naomi held up her cybernetic hand. "Really?"

Kevin held her eyes. "I'm no coward. Pragmatist, yes, but not a coward."

She shrugged yet again and shook his hand, her arm creaking. Kevin glanced down at it. "We'll get that seen to when you come in. Our hacker and our doctor should be able to get it put back in order."

"Appreciate it," Naomi agreed quietly.

Stepping away, Kevin lifted his discarded coat from the floor. "I'll contact you when we're ready to bring you in; will a day's notice be sufficient?"

Naomi nodded. "Not like I have to put in for leave or anything. Sure."

"I'll send along a new tab that you can use to contact us, via courier." Kevin called over his shoulder. "Expect it by this afternoon." He glanced back, and managed a smile at Naomi's blinking surprise. "Don't look too shocked, we're not insolvent. Our hacker emptied a few illegitimate money-laundering accounts."

"I think I'm going to like her," Naomi said. A smile tugged at the corners of the lips.

"Que será, será," Kevin replied lightly.

Kevin walked quickly once they were in the street. He made purchases with the clipped accent that got them served first in all the shops, owners assuming that anybody of his class could go slumming as they pleased and still have plenty of money on them. Kevin didn't dissuade them from their assumptions; it made things quicker.

They took a break to eat lunch and unobtrusively plug a data stick into the newly-purchased tab that removed all Corporate surveillance programs and put in Force operating systems and encryption. Once that was done, he walked briskly across the street to a courier shop. "Add a note to that please, on delivery." he added once the assistant had taken

down the details for his delivery. "It should read 'thanks, we owe you'."
Then he was back out into the street. "Time to head home, I suppose," he
remarked as his team stepped out of the cafe. "Come along children."

"Are you going to act like you're out of an old movie all day now?"
Yvonne asked sourly.

Kevin gave a laugh that sounded brittle in his own ears. "Only as
long as it amuses."

"You're the only one it's amusing," Yvonne grumbled under her
breath.

Aidan said nothing. Kevin wasn't sure whether that made him
worried, or furious.

Event File 21
File Tag: Interpersonal Relations
Timestamp:15:00-6-19-2156

Kevin was a logistical robot for the rest of the trip, navigating them through the hot streets of the Grid. Once they got past the fences and climbed onto their bikes, he was off like a shooting star. Aidan let him go.

Kevin was a fast rider; he was out of his riding gear and the garage before Aidan and Yvonne had cut the power on their bikes.

Aidan lingered in the motor pool and listened to Yvonne chat with Dozer and Topher, double checking the bikes and gear for longer than was strictly necessary to give Kevin plenty of time to get settled before he followed. The guy was pissed. He'd want room to avoid Aidan for a while, probably.

Or longer, maybe.

Aidan let the weight settle in his gut. He'd screwed up again. Of course.

When Dozer started watching him, he slunk out into the corridor and toward his room.

"Um, Commander? Aidan? Wait up." Yvonne jogged to catch up. For a moment, they stood awkwardly in the hall. "Look," Yvonne managed eventually, "I've known Kev since he was sixteen. He gets all offended aristocracy talking to the peons like this, but really it's just because his feelings are hurt. Sarah and I have dumb arguments too, maybe not this gamma—shit I said I'd stop using that——I mean not this dumb, but.... Just...well, my advice is talk about it, okay? Kevin's all about facts and conditional requirements, I mean the half of his brain that isn't a library is a logistics computer. Give him your line of reasoning for why you fucked up and he'll usually come around. I just wanted to say...well, you know. Hang in." She punched his shoulder lightly. "It'll be okay."

Aidan smiled weakly and nodded. "Thanks, Yvonne."

"Yeah, sure." The blonde woman gave him a hopeful grin. "Don't worry, it'll all be good." then she was off down the hall.

In his own room, Aidan allowed himself five minutes to sit on the bed with his head in his hands. Then he forced himself up. He washed his face, wincing at the ache of his split lip. He laid a little auto-pad over the wound. The rest of the injuries were gone. Then he got back to doing his damn job. He decrypted and checked the readiness reports from the Tearaways and the Riptides. The Tearaways were the worst off, but they were getting their positions filled. Everybody knew they needed to be ready by the end of the month.

Aidan skipped dinner. At least, he tried to. Billie brought him a plate. She was getting a little better at the cooking.

He got through his reports, his mission checks from other bases, and his general workload. He kept his head in the game. He only looked up at a knock on his door. Damian glowered at him from the doorway.

"It's nine at night, and if nobody's dying then all-nighters are a stupid idea," the rangy man remarked.

Aidan smiled weakly. "I'm shutting down now."

"Good," the doctor stated. "And go make Kevin stop for the night too. I hear that's your problem to solve."

Stones dropped in Aidan's gut. He nodded. "Guess so."

Aidan watched the doctor leave. Slowly, he went through the routine of shutting down and pulled himself out of his seat.

"Working." Kevin stated quietly when Aidan knocked on his

office door, checking one of the several tabs on his desk and typing away on his console.

Aidan noted his boyfriend's tone, but he stepped into the office regardless. He cleared his throat uncomfortably. "Damian's on us about not pulling all-nighters again. Says he wants us to sign out and think about bed."

Kevin glanced up, his eyes blank. Then he nodded, turning back. "Thanks. Be there in a moment."

Aidan waited for half an hour. But he went to bed alone.

Half an hour before lunch the next day, Aidan knocked on Kevin's door. "Coming to lunch?"

"Later," Kevin replied tightly, dragging symbols around a map. "I'm not hungry, thanks."

Aidan swallowed hard. "Kev...I...when you're done could we...talk?

"If it'll serve a purpose, we can," Kevin stated crisply. The words stung like anything.

"You haven't really talked to me since we got back," Aidan muttered. He didn't really expect a response right now, but it was worth a shot. He had to do something, try to ease the guilt that had been building up inside him. It ached a hell of a lot more than the remnants of his bruises and his split lip.

There was a gap of breathless silence. Then the wheels of Kevin's chair squeaked as he turned it. Sitting with his arms crossed, he stared up at Aidan.

"Tell me why you did this." He thawed enough to nod at the room's other chair. "Take the other seat if it'll take time."

Aidan's chest felt tight, but he lowered himself into the flimsy chair and forced himself to meet Kevin's gaze. Where could he start?

Give him your line of reasoning for why you fucked up, that's what

Yvonne had said.

Aidan drew a slow breath. "I never meant to do this. Hell, I didn't even know she got hurt, I..." he swallowed. "She was beside me when the base we were trying to settle onto got bombed out. I grabbed her and...well, I guess I did what I did with the kids. Shielded her. I don't remember. I got slammed in the head, broke my shoulder and my arm in a couple places, got pretty ripped up. My back was torn up pretty bad that time, too." He drew a breath. "They took us to different bases to recover. When I was better, I checked up on her in the record first thing. She was down as 'wounded-ambulatory.' I was still in there as ' under medical care'. And I thought then, she was..." he tried to breathe slow, forcing his shoulders to relax.

"Look. There were four high level Disciplinary Acts on Naomi's record, and a ton of low level ones. And all those big ones were because of me. She got the first one beating the hell out of my first boyfriend on the base where we were born, after the guy...beat the shit out of me and broke my jaw." Aidan closed his eyes, his nails biting into his palms. "She got the second one for knocking an officer who was in my face on her ass right after we got to our second base. She got the third one for a stupid scuffle with a guy who hassled me. And the fourth one she got when a couple guys on our new base decided to...to jump me one night and give killing me a try." He swallowed painfully.

"She should have been headed to officer training at eighteen, not getting written up because she'd had to step in for me. She spent all her life watching my back, and it was wrecking her life. She didn't get commendations she deserved. She didn't get asked on to hang out with people, 'cause she was sister to a...to a freak. And when the bombing happened, I thought..." He stared at his hands, working words past the knot in his throat. "I thought I could give her the chance to go have a good life. If I'd told her that she would have laughed in my face. She never would have done her own thing if she knew I was around. So I made sure she didn't know." He shrugged uncomfortably. "As for why I didn't tell you...I...I just...couldn't put it into words. Not that that makes it better, but…there it is. I'm sorry. I know I made mistakes. I screwed up. Again. I thought it was for the best, but…I was wrong."

Kevin stared at him for a long, long time. Finally, he sighed, pulled off his glasses and tugged his cleaning cloth from his pocket. "Aidan…" his fingers began to polish the glass as he spoke. "I love you, but I trust you as my Commander, too. You let me walk in there blind. I walked into an on-grid operation with less than half the information I needed because you were scared of my reaction, or embarrassed, or…something. What if she'd taken her disaffection out by turning us in?"

Aidan winced and twisted his fingers together. "I know. This thing, Kev—it's got me all…I…I can't think straight."

Kevin slipped his glasses back on, watching Aidan with unwavering silver eyes. "I want to ask you a few things. When you do things like this, who are you trying to keep things from? Me, or yourself?"

Aidan swallowed hard. He wanted to look away from Kevin's gaze, look anywhere but his boyfriend's face. He forced himself to hold Kevin's eyes. "I…don't know. Myself, I suppose."

"And who will you help by doing so? This base? Yourself?" Kevin's relentless voice continued.

Aidan shook his head and pressed the heels of his palms against his eyes until he saw red. He took a deep breath and tried not to feel too childish. "Maybe I should take the leave Damian wanted to put me on. Liza's better suited to leading a base. It'll be better for everyone."

Kevin's hands pulled his down. Kevin held his eyes. "Aidan. Liza led us before you came, and we almost fell apart. You're who we need. You're who I need." his hands squeezed Aidan's until both their knuckles were white as he spoke. "But you have to *stop* this. As I see it, you assume every single mistake is some sort of black mark on your character. People make mistakes. But then you keep mistakes to yourself, you lie about them, you panic over them and blame yourself and expect everyone else to blame you too. And you give that mistake time to grow worse and worse for everyone concerned. That's. Bullshit. You're making your own problems worse. You're hurting yourself, you're…you're hurting me, and you're not helping this base. Talk about things, damn it. Talk to me if you can't handle it with anyone else. But talk to *someone* who isn't a program."

Aidan bit back a sob. He knew he was hurting himself, but that didn't matter so much. Hurting Kevin was the last thing he ever wanted to do. But somehow he kept doing it, over and over again. Hurting him over things he didn't know how to deal with, how to fix, how to make right. Everyone made it sound so easy. Put words together and talk. Why could he never manage to do that when it mattered? He could find words to win people to his cause, to pull a base together, but not to tell the man he adored what had happened in his past.

"I'm not as…good with words as you." he managed eventually.

"Few people are." Kevin replied with a bleak smile. "I've come to expect it." Leaning in, he ran a hand over Aidan's cheek. "I'm not looking for poetry, love. I don't care if you're babbling nonsense. Just tell me these things."

Aidan squeezed his eyes shut, taking several deep breaths. Some sick part of him wished Kevin would shout. He knew what to do with that. But this kind of stuff made him fall apart.

Oh, he could tell Kevin was still irritated, and probably would be for a while. But he was still like this after everything. Gentle, sweet, supportive. What had he ever done to deserve this kindness?

He didn't deserve it. But he could be thankful for it, at least. He opened his eyes. "Kev? I…Thanks. I love you, you know."

"I know you do." Kevin went down on one knee beside his chair, kissing his brow. "Which is why I don't understand why you always think I'm going to go into a rage every time you tell me something. I know others did that to you." Kevin put two fingers under his chin, tipping his head up, and kissed him softly. "I'm not them. And hidden wounds don't heal." he punctuated his words with kisses. "Trust me. Talk to me. Please."

Aidan closed his eyes, relishing in the feel of the kisses. His heart pounded in his chest, and he struggled to slow it. "I'm trying."

"Keep trying." Kevin whispered. When Aidan dared to look at him, his thin face wore a smile. "And please don't make me stop people with very good reasons from breaking your nose," the redhead added. "My sympathy was rather more with Naomi on that one; fair warning."

Aidan chuckled weakly and dropped his head to Kevin's shoulder. "Yeah…can't blame you."

Kevin's arms wrapped gently around him, holding him close. "Lunch?"

"Lunch. Yeah," Aidan replied in a whisper. He forced himself to pull away from Kevin's warm embrace and take a breath, meeting his lover's gaze. "Kev…I'm sorry. For everything. I…I'll try to do better for you."

"Thanks." Kevin smiled gently. "And by the way, Aidan? Even when you're being an ass, I love you. I'll still take you to task when you're being an ass, mark me. But I'll still love you."

"Oh gag." Tweak's voice yapped at the door. "Billie says you guys eating or not? She's gonna pack leftovers. She says get there now."

Kevin burst out laughing.

Despite himself, a weak smile crossed Aidan's lips. He pulled himself to his feet and raked his fingers through his hair. "We're coming."

"People always walk in when I'm being sentimental." Kevin lamented as he stood. "Every time! It's just not fair." He twined his fingers with Aidan's. "Tweak, hold up! Walk with us and we'll tell you about your new working partner."

Aidan squeezed Kevin's fingers and took a deep breath as they caught up with Tweak. "Did Yvonne tell you anything?" he asked the little techie. She shrugged, her shoulders barely in line with his chest.

"You got a sister, you pissed her off. She fucked you up," Tweak remarked without interest. "That's all."

Aidan's lips twitched. "That's the short story, yeah. Long story: she's awesome with explosives. She'll help you get into the physical backups and out again safely."

Tweak glanced up at him. "You suck at stories," she observed after a moment. "Name? Mech? Chems? Stats? What?"

Kevin's brow furrowed. "Er...I don't think I follow."

Tweak rolled her eyes like a pre-teen. "What. Does. She. Use. How. Often. Does. She. Get. Her. Target. What's. Her. Name." she spat each word with sarcastic precision.

"Naomi," Aidan replied once he wrapped his brain around what she was asking. "Last I knew, she used anything she could get her hands on but was big on nitro and handguns. She's good with knives too. No idea when or how often she gets a win these days, but since she's a grid operative let's assume pretty often. I'll get a list of her work soon."

"So what, I gotta take orders from her?" Tweak asked. "Or is she there to get shot for m-me?"

"You're never letting that go, are you?" Kevin asked dryly. Tweak glared up at him. "I got *shot*."

"Yes, well, so have I in the past."

"Yeah, well you're crazy. I d-don't *like* getting shot."

"That, my dear girl, was a pathetic riposte."

"Fuck off, CES."

Aidan sighed and scrubbed his eyes with his free hand. "We hope no one else will get shot. But, no, you won't be taking orders from her," he stated patiently. "She'll be there to help keep you safe and help us find a plan that works better."

Tweak nodded. "Kay. But if I get caught by C-corps, I'll g-get loose and fuck your ass for it."

"Hey," Kevin remarked, all the playfulness right back in his voice, "that's my job. Hands off, Tweak."

Tweak mimed throwing up.

The teasing brought a grin to Aidan's lips. He chuckled, squeezing Kevin's fingers.

"I don't think you have to worry, babe. She hasn't got what you do."

"Yeah. I got a brain." Tweak muttered irritably. "When do I meet her? I'm n-not working cold."

"She's coming in a few days, so we can all plan together," Aidan replied quietly.

Tweak turned in front of them, blocking their way down the hall. Legs braced, she studied them both with thoughtful eyes. One finger tapped the bandages of the other arm.

"You look like you been crying," she announced eventually, holding Aidan's eyes. "Me? I got Billie. Got to take care of her. Not getting fucked over because of somebody else's f-family problems. You got problems, I want them fixed, or I want out. Not getting c-caught b-because s-s-someone else f-falls apart. G-got me?"

Aidan took a breath, and shook his head. "It won't be a problem, Tweak. I promise."

"Not getting c-caught again." Tweak stated, one foot starting to tap out a fast little rhythm. "Never. Shoot myself first."

"You're not getting caught," Aidan stated quietly. "And you're not getting shot."

If there was one thing he still knew about his sister, it was that she was an ace in every sense of the word.

Tweak's foot slowly let up on the tapping. She drew a shaky breath. "Fine." then she smiled tightly. "Had a brother. Fought, made up. It works. You pull your head out of y-your ass. Food." then she was trotting away.

Watching her walk away, Kevin shook his head absently. "You know, I never thought I was slow on the uptake before...and then I met her."

Aidan gave him a rueful smile. "I guess that happens when you're around a literal genius. Come on."

Two days later, Kevin pulled on his riding gear in their room. He'd thought Aidan was still asleep, but the rustling of sheets made him turn. Aidan lay with mussed golden hair and heavy-lidded eyes, so lovely in the pale orange night-cycle light that Kevin couldn't resist stepping over, the polyfabric of his chill vest creaking as he leaned down for a soft kiss. "I'm off to get Naomi; the truck she's hitched a ride on should be 'stopping for repairs' in half an hour. Get some more sleep; I'll be back before you know it," he murmured, stroking Aidan's wayward wheaten hair back from his eyes.

"Be careful," Aidan muttered back, leaning into his touch. Kevin chuckled. "That an order?"

"Course," Aidan murmured, turning his head to kiss Kevin's palm.

"Orders received." Kevin agreed with a last, soft kiss. "Go back to sleep." he pulled the blankets higher up Aidan's chest, kissed his brow, then turned and slipped out the door.

The cool of the air outside sang against his skin, making him feel hyper-alive as he pulled on his helmet, revved his electric motor and took off in the pre-dawn stillness, leaving only the barest of tire tracks to mark his passage. He loved dawn runs like this, racing the morning wind, the edges of his vision fringed with rainbows by the slick tech around the bike. For now, there was nothing but him, the terrain and the sunrise.

He pulled up on a ridge over the I-70, checked the time readout in his helmet and nodded in satisfaction. Right on time.

Not long after Kevin arrived, a large semi-trailer lumbered to a stop on the side of the road. A few minutes later the area repairman arrived in his personal car, a toolbox and tab in his hands. He lifted the toolbox toward the ridge, light catching on the dented metal, then rounded the truck to pop open the hood.

Kevin double checked his poncho, and carefully walked down the ridge, picking his footing in the pre-dawn light to meet his old friend the double agent.

"Morning Ed. Everything going all right?" he whispered to the repairman, tucking a holo-covered basket at the man's feet. "Basket of goodies for you and your kids; we got strawberries in a recent run. Watch out, there's eggs in there."

The man's heavy face broke into a grin as he busied himself. "Real eggs? Hot damn. Lucy's been dying to have real eggs again." Ed smiled down at his 'work' instead of meeting Kevin's gaze. "Thanks, man. Your girl's in the back. Safe and sound." Ed shifted to dig deeper into the inner workings of the truck. "Gonna take me three minutes to fix this up. Better get moving."

"Already gone. Stay out of the storm." Kevin slipped to the back of the truck, ducked under it and opened the hidden trap-door panel behind the fuselage. "Naomi? All ashore who's going ashore."

Naomi didn't respond aloud, but she moved like a gymnast as she climbed out of the small hidden compartment, her plastic fingers clicking quietly. Once she was out in the air behind the truck, she straightened and nodded curtly, her long blonde hair combed over the right side of her face to hide the scarring.

Kevin pressed a helmet into her fingers. "There's slick tech built in, and here's a chill vest and poncho. We've got two and a half minutes to be up the ridge. Bike's at the summit. Up and at 'em."

Naomi simply yanked the chill vest on and strode for the ridge. In silence, she climbed onto the back of the bike, grabbing onto the seat beneath her rather than Kevin's waist.

They rode in silence for half an hour, taking a looping route home just in case. Kevin was taking no chances this time.

It was in the interest of taking no chances that he pulled up under a thorny little tree miles from the base and cut the engine. "Routine satellite sweep's coming over in two minutes; I'd rather they didn't see any anomalies caused by moving slick tech." Reaching into his bike's saddle bag, he pulled out a larger slick tarp, flapped it open and set the struts attached to the corners, forming a small lean-to just wide enough for himself, Naomi and the bike. "Gives us an hours' or so respite. Relax." he added cheerfully, dropping down with his back against the tree trunk. The heat was starting to rise, and he was glad of the shade.

Naomi shrugged and joined him in the little lean-to. She pulled her helmet off and settled it in her lap.

"Hard boiled egg?" Kevin offered, cracking one of the half dozen he'd brought and meticulously peeling off the shell. "Perfect thing when there's no time for breakfast. Needs salt, but it'll do in a pinch and it's a great improvement on nutrient bars. A recent Fringe contact of ours has been trading us eggs for necessary supplies."

Naomi shrugged and took the egg with a nod of gratitude. Kevin opened his mouth to ask if she'd like help peeling it, then thought better of it and focused on his egg instead.

He'd nearly gotten the shell off when Naomi's voice asked, "How is he?"

"Well you didn't break his cheekbone or his nose, for which I'm grateful." Kevin remarked between bites. "I'd be even more grateful if you refrained from doing so in future. The bruising's gone, but his split lip is making kissing him difficult. I'm not amused."

Naomi snorted and polished off her egg. "Won't have to hit him if he doesn't do shit like that again."

Kevin let that pass.

The silence stretched on. The heat rose. Kevin felt his chill vest start to work under his slick poncho.

Leaning back against the tree, he flicked his player on and brought up a song. His tab's tinny speaker filled the thicket with soft, happy music that counterbalanced the quiet.

Kevin closed his eyes, waiting and listening.

And I'm feeling fine, Bon Jovi crowed, *it's nintey-nine in the shade.*

Kevin allowed himself to smile. A nintey-nine degree summer's day, nice and cool. Enough money to feel secure, and the freedom to do what you liked. The song sounded like heaven.

"How long've you been with him?"

Kevin opened his eyes when Naomi spoke, her words breaking the reverie.

"A little more than a year." Kevin met her eyes. "You spotted our relationship off the bat. What gave it away?"

She shrugged. "You were ready to strangle me over him. First hint. But then you went gooey when you saw he was hurt. You weren't just checking for injuries, you were fussing. No one does that for just any basemate."

"Ah." Kevin leaned back against the trunk of the little tree. "I really am getting sentimental in my old age, I suppose. I'll keep that in check in future."

Naomi wiped her hands on her pants. "Yeah. Probably should. He's fucked enough as it is. But...he looks good. He's still scrawny, but he looks better than he used to."

Kevin shot her an arch look, smiling thinly. "You're cruel, Naomi. I'll have you know I find him quite handsome."

Naomi studied him a long moment, her head tilted just a little to the side. It was strange seeing the living, breathing version of the holographic girl he'd come to know.

The song played on. Finally, the girl spoke. "Has he told you about his past yet?"

"Enough," Kevin replied lightly. "Enough for me to understand many of his motivations...and to help, when he lets me." He focused on peeling another egg. "Which isn't always. But we're getting there." After a moment, he raised his eyes. "Don't make this harder for him, Naomi. He made a mistake, and trust me, he's paying for it. He chastises himself enough without you adding to it."

To his surprise, she smiled, a weak thing made strange by the twist of her scarred lips. "I know. That's why I want to stay away from him for this mission. Let myself cool off before I hit him again. I'm pissed, but I know him. I know how he is. Plays it strong, but inside...not so much."

After a moment, Kevin's lips twitched in a grim little smile. "Not so much. Don't I know it..."

She smiled another moment before looking down and picking dirt from the joints of her cybernetic fingers. "So...he told you what our parents called him when he was born?"

"He did." Kevin agreed with quiet equanimity, staring out at the sun as it slowly rose over the flatland. A reminiscent smile touched his lips at the memory of Aidan's face that night. He'd been as lovely and as afraid as a deer caught in a hunter's scope.

Naomi glanced up. Kevin read surprise on that fine, damaged face for a moment. Then she crossed her arms. "Okay, he told you. You screwed him yet?"

Kevin gave a dry laugh. "My, aren't we direct."

The song ended. Something reflective from Bhi Bhiman started to play. Kevin frowned. The piece was one of the rarest in his collection and a beautiful thing, but now wasn't the time for it. Its words about the dark days of the 2020s that foresaw the Dissolution brought the mood down. He really had to turn the shuffle feature off.

He hit pause on the song. Silence filled the clearing, until Naomi spoke. "Have to be. Last guy he got involved with...I'm not gonna let it happen again."

Kevin nodded. "Ah yes. Sam. Someday I'd rather like to get ahold of that man. In a headlock, preferably."

Naomi grunted, but a curious sort of respect crossed her face. "Wait in line."

Kevin nodded his acknowledgment. "I suppose your claim takes precedence. As for the question, I haven't 'screwed him'. But, yes, we do make love whenever we can. Twice a week at least. And beyond that a polite sister wouldn't inquire further."

Warily, Naomi nodded. "Just wanted to make sure you knew what you were getting into." The young woman shrugged. "Make sure you weren't gonna bail when you got a clue."

Kevin acknowledged the words with a nod. "He had the same thought. He told me everything in that respect before he let me touch him. So, is the sisterly inquisition satisfied?"

Naomi shrugged, the joints in her right shoulder squealing quietly. "For now."

"Good, because we've still got some way to go. Come on." Kevin pushed himself to his feet. He packed the tarp and mounted his bike. A breath later, they were on their way.

They pulled up in a slight fishtail, Kevin hopping off before the wheels had quite stopped spinning. Meeting Naomi's eyes, he gave an ironic half bow. "Welcome to our humble abode."

Naomi pulled off her helmet and sized up what she could see of the base. Unfortunately, the damage was worst from this angle, and she couldn't see the wheeled planters full of crops from here. The base really was a sorry sight.

Kevin watched Naomi study the borrowed building printer as it ran its boxy grey bulk around and around the floor of what would be their new office wing when it was done. Combing her mussed hair over the right side of her face again, she asked, "How long's it been since you guys got hit? Looks like you barely had time to bug out."

"That must be why the Home Digest magazine passed us up in their latest feature." Kevin wheeled the bike inside. "Come inside if you're coming, we'll be in time for breakfast." He stretched his cramped hands, pulling off his helmet. "I know I'd like mine," he added, hanging his helmet from its hook on the wall along with his slick poncho and chill vest. He opened the door into the base as casually as pretense allowed.

"Morning!" Kevin called cheerfully as they walked into the cramped rec room, "Tweak, I've got your new best friend here. Everyone, Naomi. Naomi, the Wildcards."

Tweak raised her head to study him, glanced at Billie and rolled her eyes. "Mr. Fucking Sunshine."

"You can curse the dark or light a candle." Kevin called over his shoulder, trotting to the serving table to get his breakfast.

Tweak stared after him, brows raised. "Mr. Fucking Weirdo Sunshine." she judged. Leaving her seat, the little teenager walked to Naomi, stopping a foot away. Kevin's muscles tensed. The room quieted.

Tweak crossed her arms. "You're Aidan's sis?" The little coder raked the taller woman with one comprehensive glance. "Your arm. Needs work," she stated, like a judge awarding points.

The room breathed out. Kevin willed himself to relax. Tweak had been getting more predictable, and perhaps he'd gotten a bit paranoid around her. But apparently the others had too.

Naomi shrugged. "Yeah, I know."

Out of the corner of his eye, Kevin watched the two women as Tweak frowned. "Running weird," Tweak stated. "Needs upgrade. Needs check. Can I see?" Then she blinked. "Names. Right. I'm Tweak. You're Naom-m-mi. Need it shorter. I call you Mi? Can I see? And hi."

"Uh. Hi. You the hacker?" Naomi kept her arm at her side, sizing up the tiny woman. "Know anything about bionics?"

"Mech'n'tech!" Tweak agreed, some of that rare enthusiasm of hers bubbling up, "That's me! I could do it. Wanna?" she asked, her eyes alight. "Mech's good change up from code. Fun!"

Naomi blinked. She glanced from the little woman, down to her arm, and back up. "Um. What're you going to do to it?"

"If I'd know she was this excited about bionics, I would've gotten some in for her to program," Kevin muttered under his breath as he squeezed in beside Aidan, watching the two women.

"I think this is the only time I've ever seen her enthusiastic outside the coding chair." Aidan agreed, watching Tweak grinning like the kid she really was.

"Fix!" Tweak enthused, bouncing on the toes of her boots. "I fix it up good! Awesome! Got the stuff! Borrow the rest. Janice!" she yelped, her voice practically supersonic.

From the other side of the room, Janice's voice bawled right back. "Kid, yell that loud again 'fore my third cup of coffee an' I'll give you a roofing nail enema, you got me?"

"I need stuff!" Tweak called over, "I lost all mine. Can I come and l-l-look at what you got?"

Janice sighed. "When I'm awake an' you ain't pissin' me off."

Tweak grinned like a kitten who'd made her first kill. "That's like n-n-never."

Janice waved a dismissive hand. "Can it, runt."

Kevin sighed, then caught Naomi looking at him almost helplessly. For all her general ferocity, she looked so much like her brother for a moment. He gave her a wicked little smile and raised his voice. "Welcome to the base?"

"Gee, thanks," Naomi replied in a grumble. She turned back to Tweak and sighed. "Okay, okay! Stop screaming and I'll let you take a look later. Happy?"

"Yeah!" Tweak chirped, grinning. "C'mon c'mon. Wanna hear what you use. Got lotsa work. You talk. We talk. Mi, sit!"

Kevin repressed a laugh at the sight. "Well that's something. You know, I think we may just have the beginnings of a working team there."

"I hope so," Aidan muttered. He squeezed Kevin's fingers under the table. "How was she, coming in?" he asked under the high chatter from their coder.

"Distant and about as surly as the boyfriend of the brother who's hurt her deserves," Kevin replied lightly. "If I didn't value my skin, I'd mention the fact that she's being rather rude."

"Well, yeah." Aidan sighed. "I guess that's what I should expect."

"You could always try sitting with her." Kevin suggested between bites of breakfast.

Aidan winced. "She doesn't want to talk to me, remember?"

There was a plunk, a rattle, and Janice dropped into a seat across from them.

"You two look like somebody smacked your asses, and not the way you liked."

Kevin sighed into his coffee, feeling the heat of a blush run red banners up his cheekbones.

"Speaking of smacked asses," Sarah leaned in to hiss, grinning, "who wants to open up the betting pool? Topher's been looking Naomi's way."

Aidan choked on his coffee. Yvonne got in on it while he was catching his breath. "Ooh, you think so?"

Aidan wiped the last drops of coffee from his chin. "Um, guys? Don't waste your money. Betting on Naomi isn't going to get you anything."

"Wait what?" Sarah asked, blinking. "Is she...ohhhh, is she ace?"

"Yeah." Aidan agreed. Sarah bobbed her head. "Got it. Thanks for the pointer." Glancing down the table, she grinned, then leaned past her wife to poke Liza in the arm. "Hey Liza! Turns out we've got somebody for you to play Angry Aces with!"

Liza shot the other woman one of her patent Looks, then leveled her eyes on Aidan. "Please let me write her up for insubordination?"

Aidan chuckled. "No go, Liza. Sorry. Janice, we're just spying on my sister from across the room wondering how to get her to talk to me or, you know, stop acting like she got dumped in the nuthouse, is all." He sipped his coffee. "We've got some family stuff going on."

Janice narrowed her eyes, tilting her head to look across the room. "Well it must be some serious 'family stuff', cause she's lookin' sour as a sewed up pussy." Turning, she winked at her Commander. "I got this. You tell me what's goin' down later on, I'll see about it. I'm good with whiny little babies."

Aidan outright laughed at that. "I guess I should know."

In spite of his annoyance with the man, Kevin was glad to hear him laugh.

That night, Aidan pulled his testosterone and injector from the drawer, sitting down on the bed to prepare them.

"Hey," he murmured when the door slid open.

"Hey yourself," Kevin's voice replied quietly. Pale hands took the injector and gauze pad out of Aidan's fingers. With delicate precision, Kevin drew the correct dose, tapped the vial to excrete air, inserted it into the injector, then ran the antiseptic gauze over the inside of Aidan's arm, his fingers gentle. The injector's many fine tips sank in without a breath of pain. Kevin's fingers rested gently beside the injection site. "These small gauge injectors seem to be working well," he murmured in the soft quiet, setting the injector on its self-clean cycle and laying it aside. Aidan made a quiet noise of agreement as Kevin's hand rubbed the injection site.

With the ease of long practice, Kevin tidied the tools away and reclaimed his seat on the bed. "I did a little hacking and paperwork while we were in the city," Kevin remarked, fingers moving in circles. "Rerouted a delivery of hormonal treatments and antiseptics. A nine-month supply's going to arrive at a little clinic nearby, under one of my code ID's. It'll be good to have all the medicines we want around again.

Quality brands, too; I got lucky."

"Good to hear it," Aidan muttered, watching Kevin's fingers on his arm. He sighed and leaned in, resting his head against his boyfriend's shoulder. He didn't know what else to say, so he sat quiet.

Kevin's arms wrapped around his, and his head rested against Aidan's. "I'd do a lot more than that for you."

"I don't know why," Aidan muttered against Kevin's skin. "I'm an asshole and I don't even have a real dick. I can't give you what you deserve, and I know you hate half of what I do. I have no idea why you stick around."

There was a bare murmur of laughter. "Well, not for the self loathing, that's for sure."

Aidan sighed. "But, really, Kev…why do you stay? And don't say it's because you love me. I'm not that sappy. If it's because I'm your Commander and things would get awkward, then—"

"The word for you is maudlin. Sappy's far too inexact." Kevin replied flippantly, stroking a few strands of hair out of Aidan's face. "Maudlin, and occasionally morose. Moribund, now and then."

"You and your outdated words," Aidan muttered with a hint of a laugh. He pulled away just enough to meet Kevin's gaze. "You still angry?"

"More disappointed than angry. And a little chagrined." Kevin murmured, grey eyes soft behind his glasses. "I thought we were done lying to each other. And it is awfully hard on the girl, isn't it?"

"I didn't mean to get us all to this spot." Aidan replied softly. He leaned back against Kevin. "I just…I thought her life would be better if I wasn't there screwing it up." A breath of rueful laughter slipped past his lips. "Naomi would punch me again if she heard me say something like that."

"And we don't need that." Kevin added dryly. "It's already going to be rather difficult to kiss you."

"Want a bet?" Aidan smiled and turned his head to kiss Kevin. It still stung his split lip, but he didn't care. What mattered was that Kevin wasn't angry with him, no one had lost their life today, and they had water. He had to focus on the positive things if he was ever going to make it through.

"We'll figure something out." Kevin murmured between kisses. "And as for your other worry, if I'm allowed to get your pants off, we'll explore that little issue in detail."

"Pretty sure you still won't find a dick," Aidan chuckled, even as he attempted to kiss and undo his fly at the same time. "I keep checking, but the surgery won't be for a while."

"We make do." Kevin murmured in his ear, hands moving in a newer, slower rhythm. "We can certainly make do."

Aidan hummed quietly and kissed Kevin again, guiding his lover's hand elsewhere. "Oh my. And here I'd thought you'd be tired." Kevin quipped softly, grey eyes sparkling. "If this is an apology, I'll have to scold you more often."

"Oh, am I going to get another scolding?" Aidan asked, a hint of laughter in his voice.

"Only as much as you deserve. The question is how much you deserve. Now let me think..." Standing easily, the wiry man paced the room for a moment, miming deep thought. He leaned against the wall, looking back at Aidan. Raising a hand, he crooked a finger. "Come here."

Aidan shuffled forward obediently, a sheepish smile on his face. When he reached his boyfriend, he was grabbed into a hard kiss, fingers buried insistently in his hair, tugging with a force that walked the line just under pain. "You realize you've worried me nearly to death, and lied to me twice in the last two months?" Kevin whispered, running his lips down Aidan's throat.

"I'm sorry," Aidan whispered, tilting his head back to give Kevin better access to his throat and pressing into his lover. "I didn't mean to scare you. Really."

"Too bad. You did." Kevin growled, sucking at the thin skin on Aidan's collarbone as his fingers undid Aidan's jacket.

"And, may I add, you broke a promise. We said we weren't going to keep secrets any longer. Now, would you like to atone for that?" Kevin whispered in his ear, nibbling on the ridge of it.

"What can I do to make it right?" Aidan asked quietly.

Kevin laid a line of kisses down the other side of his throat. "Well. What you do to atone with your sister is your affair, and I'd advise that it happens soon. But if you want to make it up to me? Tonight, you give up the right to choose what's best for others. Tonight you don't get to decide what's going to happen. Are those terms acceptable?"

"My turn to feel helpless and clueless?" Aidan asked, his body tingling.

"Yes." Kevin almost growled the word as he pulled Aidan's shirt over his head.

"Sounds like I owe you that," Aidan whispered. "I'll take your terms."

He felt Kevin grin against his skin. "Well then, undress for me if you would, love."

Aidan got out of his clothes with butterflies in his stomach. When he was naked, Kevin sauntered over and leaned him against the wall, kissing him. Kevin ducked his head, and his teeth grazed a nipple. Aidan inhaled sharply and slid one hand down Kevin's hip. But Kevin's hand caught his.

Aidan whined in the back of his throat. "I can't do *anything*?"

"No, you can't. It's your turn to feel like you're not being told what's going on." Kevin retorted, hands sliding down Aidan's hips. "And tonight nothing is under your control. You did agree, yes?" Kevin murmured.

Aidan closed his eyes. "I guess I did. Yes."

"Good." Kevin stepped back. "Now, you are allowed to get me out of these pants, and after that, well, we'll see."

"Yessir," Aidan chuckled as his breath hitched. He reached eagerly for Kevin's fly, fumbling with the buttons until he could slide the pants and boxers off his guy's hips.

Kevin drew a breath as Aidan's hand traced his balls, the head of his shaft. "Now who said you could do that?" he growled playfully, stepping out of his pants and pushing Aidan against the wall in one smooth motion, his shaft resting between Aidan's legs as they kissed. Aidan shifted to press his thigh against Kevin's dick.

Then Kevin's warmth was gone. A hand pressed against Aidan's chest. "Now, stay here, and close your eyes."

Aidan did as he was told, leaning against the wall and squeezing his eyes shut.

There was a rustle and a thump, and then there was the pinch of the strap on attaching.

"Open your eyes," Kevin's voice whispered. Aidan did what he was told; after all, he'd promised. Kevin was grinning, grey eyes glittering. "I think it's a night for new experiences. A bit of a lesson, as well. And the lesson is this." A hand stroked the strap on and the flesh around it. "Sometimes, other people do care enough about you to do the right thing for *you*. Sacrificing yourself in the hope that you'll make others happy is not what you're here for. You make others happy. You make me happy, when you're not trying to play Saint Lawrence. I much prefer Saint Jude." Kevin's fingers teased him, running goose flesh up his sides before wandering back down. "I love you enough to *want* to help, when you *let* me. I love this, and this." the soft voice added, long fingers reaching around to run fingers tenderly over Aidan's ass. "But I also love this." Kevin continued, and two fingers very lightly tapped the side of Aidan's head. The fingers trailed down to tap over his heart. "And this most of all. Mistakes, problems, idiocy and all. I love every inch of you, and if you'll let me, I'll prove to you that what you are can be quite an advantage, not a problem."

"What do you mean?" Aidan asked in a breathy whisper, leaning back against the wall. "What I am is an advantage?"

"I know for a fact that I can bring you to climax more than once. Which means that I can take my time with you." Kevin murmured in his ear. Aidan shivered as Kevin's hand stroked him softly. Tingling heat ran up his body.

"And I intend to do exactly that." Kevin continued, hand busy on the prosthetic flesh. "I have such a lot of plans." Kevin's teeth added a new mark to Aidan's collar bone.

Aidan swallowed. He reached for Kevin, hoping to wrap his hands around his guy's shaft.

Kevin caught Aidan's hands and pinned them against the wall, Kevin's mouth kissing him hard. The taller man pressed himself against Aidan, their dicks pressed together.

For a moment, panic raced through Aidan, but warmth filled the place it tried to occupy. Kevin holding him wasn't a danger. Kevin, he could trust.

The pale man leaned back, hands still holding Aidan in place as he admired the view. He grinned. "Hmm, tuppenny upright may work out well, for what I have planned." Releasing one of Aidan's hands, he reached over and lifted something from the table beside them. "Ever seen one of these? I'd originally picked the printer schematic for it up as a treat. But I have heard it's sometimes used as a form of discipline."

The object looked a little like a pear stuck to a vase stand in shape, made from soft black silicone. Kevin grinned invitingly, waggling the toy slowly. "Know what this is?"

Aidan studied the object, blinking. "Isn't that a butt plug? I saw an article about them, one time… never used one though."

Kevin's grin widened. "We'll remedy that little oversight tonight. Now, your orders are to hold still, and close your eyes."

Aidan wasn't completely sure he liked where things were going, but he had said Kevin got to make the decisions tonight. He'd left Kevin feeling unsure and out of his depth plenty of times. It was his turn. That was the point of tonight, he was pretty sure.

He leaned against the wall for support and closed his eyes, waiting.

For a moment, fingers ran up and down Aidan's prosthetic shaft, teasing, coaxing. Then two fingers slick with the prosthetic's lube explored Aidan's body, slipping inside his opening. "This is self lubricating too." Kevin whispered into Aidan's hair, as something strange and cool slipped inside him. "And you know what? It vibrates." There was a click, and a very quiet whir began, along with a bone-deep vibration running through Aidan's body. He could feel the device tracing tight circles inside him. Kevin's breath ran over his throat. "Now, I'm going to tell you something I've been keeping from you."

"Yeah?" Aidan asked, his body tingling.

Smiling slyly, Kevin slid two small black rings onto his pinkie fingers. "Both the toys you're wearing have remote controls. And I'm going to use them tonight."

Aidan swallowed. He was already tense as a wire. If the toys did much more he'd…

Kevin tapped the ring on his left hand with his thumb. Aidan's prosthetic started a long, slow pulse that pulled a whimper out of him. Every muscle in his groin tensed.

"Now, the art of this little toy around the back is to move it deeper, little by little, like a screw...if you'll pardon the pun." There was a gentle twist, and the tight vibration sank a little deeper inside Aidan. "Encourages heightened sensation." Kevin chuckled, both hands fully occupied, one on either side of Aidan's body. "But not too fast..." the redhead's voice murmured. The slow, massaging pressure inside him eased down to sync with what the prosthetic was doing.

Aidan could barely breathe. The vibrations tickled his bones, made his muscles twang, and he swore his knees would give out if it went on too long.

There was another twist, and the pressure settled deeper inside him. Kevin's fingers twisted the toy from one side to the other, and Aidan's opening shot sensation through his body. He dropped his head, panting. Then Kevin's hand left Aidan's shaft, and a breath of laughter ran over his skin. "Now love, I'd like you on your knees, with your mouth open, if you would." Kevin murmured, red hair tickling Aidan's cheek.

Aidan dropped to his knees. They were wobbly already; it was probably a good thing. He knew he was good with his tongue and he certainly didn't mind using it. He just hoped he could, with the pleasure still building in his own body, the vibrations rumbling through him.

Kevin's fingers tipped Aidan's chin up. "Open your eyes, Aidan my love. Look at me."

Aidan opened his eyes and tilted his head to meet Kevin's gaze. Kevin smiled down like some angel of lust. He waited until Aidan was looking him in the eye. Then he touched both rings. The vibrations of both toys intensified. Aidan groaned.

"My, I'd best give you something to put in that mouth," Kevin whispered. "Otherwise we'll wake our charming neighbors. Would you like something in your mouth?"

Aidan tried to say something smart, but it came out as a squeak. He wrapped his lips around Kevin's shaft, swirling his tongue around the head before settling into an insistent rhythm. The vibration of the toy inside him almost had him on his edge all on its own.

"Look at me, Aidan." Kevin's voice was low now, smoky.

Aidan raised his eyes to Kevin's. The redhead grinned, and touched one of the rings again.

Aidan's prosthetic tightened and heated as if a hand were touching it. The butt plug's gyrations got stronger.

Aidan's climax overtook him before he could think. He gasped, his entire body shuddering as he struggled to keep Kevin in his mouth, struggled to give his incredible guy pleasure as it burned through his own body. That was all he had to do now. Feel and give pleasure.

"I think that will do nicely." Kevin's husky voice glided over the words. He gently pulled away and knelt behind Aidan, twisting the plug a little deeper. The sensation arched inside him. He was shivering in the wild place between one orgasm and the next. Kevin stroked his prosthetic, and he felt the pulsing wave come curling up his body again.

Then Kevin was wrapped around him. His fingers were carefully pulling out the butt plug. Kevin was sinking his own body down inside Aidan, gasping. His boyfriend thrust deep and fast.

Aidan dug his fingers into Kevin's thighs as his entire body exploded into drumbeats and fragments of pleasure. He couldn't think, couldn't breathe, couldn't believe these thrusts that drove him crazy. Instinct pushed him to go down to hands and knees, but Kevin had one arm across his chest and one hand on his dick, holding them tight together. Kevin thrust faster, harder, stroking him relentlessly, and Aidan cried out at the sheer overwhelming pleasure of it. Fireworks went off in his head. Kevin's voice mixed into his.

The thrusts grew gentler, easing them both down into reality.

Kevin leaned his head on Aidan's shoulder, a lazy hand pushing Aidan's sweaty hair out of his face. "That...was really quite...that was...wow..."

"Yeah...didn't get to use my dick, but yeah," Aidan whispered back, barely coherent. He grinned like a fool, shifting as much as he could to tuck his head under Kevin's chin and press their bodies together. Even now, he still shivered with the aftermath, but he wouldn't complain.

"Payback." Kevin murmured languidly. "That's your payback. You don't always get to make decisions for everybody else. So there."

"Mmmk." Aidan barely had enough energy to smile and kiss at Kevin's cheek. "I can live w'that." He curled into the warmth that cradled him, murmuring incoherent sounds of pleasure in the back of his throat. "Love it when you touch me..."

"Mm." Kevin agreed, a little dry humor in his voice. "If you'd kept fewer secrets with me, we would have found *that* out a great deal earlier. Just a point to remember." he added, taking the sting out of the words with a soft kiss. Aidan couldn't exactly argue with it anyway: they would have been together months earlier if Aidan hadn't been such a chickenshit.

"I don't think I have any secrets left," Aidan murmured as he let his body relax.

"Good." Kevin muttered dryly, "Because untying Gordian knots isn't a hobby of mine."

Aidan tried not to wince. "Sorry. I don't try to be difficult, I just...."

Soft fingers covered his lips. "Stop that."

He smiled against Kevin's fingers. "Trying."

"So *now* can I see?"

Tweak planted her fists on the table. Naomi blinked at her. "Um...hi?"

"Can I see your arm today?" Tweak repeated as the team around her ate their breakfasts. Across the table, Billie caught her eye and made a 'turn down the volume' gesture. Tweak blinked. She hadn't realized she was overdoing it.

She took a seat and a bite of breakfast. "I can fix it, we can plan. We're on a d-deadline. Got me wired. Sorry. We go and hang out with j-j-Janice after b-breakfast, okay? She's got s-spare parts I need. You read up on all this yet? J-Janice, that work?"

"Christ shoving his cock in a koala, yes you can come an' see what I got for spare parts. Eat somethin', girl, 'fore you jitter off the table," Janice grumbled. Tweak sighed. Alphas wasted so much *time*. They needed so much food, so much sleep. It slowed everything down.

Janice glanced at Naomi, then down the table at Aidan. Out of the corner of her eye, Tweak saw the older woman wink. She grinned. Perfect. Janice got where she was going with this.

They needed to work like a machine to pull this mission off. They needed to kick ass. To do that, they needed to get personal crap settled fast. And besides, Tweak liked Aidan. She wanted to fix stuff for him. That meant figuring his sister out, and fixing her beef.

"All right," Janice muttered twenty minutes later, 'c'mon ladies, let's go see what I got that you can use. Dozer? If I ain't got the stuff, can I send them to you?"

The big mechanic shrugged. "Sure. Me'n Toph are gonna be babysitting the module printer and working on wiring up the new office module most of the day, though."

"Roger," Janice agreed, waving a hand in their direction as she sauntered over to dump her plate into the recycler. The machine shredded away the plastic with a quick, rough grinding that bothered Tweak's ears. She couldn't wait until they had a sink again. Everybody was using crappy plastic plates and stuff until they had a kitchen again, grinding them up and melting the plastic at a temperature that burned the food stuff away before they put it back through the printer to get recycled. They weren't printing anything good until they had a sink to wash things in again. It meant all the food smelled like burnt plastic from the plates. Tweak hated it.

Shoving her plate in the recycler, she trotted after Janice and Naomi. They were half way down the hall before Janice slowed down. She paused for a second. Then she turned fast. "Git you two!"

Dilly and Donny took off in the opposite direction, their boots clattering on the pre-fab floor. The engineer turned away, smiling ruefully.

"Little shits. Noses in everything. Either they're gonna be the greatest Dusters we ever had, or they're gonna blow themselves to hell."

Naomi actually laughed at that. Tweak blinked.

"Aidan and I were the same when we were younger," the blonde woman remarked. "Follow all the big kids and the strangers, try to sneak into the classified meetings. Blow shit up. It's part of being a Duster kid."

Janice grinned. "You got that right. Why this stays locked." she added, opening her maintenance room door. Dropping into a chair inside, she sipped coffee as she brought up her screens. "Tweak, I got my inventory up. Holler when you're ready."

"Kay." Tweak agreed, spooling a line out of her tab. "Mi? Where's your port?"

"If you have to call me something short, go with Omi." the woman grumbled. "It's in the wrist."

"Got it." Tweak felt along the plastic. "Your model's CPS. Why'd you get this?"

Naomi sighed. "Anybody tell you you're rude?"

Janice snorted quietly as she worked on something. Tweak brought up the schematics and diagnostics on the arm. "Yeah. I don't waste words. Deal."

Naomi blinked. "Okay then."

"Hear you're a whiz kid with blowing shit up. Brother talked a bit about you when he said you were coming in," Janice remarked from her work station. Naomi shrugged. "I do what I can. Something about the smell of explosives, feeling the boom. I get into it. Is this going to take all day?"

"Nope!" Tweak chirped, digging into the details. She'd missed doing mech work for Jazz.

Janice blinked. "Boy, you've got your shorts in a twist, don't you?"

"I'm supposed to be working," Naomi replied, as if it ought to be obvious.

"You work better with two hands." Janice replied.

"And it takes longer when you m-move," Tweak added, pushing her hand against the cybernetic shoulder. "Hold still. Thing's shit and you d-didn't do m-maintenance. Looks like crap."

"I'm not trying to look good," Naomi groused. "And I haven't been anywhere that could get me a quality arm. Looks like Aidan got lucky with bases. All they could do where I got sent the time this happened was keep me alive."

Tweak studied the readouts, frowning. The joints needed lubricating, that was for sure. The cables to the EM charger needed some work; the thing was slow and squeaky because it wasn't charging right off the electricity from the friction Naomi's body made. And there were 'please maintain' notes from sensors all over the thing. There had to be dirt and junk in all the joints.

"What d'you need tool wise, Tweak? We can scrounge up a thing or two," Janice's voice asked over the soothing shush and grumble of the hydraulics and climate machinery.

"First, detach and de-grease," Tweak stated, thinking as she worked. "I work on that and we talk. Got de-greasing wipes? Injector? T-toolkit? S-solution?" Tweak asked, rattling out the words and almost beating the damn stutter to the end of the sentence.

Janice nodded. "I got all that. Black box by your head's a micro-utility case, ion cleaner works better than liquid solutions. Across the room, box with a big red I on it."

"Good." Tweak bobbed her head. "Omi, take off?"

"Hunh?" The woman blinked at her. Tweak rolled her eyes. Why were alphas so slow?

"Take the arm off."

"Oh."

Naomi put her natural hand under her cybernetic elbow and closed her eyes, whispering something under her breath. There was a soft snick, and the arm detached. The woman gingerly held out her arm. "Uh. What am I supposed to be talking about?"

"Whatcha do. Second thought, hold that. Gotta get stuff." Bouncing to her feet, she grabbed what she needed off the walls.

"Okay! Awesome. Okay. You tell me, I tell you, we work it out, we tell them what we do. How good are you? Stats?"

"Stats?" Naomi asked, bewildered. Tweak tried to fight down her irritation. This was not that hard.

"I'm guessin' she means, what's your success rate." Janice explained. Tweak nodded as she fitted the ion cleaner together. "Yep!" She'd start with that, using the ion cleaner's beam to shake loose all the crap in the joints.

Naomi blinked. "Wow… you wanna go there right away, kid?"

"All the way!" Tweak chirped.

Naomi grinned. "All right, out of the last nine missions I've run seven were completely successful. One was a bust. And one I had to ask for help on, so I count it as a partial. Sector counts it as successful."

"See we got ourselves a winner. Brother's gonna be glad you're around." Janice remarked. "Sides, I hear just havin' you around makes him happy. Might make you happy too, never know."

Naomi snorted at that. "Yeah, he missed me so much he made sure I thought he was dead. Must've *really* wanted to see me."

"What we want an' what we think we deserve ain't always the same," Janice suggested. This time, Naomi didn't say anything.

"Oh shit, you mope just like your brother, don't you."

A thrill of guilt and panic ran through Tweak at the sound of Janice's voice. She raised her head, but Janice was looking at Naomi.

"I do not!" Naomi snapped. She glared at the older woman. "I'm just antsy. That's all."

"Riiiight." Janice took another sip of coffee.

Tweak gave the blonde woman a skeptical look. "Your brother. He's an asshat."

Naomi snorted. "Understatement."

"But he's a *good* asshat. Does stupid stuff trying to do good stuff." She watched as dust and grit cascaded down out of the arm under the tool's slow-moving wand tip. "We get back to work this week, you be ready for the job?" she asked.

"Better than sitting around here doing squat," Naomi's voice remarked.

Taking a breath, Tweak looked up and met the woman's eyes. "Question."

"Answer," Naomi replied dryly.

"You always a pill?" Tweak demanded.

Naomi gave her a shit-eating grin. "I've been told that, yeah."

"They weren't kidding," Tweak retorted waspishly, looking back down at the cybernetic arm. "Question: can you focus and do this? If you can't, I'll d-do it alone."

The chair Naomi sat in creaked. "I may be a jackass, but I'm not a traitor. I do my job, and I've signed on for this, so I'll do it."

Tweak glanced away. She needed a break from emotions written on other people's faces in order to put the words together right."Yeah, but you need to do it good. No t-teenager shit. Get over it before we get in there. I don't want to die."

She managed another glance. Naomi's eye had narrowed ever so slightly. "I'm not a screw-up, Tweak. Drama doesn't happen on the job. And as for teenager shit, what are you, fifteen?"

"Eighteen. Twat," Tweak spat. Janice fake-coughed the word 'liar'. Tweak shot her a glare. "Fuck off."

"Only after duty, lil'un. With the *good* porn on," the older woman replied with a slow smile. Tweak looked away. "Gag. Okay. This takes time. Omi? Talk. First problem. Snitch. Intel l-leak."

"Yeah, I read about that in your briefing." Naomi agreed quietly. "Somewhere there's a leak, and it got a hell of a lot of bases hit. It probably isn't on this base—"

"It's not," Tweak stated flatly. "I'd know."

"So it's somewhere on one of the other bases. Probably one of the ones on this op, if they knew enough to let your people walk all the way into the Broomfield trap before they sprang it. And it's hard to talk about hunting it down, because—"

"Then the snitch gets the intel too, I know." Tweak finished, irritably flicking the ion wand. "Can't figure out what to d-do. Fake intel, sure, see who acts on it. But if they're s-smart and they d-don't?"

"Yeah. There's that," Naomi agreed quietly. "Do you know if it's a human actor or a digital one? Or even a nanoid mimic?"

Tweak shook her head, irritation running itchy lines through her brain. "N-no. I tried a c-couple times to f-fake it out. Used some fake intel. No bites. And we don't have time for me to go in depth on all the b-base systems and t-trace it."

"Tell me again why we don't have time?" Naomi asked.

"'Cause your brother got us a nation-wide protest march, organized for a month from now. It's the best cover we could ask for, takin' all the Corps' attention," Janice explained. "An' if we're askin' people to risk their lives for us, we better fuckin' deliver for them."

Naomi sighed. "My brother. Of-fucking-course he got us into this."

"Kinda his job as Commander." Janice observed dryly. Naomi grunted, noncommittal.

Tweak set down the wand. 'Kay. Gonna get into the c-connections. Janice, g-got anti-dust c-cloth?"

"Top drawer on your right," the specialist remarked as she worked on the solar panel at her station. Tweak pulled out the white sheet and laid it down, her fingers fizzing with the static charge of the cloth. Everything that had been gunking up the insides of Naomi's arm stuck to the underside immediately. She set the arm down on top and opened the casing.

"Hm," Naomi muttered.

"Hm?" Janice asked.

"Mm..."

"You really ain't one for conversation, are you?" Janice remarked.

"I'm trying to think..." Naomi's voice sounded far away. "Tweak?"

"Yeah?" Tweak asked, setting the box half as long as her pinkie finger holding the micro-repair kit inside the arm. The tool's control program popped a new window up on her tab, and she carefully navigated the miniature world through the screen, tapping to give the tools instructions for repair.

"You tried a QR code in a vid message?"

Tweak raised her head, electricity shooting up her spine. "Q...R..." She could feel her brain starting to kick up a notch.

"QR...QR c-code..."

"Well if you think it's a bad idea just—" Naomi began, but the idea burst onto the screen of Tweak's brain like the best vid ever. She jumped up. "Stupid stupid I've been s-s-stupid! QR code! V-virus! P-p-perfect!"

She leaped for the door, electricity in her blood, and took off down the hall. The guy she needed wasn't in the garage. She took off outside, skidding to a stop in front of the printing module. "Topher! T-t-topher!"

Topher's fedora popped up over a building wall, already four feet high. "Hey Tweak, what's—"

She vaulted the wall to land in front of him. "I need you, c'mon c'mon!"

"For what?" Topher asked, blinking. Tweak grinned. "You gotta help me print a shirt."

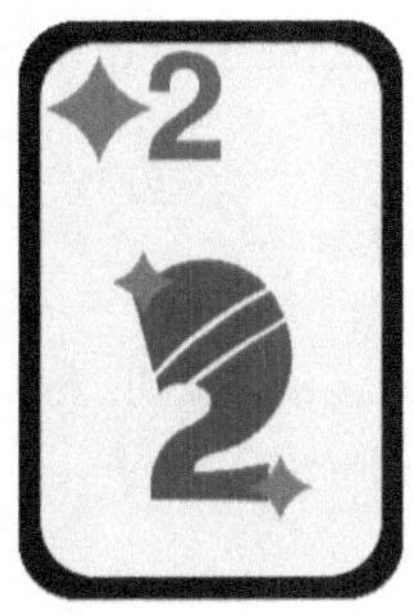

"So you want me to wear...a shirt?"

"Yep!" Tweak replied, grinning up at her Commander. He glanced from her to Topher. The look on his face told her that he wasn't getting it. She sighed. "Kay. Look. R-record a vid telling everybody that we're back on t-track. Set a meeting time, couple days away. All Dust m-machines use secure OS and code from Europe, r-right? C-corps all use Techo's machines and their p-programs. So, I got a QR code that translates into a v-virus when Techo's tech parses it. We print it on a shirt. A j-jacket. S-something. When your snitch tries to parse it or reformat it to send, it'll c-c-crash their gear." She planted her hands on her hips. "Bang," she finished.

Aidan blinked. "Okay, 'bang'. You're sure you're not going to frag somebody's legit stuff?"

Tweak crossed her arms. "You. Gonna ask me. If I'm sure. About *code*."

Aidan smiled crookedly. "Okay. You're sure. Then I guess we give it a shot."

It took two hours to code a shirt that would do the trick and was subtle enough that the human eye wouldn't spot it. Aidan pulled the blue long-sleeve shirt on and closed the door of his tarp-walled office to make the secure video.

And then they waited.

And waited.

By dinner, Tweak was pacing the rec-room, tapping her fingers on surfaces in an effort to burn off her nerves. Damian pinned her with a long look. She looked away.

She jumped a mile when Liza's voice spoke behind her.

"Tweak. Step out in the hall with me for a second."

Tweak glanced at the taller woman, feeling her body tense. Her scales shivered under the bandages.

Liza smiled tightly. "You're not in trouble, Tweak. Just come out and talk."

Warily, Tweak followed the woman. Liza moved like a guard dog. She'd freaked Tweak out since day one.

"Yeah?" she asked, crossing her arms when the taller woman stopped walking. Most people got the message not to fuck with you when you did that, but it also let her hug her arms around her body, and that helped with the feeling that her skin was crawling.

Liza studied her for way too long before she spoke. "How're you doing?" The tone of her voice made Tweak raise her head. She sounded...nice.

"Hunh?" she asked, cocking her head. Liza smiled, which made her look a little less like a guard dog ready to bite.

"There's a lot on you, with everybody expecting your code to catch our snitch and solve our problems. I'd be freaking out, if it was me." Liza gave her a quick, almost low-key once over. "Did you take your meds today?"

Tweak shook her head. "I gotta move fast r-right now. The stuff s-s-slows me down."

Liza frowned. "Tweak, you already moved fast. We have to wait for things to play out now, right? You did a lot already. And you're shivering. So, maybe you can go take your meds?"

Tweak glanced down, unfolding her arms to look at her hands. They were trembling.

"Fuck," she snapped, disgusted with herself.

"I hear that," Liza agreed wryly. "I've felt shaky for weeks. Nice thing is, there's meds for that. I'll save you a plate, okay?"

Tweak glanced up at her, eyes narrow. "Why d'you care? You d-don't even want me here."

Liza's shoulders tensed, but she managed a smile. "I don't want anything messing up my family, Tweak. Thing is, you stopped being a threat around last Christmas. You got your card. You're a Wildcard now, right?"

"Right?" Tweak asked, watching her. Liza shrugged. "Well, now you're family. I don't want anything messing up you. So go take your pill. And you're getting a haircut this week. You look like more like a dust bunny than a Duster right now."

Tweak snorted, looking away. Something warm was cracking open inside her chest, and she wasn't going to let Liza see her get all gooey over something as dumb as getting told she needed a haircut.

"Lame, Liza."

"True," the officer replied with her tight, professional smile. "Go on, before the food gets cold. It's bad enough hot."

Tweak took her pill. It did make her slower, but it made it easier to eat dinner and talk too. She wasn't so angry at the rest of the world for taking too long when she took the stuff. And it meant she got to sleep.

The pill didn't stop her from jumping out of bed when the knock came on her bedroom door. In the other bed, Billie gave a whimpering little scream of fear. Tweak stepped across, grabbed a fistful of blanket and used it as a glove to hold her friend's hand. "Hey, 'sokay. Our people. Just our people."

Billie nodded, still wide-eyed with the sudden terror of a knock on the door in the night.

Tweak didn't have time to wrap her arms, so she tugged on a sweatshirt and heavy pants. "Better be good!" she called through the plastic as she shoved the door open.

On the other side of the door, Aidan was grinning like a loon, his hair all over the place.

"I got a message. We got the snitch. Come on, I want you in on the call." He gave her a quick once over. "Um… you covered enough?

She glanced down. The sweatshirt was Billie's; she looked like a little kid in it, her hands lost somewhere up the sleeves. She held up the flopping tubes of cloth. "You see any s-scales? No? Then I'm covered."

Aidan laughed quietly. "Okay, you're covered. Come on."

Tweak watched Aidan run through all the security levels that let him place the call. When it went through, a man's pale face appeared on the screen. His fluffy white hair looked weird enough that Tweak almost laughed, but he was way too freaked to be funny.

"Headly," the man gulped down a breath. "Thanks for the call."

"Course. What happened?" Aidan asked. The guy straightened up in his chair.

"It was Possum. Paulson, I mean. My personnel man. Turns out he was a fucking mimic. Watched the vid you sent, and he just..." the old man mimed an explosion with both hands. "When they replaced him we can't tell. But no wonder they had all those base coordinates."

Aidan nodded once, slowly. "Condolences to your team, Anderson. That's harsh."

"It's a knife in the back, is what it is," the words came out of the old man raw, rough edged.

Aidan nodded. "Yeah. It is."

The old man ran a hand over his face. Then his red-rimmed eyes pinned Tweak. "Take it you're the coder who pulled this off?"

"Yeah," Tweak looked away, unable to stand the emotion burning in his eyes. "Sorry."

The old man grunted. "Should be me apologizing, sweetheart. And saying thanks. My team dropped the ball. My people take all responsibilities for this one." Tweak heard him suck in a breath. She didn't usually put up with that 'sweetheart' shit, but the old guy was wrecked. She let him talk. "Okay, Headly. What do you say to a meeting in the morning?"

"I say yeah." Aidan agreed, "and let's make it full operating teams. I want our technical officers and our logistics people talking to each other real time; now that we can talk, we need to get our asses in gear."

The old man gave a hacking laugh. "I hear you, boy...scuse me. Headly. You'll see my team. Time?"

"How's eleven-hundred for you?" Aidan asked. Tweak flicked her eyes to the screen, watching the old man nod.

"Eleven-hundred. We'll see you. Signing off."

"Hang in there," Aidan murmured. Anderson nodded, wordless. Then the screen flicked to the Force logo.

Aidan turned the screen off. He sat still for a moment. Then he stood slowly.

"Boss?" Tweak whispered. Aidan glanced at her, smiling a tiny, trying-to-be-brave smile.

"Yeah, Tweak?"

"We did good, right?"

"Yeah Tweak. We did good. Go ahead and get some sleep. We've got a lot to do tomorrow."

Tweak hated seeing the way he looked. He looked like her dad when he smiled like that, sort of sad. Forget that he was white and her Dad had been Chinese. It was the eyes. Stepping in, she crossed her arms, looking up at him.

"I got some new ideas. Better stuff. They fucked with us, right? We fuck them over. Sideways. With a c-cactus."

Aidan gave a tiny little laugh. "Sounds like a plan."

Event File 26
File Tag: Operational Retrenching
Timestamp:11:01-6-24-2156

The projections of three working teams fizzled into life at 11:01. Aidan rested his shoulder against Kevin's as the room crowded with holographic people. The three projectors he'd set on the floor whirred, the little machines working hard. He'd worry about whether they could handle this kind of workload later. On his other side, his sister leaned forward, getting a look at the other teams. Tweak leaned out of her way.

"Hey." he remarked, nodding to each of the team leaders in turn. Everybody was a little worse for wear. But everyone looked like they had their heads in the game.

"Good to see everybody," he continued. "Thanks for making the time. I've brought on a new munitions officer, and she and my technical specialist have some new ideas."

"We've been working on some things ourselves, in the downtime," Seattle added. They nodded at a huge man on their left. The guy had to be six and a half feet when he was standing.

"Deniki?"

The big man nodded. "Officer Deniki, Technical. I've been thinking. We need a distract, we all know that. And we all want to do some fucking over, I think."

The feed from three rooms full of people agreeing sounded a little like the growl of a dog pack. It was hair raising, but it made Aidan's lips twitch grimly.

"Well, we got a virus into Natbank and EagleCorp systems, right? You guys have been talking about running a big fat DDOS to cover us, but nothing we're going to do is going to be more than a fly in the Corporate ears. The protests that are getting together, that's going to work a lot better. But if we really want them scrambling, what if we just use our nifty little virus as a back door and mess with the DNS of the systems a little. Get them looking a little funny, maybe?"

For all the good the guy's explanation did Aidan it could've been Greek. But Kevin laughed, and Tweak jumped out of her chair and bounced like somebody doing an exercise routine.

"Yes yes yes yes! Oh fuck YES!" The little coder exclaimed. Kevin caught his eyes and grinned.

"Can I get an explanation on why this is good?" Aidan asked. Tweak turned on her heel, laughing. "Eagle! Natbank! R-r-read each other as malw-ware! Systems attack each other! Oh YES!"

"Oh my ears." Kevin remarked, but he kept it down.

Hagge was actually smiling. "Well holy shit… you may just have something."

Deniki grinned, looking from Aidan to the Tearaways team. At least Anderson was just as confused.

"If we can mess up the system credentials, the Natbank systems and the EagleCorp systems will flag every packet they send each other as malicious." Deniki explained. "Their antivirus softwares will basically start trying to take each other apart."

"Like an auto-immune disease in a human body," Kevin agreed, nodding. "That, my friend, is truly breathtaking. And it will certainly act as a distraction."

Aidan grinned as he caught on. "Like getting two guys to punch each other in a fight. Wow...how long will it take to make it happen?"

Tweak snapped her fingers. "We gotta patch the v-virus. D-dead easy. A day. Tops." She shot the tall Native guy a grin. "This is great."

The moon-faced man shrugged, giving a dismissive smile. "Eh. I got pissed off. Decided to fix it."

"And this's why you're Deniki," Seattle observed, smiling like a parent with their smartest kid.

"Hunh?" One of Anderson's people added. Seattle shrugged. "Deniki means 'Moose' up here. Something gets in his way, he flattens it."

A little eddy of laughter ran around the room.

"Okay, so they're good and distracted," Naomi cut in with the grin Aidan had missed. It was her battle grin, all feral and ready for a fight. "That'll keep them busy while we throw our next trick out there. We figure they'll be watching the backups, right? Of course they will; we went after them once. But they won't be watching the code. So we write an OS patch. We get into a software developing team's workspace assigned to EagleCorp, the night before the protests. We put this thing out as a software upgrade. The system auto-upgrades. And what does it do? Instead of fetching the information from hard drive and using it as backup, the compiler in the system over-writes the backup with garbage code and then deletes it."

The room went silent.

"Well holy shit," the raw-boned woman beside Anderson murmured. "That'll surely do it."

"Wait, don't developer's centers use biometric locks?" The tall woman beside Hagge asked, leathery brow wrinkling.

"So?" Tweak asked, grinning. "We print synth, right? We print g-genome with a v-virus in it. V-virus tells the computer it's unlocked."

"Wait, we can do that?" a dark man on Anderson's team asked, black eyes wide.

Tweak crossed her arms. "*You* can't. *I* can. Me'n' Topher t-t-tested it. Works great."

"One of my transport guy's a printing wiz." Aidan explained, grinning at Tweak as he spoke. Man, she really was getting good at this.

Aidan glanced between his sister, his coder and his guy. "So you guys are going to take that part of it?" he asked.

"Fuck yes!" Tweak just about shrieked.

"It's on Techo grounds," he warned, wishing he could cover his ears.

Tweak grew still for a moment. Turning her head, she met his eyes, then glanced from Naomi to Kevin.

"You guys get me in? Get me out?"

Naomi nodded. "We got your back."

"I've expended far too much effort to waste it letting you get arrested now," Kevin added with a grim little smile.

Tweak glanced around the room. Then she crossed her arms. "Kay. It's ours."

Catching Aidan's eye, she gave him a knife-sharp grin.

"Nice way to finish out my contract with you guys," Naomi added, leaning back in her seat with a grin.

A lance of pain shot through Aidan's chest.

"Here we are then." Kevin remarked several hours later, drawing up a screen. "Getting the details on this development team's office was refreshingly easy. Now that we've got building schematics, I'll get a run organized for...Tweak, how much time do you need to work the OS patch into the system?"

"Gimme three hours," the little coder decided, cocking her head to one side like a crow. "N-not d-dead easy, but n-not that hard."

"We'll head in the Friday before the protests, then." Kevin agreed, giving her a nod. He gave Aidan a quick smile. "Paperwork on your desk by the end of the week for a three-person mission, scout's honor."

"Thanks Kev," Aidan murmured, not really sure what a 'scout' was but almost completely sure it didn't matter.

Kevin straightened, brushing his hand over Aidan's as he stepped away. "I'd best get at it then. See you at dinner."

"See you," Aidan agreed. On his right, Tweak snorted. "You guys. All g-googly eyes."

Aidan shrugged, giving his coder a small smile. "It happens."

Tweak rolled her eyes, half smiling. "Whatevs. Code." For a small person, she could clomp incredibly loudly in those big boots she wore.

Naomi moved to leave her seat too. Aidan scraped his courage together. Reaching out, he touched her hand. "Omi? Can you stay for a second?"

Naomi blinked. Wary, she settled back in her seat. "Yeah?"

"Your contract with us is up in a couple weeks. I wanted to know if you were going to stick around, or if I should start looking for another Munitions officer." He chose his words carefully. "And...on the personal side of things, we both know what I decided to do turned out to be pretty screwed up, looking back. I tried to protect you, and I ended up hurting you. That's on me. But if you want to hear what I was thinking..." He shrugged. "I can answer questions. If it helps."

Naomi's eyes narrowed. Silence thickened like dust in the room. Aidan's throat was dry.

"I was eighteen. I saw the bones of your ribs through your back. I thought you died shielding me from a blast. And you left me alone." Naomi's words were tight. "How do you explain that?"

"I was ruining your life, Omi," Aidan said softly. "Look back at your record. You kept standing up for me and getting written up for it. Dad...Dad broke your arm because of me, and—"

"Dad broke my arm because he was a sick son of a bitch who couldn't tell the difference between 'discipline' and abuse," Naomi snapped, eyes fixed on his. "And if you're still letting him guilt you when he's been dead nine years, you are a dipshit."

"Omi." He swallowed hard. "You found me in a pool of blood twice in one year. I was seventeen, but you were thirteen. Just thirteen. You had to be my rock, right when I should've been looking out for you." Staring into her eyes, he tried to smile. "You're my baby sister, but you got stuck with all the big sister jobs. Cleaning up the blood and the bad days. Fighting for me. Standing up for me. Those should have been my jobs. I didn't want to keep doing that to you. I thought you'd be happier if you didn't have to deal with my problems all the time. I knew you didn't want to hear it. I tried to talk to you about assigning to separate bases, remember? You laughed me off. I thought that if I was out of the picture you could go have a normal life. Well, Duster normal, but yeah."

Naomi snorted. "And how did that work? Do I look nice and 'normal'?"

Aidan didn't let himself look away. "I didn't hear about you getting hurt. Can I ask what happened?"

Naomi rolled her eyes. "Being a Duster who works munitions happened. What else."

Aidan tried for a smile. "But hey, Officer by twenty, right? That's something. I...um...I read about your promotion when it happened. And your commendations. I was...I'm really proud of you."

Naomi's eyes narrowed. "Aidan? You really are a dipshit some days."

Aidan glanced away, feeling the storm clouds building in his chest. "Guess that hasn't changed."

Silence.

"If that was all true then, why do you want me here now?" Naomi asked. Aidan held her eyes. "Because now I can give you something good. I got to a good place; I can offer something that isn't shit for once. This crew's good. I think you'd...um...I think you'd be happy here. I couldn't give you that before." He drew a long breath "I can now."

Naomi blew out a long, hard sigh, looking away. After a beat, she raised her eyes. "Okay Aidan. Why am I angry?"

That brought Aidan's head up. "Hunh? Why are you...because I lied to you."

Naomi shook her head. "Nope. Guess again."

"Because I left?" Aidan tried. Naomi shook her head.

"Wrong answer." She stood. "I'll give you my final decision after the mission's complete."

Then she was out the door. Aidan closed his eyes, groaning to himself. "Fucking hell..."

The lock snicked open, biometric key faked out. "Okay," Naomi sub-vocalized into her mic, "we're in."

Tweak's skin fizzled with nerves. They were in an EagleCorp-contracted office. They were in a TechoCo office. If anything went wrong, they were so dead. Worse than dead.

"You're clear, Tweak. Just walk in," Kevin's voice murmured in her ear. "The area's clear."

Get some guts, she snapped at herself. But she was still shaking as she stepped inside. Her fingers ran over the data stick in her pocket, pleasantly easy to touch under the Synth covering her skin.

The consoles sat around the room, still and dark. Naomi took a stand beside the door. Tweak gulped. Her bones were shivering in her skin.

Cat-footing into the room, she took a seat at the nearest console and pressed her Synth-covered hand to the palm reader. The system took longer to read her virus-laden genome off the Synth's skin cells than it usually did, but it bought the virus. The holographic screen slid up, the TechoCo logo shining bright.

Tweak's blood froze.

The white circle stared back at her, an eye with a wavering red pupil.

She'd been in this chair so many times, with that logo staring at her. Cold. Hungry. Waiting for the electric shock to run through her fingers when she made an error. Hurting. Hurting. Hurting.

The logo stared at her. The controller would punish her for being too slow. But she couldn't make her fingers move.

Her heart hammered in her ears.

Somebody was talking beside her. No, somebody was talking in her ear.

She wasn't being given a task. She had to get her task and carry it out, or the pain would start.

"Tweak, what the hell are you doing?" A man's voice. Hissing. Angry.

People shouldn't talk. Controller was going to make them hurt.

They hadn't given her the task. She needed to complete her task, but they hadn't given her a task.

She was going to hurt again.

Tears prickled behind her eyes.

"Tweak? Hey Tweak? I'm going to touch your back, okay?"

A hand sent burning arcs along her skin. Not really painful. Not yet. But soon. She flinched.

The pain didn't come.

"Tweak. Can you breathe real slow for me? Count to five breathing in, okay? Count to five breathing out. You can do that, okay? Breathe in for five. Breathe out for five. In for five...out for five..."

Tweak's breathing fell into the rhythm the voice set. In for five. Out for five.

The hand on her back was like the warm, wet sponge her mom had used to bathe her and Bao Li.

"In for five...out for five..."

Her heartbeat slowed. The words were easier to hear now.

Tweak moved her cramped fingers. They ached.

Turning her head, she met Naomi's eyes. She took a shaking breath. "I f-f-freaked. Y-yeah?"

Naomi nodded. "Yeah. You're shaking."

Tweak nodded, hating herself. Goddamn, this was fucking pathetic. This was…

This was trauma. That was what Psych kept saying. She'd been traumatized. Turning her head, she glared at the symbol that sent ice down into her belly. "F-f-fuckers."

"They had you, hunh? Conditioned you?" Naomi asked softly.

Tweak nodded, making the wordless sound of assent her throat allowed her.

"Sucks. I've seen it before," Naomi murmured. "Right now, you think you kicked it?"

Tweak swallowed a few times, working her throat open. "Y-yeah."

Naomi's flesh hand gently rubbed her back. "You ready to fuck them up?"

Tweak gave her a grin. "Yes." This word hissed from her lips like a throwing knife, all quick and clean.

Naomi grinned. "Okay then. Go for it."

Turning her head, Tweak started to type.

It took even less time than she'd planned to load the updater she'd spent the last few days making. Once it was in, she got down to process the deltas, inserting them carefully. The changes clicked into place, dancing into life under her fingers.

She stayed focused on the authentication and data-retrieval areas of the OS, stuff that hadn't been changed in ten years, maybe more. That was shitty OS maintenance, but it did save cash to ignore something that almost nobody could get at anyway. And the Corps loved to save a buck.

"How are we doing, Tweak?" Kevin's voice asked in her ear.

"Good on time," Tweak murmured, "N-no problems."

She told the updater tool to generalize across all versions of the OS. Figuring out how to do that alone had been a hell of a trick.

The 'changes successfully made' window popped up. She took a checksum of the OS. Taking the checksum number, she inserted it into the updater.

An update window popped into life. 'Processing...'

Breathe, Tweak told herself.

One minute.

Two.

Three.

The window flashed green. 'Update Completed Successfully! Thank you for your work!'

Tweak grinned. "F-fuck yes."

"Is that it?" Naomi murmured. "Yep!"

Just for the sake of it, Tweak added her own last-minute touch: she got into the settings and turned the screen saver for every computer in the facility into a roaring luck dragon. They didn't know her, but they'd remember the Lucky Dragon.

"That went off surprisingly well," Kevin remarked, slipping a stay-wake under his tongue. He held the bottle out to Naomi. "You'll want to be sharp for our trip home."

The blonde woman took the pill in her cybernetic hand. The joints didn't squeak anymore. She'd done a good job on that thing. Tweak was just a little proud of that.

"We'll be back by dawn, yeah?" Naomi asked once the pill was down. "Only it's fucking hot right now."

"Should be, yes," Kevin agreed, dropping to the hotel bed and pulling up a screen to float at his eye level. "I'll check the drone patterns while we're here and make certain we won't have any surprises...good work on getting the trackers on the freelance drone swarms into our threat-mapping programs by the way, Tweak."

Tweak shrugged. "I'm n-not getting shot again."

Naomi offered her the bottle, but she waved it away. She didn't need the things to stay sharp.

Kevin chuckled, shaking his head as his fingers tapped the slick surface of his tab. "No arguments from me on that count, it's..."

Tweak looked up as Kevin trailed off. The High-Standing man's face had gone scary white.

Fingers moving fast, he brought up another map, eyes flicking between the two. His words came out a whisper.

"Oh dear Lord..."

Tweak's heart started to pound. Stepping around the bed, she studied the screens.

Clusters of red drone lights hung over two parks. Smaller ones hung stationary over a handful of houses across the map.

She let her eyes slide to the map beside it. The houses were marked with addresses and the words 'Check Point'. The park on the map was marked 'rallying point'.

She met Kevin's eyes. He swallowed hard. "The protesters. They're scheduled to gather today and rally in the morning. This is every house where they're camped tonight. The drones have them all in sight. They must be waiting until everyone's at the rallying point tomorrow. When they spring that trap it'll be a *slaughter*."

Tweak's heartbeat kicked up a notch. "Okay, let's g-go. Warn them. Now!"

Kevin shook his head. "We don't dare go in person, but maybe..." Feverishly, he tapped keys and brought up a messaging window. Tweak leaned back as the taller man growled. "Damn it! Everyone in the direct contact list I was given has done the smart thing and left devices at home! Of all the times for people to actually follow security protocol...all right, the organizers at least must have a device on them." He typed fast. Tweak watched the deadly little red dots on the map.

"How many p-people?"

"Over fifteen thousand in Denver. At least a few thousand in all the big cities on the CO-WY grid. Same on the national." Kevin rapped out. "Now don't talk to me, Tweak. I'm working. Damn it, somebody's got to answer me!"

Tweak watched him flicking screens and panicking, his fingers flying. She should be doing that.

She glanced up at Naomi, who sat still as a statue. The other woman shrugged.

Tweak's blood fizzed in her veins. Standing, she tried to work out the feeling by pacing.

Fifteen thousand people.

"Shit!" Kevin hissed. Tweak jumped. "What?" Naomi demanded.

Kevin carded both hands through his hair. "Techo's got an internal alert out! One of the Grid operatives working inside just leaked it. Techo knows what they're watching for! Any messages we send, through the Greynet or not, they're going to see. *Shit!*"

Tweak watched him, feeling her body starting to really shiver. She could feel her scales standing up on end, cutting through the bandages that covered them.

Fifteen thousand people.

And that was just here.

The drones were going to shoot so many people. Eagle wouldn't even need to bother sending Peacekeeping Officers in. They were just going to shoot everyone.

The thought snapped something inside her. Moving, Tweak grabbed Kevin's tab and typed. She studied the maps. The area around EagleCorp headquarters was still clear of drones. Of course it was. Who needed drones when you had a whole building full of assholes?

If they didn't have drones around the entrance to the maintenance tunnels, they could still get in.

If they could get in, this could work.

She raised her eyes. Kevin and Tweak were both staring at her.

"If you can g-get me b-back down into the Eag-g-gleCorp tunnels, I can f-fix this," Tweak stated. "I already w-wrote the code to use for the IR emitters, r-r-right? How about if I inject it into the whole system?"

Kevin blinked. An amazed smile crept across his face "Do you mean..."

Tweak grinned, feeling a fizz like soda pop starting in her chest.

"Oh yeah!"

"Can we get an explanation for the rest of the class?" Naomi asked. Kevin turned to her with a laugh. "We're going to take every drone in the country down tonight. That's an explanation for you! But the surveillance on the maintenance tunnels will still be on, we don't have the time to re-route the cameras or prep." Standing, he paced the room, his eyes far away. "We'll use an EMP, that will short out the sensors and such, but that will set off a whole set of alarms...oh balls...we need a distraction."

He leaned back against the wall, tapping his knuckles against it methodically. Then he crossed back to the bed and snatched up his tab, typing out a message. "I'm letting Aidan know what we're going to try," he muttered distractedly. He waited and paced until a message came back, snatched the tab, nodded at the screen, then snapped out a vid-call window. "Stay out of camera range, ladies."

"Yeah?" A hard-looking woman demanded when she answered. Kevin grinned. "Evening Lainey. I need a word with Blucifer. At his very earliest convenience."

"You mean now, right?" the woman asked, overly made-up eyebrow raised.

Kevin nodded. "Now would be best."

The guy who came on a moment later was weird: he had dreads piled up like messy spaghetti on top of his head, the color of dead grass. His eyes were crazy-pale blue. She felt shivers run up and down her body. A gang guy. Had to be a gang guy. Nobody else got that look.

The ganger watched Kevin through the screen. "Late at night for a call."

"It is that," Kevin agreed, "but I have an offer for you. If we could take every EagleCorp drone down for a period of..." Kevin glanced at Tweak, holding up ten fingers. Tweak held up seven. Kevin nodded, turning back to the vid. "Seven days. We can promise you seven days without a security drone in the sky. What would you say to creating a distraction in order to get it?"

Event File 28
File Tag: Actions in the Field
Timestamp:1:00-6-27-2156

The first bomb was lobbed at one in the morning. Tweak heard it whistle and thump. The ground shook when it exploded.

"What are they using to launch those things?" She asked, wishing she wasn't shaking.

"Modified bazooka shooting bottles full of bio-gas with a fuse, from the sound of it," Naomi replied, grinning. "Maybe a mix of a couple drain cleaners too, if that second explosion's what I think it is. Wish we could see from here."

Tweak took a second to study Naomi, impressed with that grin. Turned out she really did get into explosions.

"Not our job, ladies," Kevin remarked quietly, levering up the maintenance hatch. "Now that the Kings and their friends have kicked the hornet's nest, it's best we got on our part of the bargain. Naomi? Go ahead with the EMPs, if you will. Your arm is protected, isn't it?"

"Double walled lead foil in the casing." Naomi murmured, tapping her flesh and blood knuckles on the casing of her cybernetic arm. "I'm good." She palmed the black hemispheres, grabbed one pole of the maintenance tunnel's ladder and slid down into darkness.

"I'm sure we're all very impressed," Kevin muttered under his breath. "Right Tweak, your turn."

Tweak wasn't stupid. She climbed down. The noise of the attack shut off as Kevin closed the hatch above.

Naomi came jogging back. "Everything's fried. We're set," she announced, grinning. Kevin nodded. "Lovely. This way then. Got your mics in?"

"Now I do." Naomi agreed. Tweak sighed when Kevin eyed her. "Fine. I guess." Reluctantly, she slid the throat mic and the earpiece from her pockets, putting them on. They were irritating as hell to wear. Her throat itched already. "Hate this thing," she muttered.

"Better than getting caught," Kevin remarked, nodding down the tunnel. "Keep between Naomi and I. Once we reach the juncture I'll hang back and watch the tunnels under a slick tarp. Tweak, you work your magic. Naomi, watch her back."

"Roger." Naomi agreed, pulling a holster from the pack on her back and slipping it around her waist. She slid two pistols and one dart gun into it.

It felt surreal, being right back where they'd started. Same gritty concrete. Same stink. Same fiberoptic bundle, nano-clamps between her fingers sliding needle legs through the plastic of their casings. Same fear.

No, worse fear. She wasn't the only person who'd die this time.

Pulling out her tab, she got to work. Sliding through the system was faster this time. She knew where everything was now. She knew how to get around the security setup. But she wasn't aiming for storage. She needed the active drone direction systems.

This would never last long. When the drones went down, EagleCorp would go insane. They'd have the things back up in a week at most. But the heart attacks they'd have in the meantime were going to be great to watch. They'd be so busy with this that they might take the whole week to have a stroke over what was about to happen to the Social Scores.

She slid into the OS easy as a snake. This was everything she'd been trained for. This was easy.

She got into the main command systems for drones. The web of drones spread itself out across the country like a city seen from above. So many damn drones.

Well, she'd fix that.

"Tweak, Naomi. Cover. We've got movement," Kevin's voice murmured in her ear.

Tweak froze.

"Slick poncho, Tweak. It's in your pack. Just pull it on." Kevin's voice added softly in her ear.

Skin tingling and heart in her mouth, Tweak pulled out the slick poncho. She minimized her screen and slid up against the wall, yanking the nanomesh weave with its heavy coolant lining over herself.

Four EagleCorp officers came into the room, guns at the ready. Tweak put a shaking hand over her mouth. *Shit. Shit. Shit.*

If they heard her breathing, she was dead. They were all dead.

Closing her eyes and ignoring the feel of her scales trying to stand on end under their bandages, Tweak listened.

The sound of creaking poly-weave and heavy boots. The men muttering to themselves.

"—mess upstairs and they send us down here? Fucking stupid."

"Hey, I'm not complaining. I don't want a flaming bottle to the face."

"Fucking crazy night, and… what the?"

There were two quiet gasps. A little yelp. A thump.

Naomi spoke. "They're tranqed, Tweak."

The rush of relief made Tweak's muscles feel like jelly. "They g-gonna sleep a while?" she asked, eyeing the officers laid out side by side as she pushed her slick poncho off. Naomi shrugged. "Couple hours."

"Kay. B-body cams?" Tweak asked, crossing her arms to slow the shivers.

"Not anymore." Naomi remarked, pressing a taser wand to each vest. Each one fizzed and sent up a thin tendril of smoke.

Tweak nodded, trying to catch her breath. Her fingers were still shaking when she brought the screen up. Her chest hurt.

"Omi? Bottle of pills. In the bag." Tweak stated as she worked, eyes fixed on the screen. "G-get me two?"

White pills shone in the black plastic hand. Tweak slipped them under her tongue, tasting the slight sweetness as they melted away.

Slowly, the static in her head eased up. She got back to focusing on the job. Pulling the code snippet she used in commands for the IR emitters from her file, she placed it in the command code matrix that ran the drones.

'Propagate?' A query window asked. Tweak hit 'yes,' grinning wide enough to make her face hurt. The code was propagating across the system now, telling all drones to turn off. That code would spread across the country, dropping EagleCorp drones out of the sky.

Perfect.

"Fuck yes. Fuck you," she whispered.

"I take it we're good to go, then?" Kevin murmured in her ear.

"Based on how she's grinning, I'm guessing yes," Naomi chimed in.

"One sec," Tweak whispered. With a careful set of keystrokes, she signed her work, her lucky dragon glyph burning on the screen.

<(-_-)>^^^^^/__________

Then she shut down her tab and grabbed her clamps. "Okay. We go."

There was a thump and a yelp above as Kevin climbed out of the maintenance hatch. A Peacekeeper went sailing past Tweak where she was plastered onto the ladder, hitting the concrete below with a wet smack. Tweak nearly lost her dinner at the sound.

Naomi shoved at her leg from below, sending electricity burning up her spine. "Go damn it!" The blonde woman hissed.

"In a s-sec!" Tweak snapped back. Above them, somebody just missed following the Peacekeeper down the hole, leaping it at the last second.

The noise poured down on them like a waterfall. *Just like a prison riot. Fuck fuck fuck I never want to be in one of those again. FUCK!* Tweak's mind chattered at itself. She remembered riots way too well. She remembered hiding in a corner with a meal tray for a shield, scuttling back to her cell to hide under the bunk.

But there were no corners here, and no cells. The only safe place was on the other side of the noise.

"Two seconds!" Tweak called up to Kevin. Hanging onto the ladder, she zipped her jacket up with one hand, pulled out her 'buds and stuffed them into either ear. It wasn't perfect, but it was something. Digging in her bag, she pulled out her old buddy, the tase knuckles. Then she started to climb.

The first guy to come at her got tased in the groin. He went over like a flipped car.

"Nice shot!" Kevin called over the mess, grinning and bloody-knuckled. He leaned on the piece of rebar in his hand as if it was a cane. Where had he gotten that?

"Duck!" Naomi shouted behind her, and Tweak dropped. A baton whistled over her head. She tased that Peacekeeper too, right in the nuts.

"Remind me not to irritate you ladies!" Kevin shouted. Tweak shot him a wide-eyed look. Did he think this was some kind of game?

Naomi tossed her head, her blonde hair catching the light. "Yeah well! You got an out for us, bookworm?"

"Oh definitely. Let's rock and roll, ladies!" The logistics officer shoved the piece of rebar ahead of him like a sword, pushing their way through the yelling clusterfuck. There was a loud crash and a scream off to the left, and Tweak caught a glimpse of a ViperDrone splayed broken across the roof of a car. Kevin swung his rebar like a baseball bat and knocked a Peacekeeper flying. Naomi punched one with her cybernetic arm on the other side, and the man fell as if he'd been broken in two. Maybe he had. That arm was strong when the settings were right.

"NET!" Someone screamed as a gravometric pressure net came

hurtling out of the sky, micro-steel wire mesh cutting through the air. It flattened everyone within its radius, pressing them to the earth like a giant's hand.

"Let's move!" Naomi shouted, shouldering the crowd around Tweak. "Roger!" Kevin called back on her other side, ducking a fist and returning a hard uppercut that sent the guy he hit to the ground.

A pale cloud of dreadlocks loomed up on one side, the big man laughing. There was blood around his mouth. "Hey Duster, welcome to the party!"

"Thanks for starting it!" Kevin yelled back, "What do you think of the party game we got together?"

"Fucking awesome!" the ganger shouted, slamming an aluminum bat studded with nails into the gut of a Peacekeeper who'd tried coming at him. He turned, baring bloody teeth, and caught Kevin's hand in a grip and a handshake that moved the thinner man's whole body around.

"You gave the Kings a gift! We'll remember!"

"Good to hear!" Kevin laughed, his eyes a little crazy too. "I'm going to go have some fun of my own now! Enjoy!" He saluted with the length of rebar, grinning. Nobody should look that happy in the middle of this craziness.

The next ten minutes were a blur in Tweak's memory for the rest of her life: screaming, fists, feet, bodies pushing on every side. Naomi with her boots and fists, Kevin swinging the rebar like something off a ninja film. And hands and faces coming for her, all the time. She tased so many people.

Kevin was laughing in the mess, she remembered that. It was official. He was batshit. Tweak was desperately trying not to throw up, not to pass out from the lightheaded terror that was crushing her, and that bastard was laughing!

Naomi was grinning too. What was with these crazy alphas who thought it was fun to fight?!

Then they were at the edge of the crowd and away down an alley.

All three of them leaned against an alley wall, gasping for air.

Over her head, Naomi and Kevin turned their heads, looking at each other. Then they both started laughing in wheezing gasps.

Tweak raised her eyes to glare at them both. "You guys. Are. Fucking. *Batshit*!"

"True enough!" Kevin agreed, finally letting up on the stupid snickering. He gave himself a shake. "Well, that was fun. Now, let's go home."

Event File 29
File Tag: Mission Success
Timestamp:16:00-6-29-2156

For two days, Aidan watched the news with a grin on his face. The Corps tried to cover it at first, but the NatBank revolving doors spun insanely fast, the EagleCorp gates were stuck, and the billboards for both companies all over town flashed gibberish. It couldn't be ignored for long. Every news channel had at least a segment on it. And even that story got pushed down by the falling drones. The stuff about their actual objective was barely a ripple in the news feeds by day three. He double checked one more time as he sat in his new office and prepped for the meeting. Yep. Same headlines.

He couldn't have asked for more.

His tab bleeped. Meeting time. Bringing his work computer online, he flicked on four holo-emitters. His fellow Commanders' images flicked into view. This time, Hall and three other Regional Commanders appeared as well.

"So who came up with the drone trick?" Hall asked once the saluting and the greetings were over.

"My technical specialist," Aidan explained, "though it was kind of at the last second. She's the one who created the IR emitters, so she had the codes on hand. And I guess she kind of...went for it."

"And she'll be going up for Officer after this week," Commander Hall announced.

Aidan gave her a smile and mouthed "yes, ma'am", though he really wasn't sure asking Tweak to take an officer's duties was a great plan. Worry about that later. "Would you like the operation report in person, ma'am?"

Hall nodded. So Aidan walked the gathering through what his team had done earlier in the week, step by step. There were a couple whoops when he finished the story.

Commander Hall glanced at her colleagues, who nodded. Turning back to the assembled teams, she stood, smiling.

"People. What you've collectively done has exceeded everyone's expectations. To begin with, our commendation and our congratulations. Ours and National Command's. This mission has done more to put a dent in the Corps than we could have imagined. Your teams will each be receiving awards. Posthumously, where needed. We've got hundreds of operations fast-tracked during this window of opportunity. That being said—" the woman actually grinned. "Your teams are on leave with honors for two weeks. And with our thanks. Go get rested up. Take care of your people. And tell them they have the Force's gratitude and thanks."

That night, the rec-room was crowded and noisy with groans and laughter. The minute they'd heard they had two weeks' leave, everyone had yelled 'movie night' almost in chorus. Things had gotten funny from there. The shitty sword and sorcery movie played on, everybody adding their own commentary. Aidan thought the vid was crap, but his team was into it. And they were having some time together; that was what really mattered.

In the flickering light, he glanced across and watched his sister shake her head, grinning. She was sitting on his right, and her scars looked worse when the light and shadows cast them in relief.

Scars. He should have stopped that from happening.

He'd thought he was protecting her by leaving. He'd meant to protect her.

Naomi glanced his way and flashed a small smile. Then something stupid happened on-screen, and she was back to watching that and laughing.

She didn't need him to protect her anymore. But maybe she didn't need him messing up her life either.

He really needed to settle this stuff in his head, before it drove him nuts.

He kissed Kevin's shoulder and slid from his arms. "Back in a sec, need to check stuff."

Walking down the hall, he slipped outside to sit between their wheeled planting boxes. Breathing in the night air, he watched their crops wave leaves against the stars. The all-nutrient potatoes were taking off. The tomatoes weren't doing great, but they were getting better. The corn was getting tall, along with the bean plants in the box with them. The strawberries and the carrots looked pretty pathetic, but there were a couple of tiny red fruits. The amaranth, golden rice and quinoa plants looked like they were loving life.

Aidan studied the plants until he felt his mind start to settle. It had become his new place to get his head on straight, here in the early mornings and late evenings, between the planter boxes. It was harder to find time to himself these days; now that he shared a room with Kevin, his evenings weren't as quiet. It made doing stuff like this without feeling embarrassed as hell a little more work. Of course, it made getting through his dark days easier too. It wasn't a trade he'd pass up. But right now, he needed to get this straight in his own head.

"Good evening, Aidan," his psychological wellness coaching program's modulated voice murmured. Aidan leaned against the wheel of the corn box, smiling at the image of his sister as she had been and fighting the lump in his throat.

"Hey Omi. So...I need to figure out...the real Naomi...she said she wanted to finish her contract with us. And I...I really don't want to lose her. I want her to stay. But maybe I don't get to make that call anymore, not after what I did. And I just...I don't know. I need to get it straight in my head, okay?"

"That's what I'm here for," the program agreed quietly. "Have you explained your thoughts to your sister?"

Aidan closed his eyes, listening to the rustle of the night wind in the leaves. "Is it fair for me to put this on her? I mean, I'm the one who got us into this. I thought I was helping, but...she was eighteen. And I left her alone. I don't know if I get to just say 'I want you back now that things are good'. And I..." His voice cracked. He pressed his fingers against his brow. "Fuck..."

"Try to look at it as a simple equation." his holographic companion murmured. "Let's lay out the pros and cons."

A facsimile sheet of paper appeared beside her. Aidan drew a slow breath.

"Okay. So, I guess a pro is emotional stability for us both."

The words appeared on the paper in one column. Aidan forced himself to take long, slow breaths. "Omi will be safer here. She'll have a support system. It's a big career boost to get a base Officer position. And...we can get her fixed up. Medically, I mean. If she wants."

"And what do you see as the negative elements?" the program asked.

Aidan laughed weakly. "Feeling like an asshole, mostly."

"That is a very vague answer. Can we solidify it?"

Aidan swallowed. "Feeling like I'm guilt-tripping her. Re-traumatizing her. She built a life and had a position without me. I don't want to take it away. So there's that. And there's a few worries about nepotism I guess. I worry about conflict down the road." He shrugged. "I guess that's it."

The program's paper filled itself out. The 'pro' list was a lot longer than the 'con' list.

"Based on the exercise, it appears that this is to your net benefit.

Long term, she will have higher quality of life and a lower risk factor. It appears mutually beneficial," the program suggested.

Aidan's chest ached. "But what if…" he cut himself off, shaking his head. Too many what ifs. What if he got Naomi killed? What if the base got hit again and he lost everyone, now that so many people he cared about were in one place? What if Naomi decided that she hated it here and resented him later for trapping her in this? What if the shit he'd pulled was something they couldn't get past after all? What if?"

"Are you avoiding discussing it with her due to fears of rejection?" Omi asked gently. The tab projecting her image kicked over into a cooling cycle, whirring loud.

Aidan nodded. "Yeah. I mean she has every right to kick me to the curb. I tricked her into thinking I was dead…"

"Her sense of betrayal will be much better balanced if you explain your motives, and sincerely request the chance to be a part of her life again."

Aidan shook his head, fighting to ease the storm in his chest. Finally, he sighed. "Sometimes I wish Jackson had given you better emotional mimicry programs."

The program gave an odd, modulated blip. An easter egg appeared in Omi's hand, brightly painted, and cracked open. Inside was a message screen.

Recorded Message For Aidan Headly, it read. Jackson's voice came out of the screen below Naomi's holographic form. Aidan jumped as the voice spoke.

"Hey man. I know neither of us knows where we're gonna be in a while, but I left this easter egg to get triggered by a couple of possible comments, because one of these days, you're gonna get sick of talking to a machine. And you should. I made this thing as a crutch, but you toss crutches out when your bones heal, you get me? So if you're sick of dealing with shit grade AI, go talk to a real person. I'll talk if I'm around, but talk to somebody, okay?

I love you like a brother man. Don't be an ass; talk to someone.

This is Jackson, signing off."

Aidan felt tears prick behind his eyes as a voice he'd thought he'd never hear again finished speaking. He wiped a hand across his face, smiling. "Goddamnit Jackson. Stupid son of a bitch. You were always smarter than you looked."

"I'm instructed to ask if you'd like me to switch off at this point." the hologram added quietly in her own voice.

Aidan sucked in a sharp breath. Talk to someone. Someone who wasn't an AI. Jackson had been right. The man he'd loved like a brother had told him to stop being a dumbass. Again. And he wasn't going to ignore that last message.

He drew a slow breath. "Yeah...that'll be all. Thanks, Omi." He swallowed. "Program command. Next time you turn on, reset your appearance to default."

The holograph of his sister smiled gently, dissolving in light.

The movie was ending as he slid back into the room, the crew catcalling it long and loud.

"What the fuck is the point of armor that leaves all the artery points open?"

"Watch, he's gonna...I knew it, there goes the head!"

"There goes shitty CGI you mean. Heads seriously don't bounce."

"Tell me this thing's nearly over?"

"Suck it up Kev, you made us watch worse!"

The sight of everyone piled over each other and goofing off brought an unexpected lightness to Aidan's heart. He felt himself smile.

A cheer went up from his gang as the villain got himself gutted and beheaded. Tweak rolled her eyes. "I could code better CGI in m-my sleep." But she was grinning all the same.

"Okay, so what's next?" Topher asked, flipping onto the menu screen "We've got The Bad Day, we've got City of Cats, we've got When the Stars Fall Dow—"

"No!" most of the room chorused, united against a truly awful romance flick that Topher liked for some reason. Probably because the guy who got the girl in When The Stars Fall Down was a mechanic, if Aidan guessed right.

Liza cleared her throat. "Guys. What we've got is a hell of a late night. Let's hit the sack."

That got a whole new series of catcalls, and it got Liza giving everyone 'the Look'. Laughing, the crew broke up as people headed for their rooms in ones and twos. Kevin sauntered over to join him in the doorway, pressing a kiss to the top of Aidan's head and resting his hands on Aidan's shoulders. "Come to bed?"

"I'm going to check in with Naomi for a sec," Aidan replied quietly, turning his head to nuzzle Kevin's throat.

Kevin brushed a hand over his cheek. "That's good to hear. Fingers crossed, love."

Then his boyfriend was off down the hall, getting punched in the arm by Sarah for something or other and pretending to yelp in pain.

Quietly, Aidan stepped over to Naomi's side. "Can you stay for a second?"

Naomi eyed him warily. Her nod was almost too small to see. But she stayed in her seat.

Janice gave Aidan's shoulder a squeeze as she passed, putting an arm out to snag a curious Blake by the elbow and tow him out of the room. Soon enough, they were alone.

Aidan wet his lips. His sister pushed her long bangs back, staring at him expectantly.

"Yeah?"

The word was clipped, but the tone was neutral. That was something.

Aidan nodded at the blank vid projector. "Pretty shit vid, hunh?"

Naomi held his eyes. "You missed most of it," she observed, deadpan.

Aidan shrugged. "I signed up for Command. Comes with the job. Can I sit?"

Naomi rolled her eyes. "You're the commander here, not me."

Carefully, Aidan took a seat a little down the couch from her.

"What're you thinking of the crew so far?" He asked, starting on something easy. Naomi eyed him.

"That's not what you held me up to ask, is it?"

Aidan chuckled. "Your bull meter's still good." He drew a slow breath. *In for seven. Out for seven. Relax.*

"I wanted to ask if you...um...if you made a decision. About your contract."

Naomi studied him, long and slow. She shifted into a more comfortable position on the couch, folding her arms.

"Same question," she stated eventually, "why am I angry?"

Aidan sighed. "I can think of a lot of reasons. But I don't want to tell you why you're angry. I want to find out, and fix it if I can. If you want me to. So why're you angry?"

Naomi held his eyes. "I'm angry because my big brother, who I *love,* who was one of three—count that, *three* people who ever gave a *flying fuck* about me as a kid—my big brother really thought that I'd be happier thinking he was *dead.* I spent the last four years thinking you died saving my life. Fuck Aidan, I've been carrying *that* around. You thought a good duty record was going to make me happier than being with the only part of my family who's worth shit and *alive?*"

Aidan glanced away from her eyes. "Okay, so it sounded good in my head."

Naomi snorted. "Do me a favor and don't listen to what's in your head. Dipshit. You're my big brother. You're about the only other human who doesn't piss me off."

Aidan rubbed his jaw. "For somebody who doesn't piss you off, you sure hit me hard enough."

Naomi smirked. "You're the one who showed me zombie flicks when I was nine, remember. And then you showed up at my door after you were dead. You're lucky I didn't use a baseball bat."

Aidan chuckled. "Guess I am," he agreed quietly.

They sat for a long, long time in silence. Then Naomi reached over and put her flesh hand on Aidan's shoulder. "So when I sign with you, I'm not going to get 'punched a superior officer' on my record again, right?"

Aidan's heart felt like someone had expanded a balloon in it. He grinned at his sister. "I think I can get your commander to waive it, yeah."

"Good," Naomi retorted, giving him a cockeyed grin. "And heads up? You're a commander now, so I'm not your 'baby' sister. Don't start that 'be careful' stuff you used to do on me."

"I don't think I'll forget," Aidan agreed. Reaching up, he squeezed Naomi's hand. "Come down to my office in the morning. We'll get the paperwork filled out with Sector."

"So can I be Queen of something?" Naomi asked. Aidan blinked. "Hunh?"

"For my handle, I mean." Naomi grinned like she'd won a prize. "It's supposed to be a playing card, right? I want a Queen of something card."

Aidan laughed. "Sure. How's Queen of Spades?"

A Wildcards Playlist, Part 3

- Buffalo Springfield, "For What It's Worth", Atlantic Records Time Capsule,1966
- Bhi Bhiman, "Can't Nobody Stop Us", Peace Of Mind, 2019
- Imagine Dragons, "Thunder", Evolve 2017
- Social Distortion, "Telling Them", Mommy's Little Monster, 1983, ***Quoted Chapter 8***
- The Elders, "Who Are the Seventeen", American Wake, 2004
- The White Stripes, "Seven Nation Army", Under Great White Northern Lights, 2010
- Rise Against, "Prayer Of The Refugee", The Sufferer & the Witness, 2006
- The Offspring, "Defy You," Splinter, 2001
- The Interrupters, "Take Back The Power",The Interrupters
- The Gaslight Anthem, "Wherefore Art Thou, Elvis", Señor and the Queen, 2012
- Tim Cappello, "I Still Believe", The Lost Boys Original Motion Picture Soundtrack, 1987

- Rise Against, "Satellite", Endgame, 2011
- Flobots, "Dancing in the Light of a Burning City", NOENEMIES, 2017
- Don McLean, "American Pie", American Pie 1971
- Blue Öyster Cult, "Don't Fear The Reaper", Agents Of Fortune 1976
- The Gaslight Anthem, "The '59 Sound", The '59 Sound, 2009
- Alabama Shakes, "Future People", Sound & Color 2015
- The Gaslight Anthem, "Get Hurt", Get Hurt 2014
- Peter Seeger, "We Shall Overcome", We Shall Overcome 1963
- José González, "Stay Alive", Soundtrack: The Secret Life Of Walter Mitty, 2013
- Mischief Brew, "A Rebel's Romance," Smash the Windows, 2005
- The Police, "King Of Pain", Synchronicity 1983
- Soul Asylum, "Runaway Train", Grave Dancers Union 1993
- Simple Plan, "Welcome To My Life", Still Not Getting Any 2009
- The Doubleclicks, "Sensitive Badass", Love Problems 2017
- Mumford & Sons, "Little Lion Man", Sigh No More 2009
- The Tragically Hip, "Ahead By A Century", Trouble at the Henhouse, 1997
- Ben Howard, "Under the Same Sun", Every Kingdom 2011
- Ben Howard, "The Fear", Every Kingdom 2011
- Jose Gonzalez, "Step Outside", Soundtrack: The Secret Life Of Walter Mitty, 2013
- Lindsey Sterling, "The Arena", Brave Enough 2016
- The Verve, "Bitter Sweet Symphony", Whatever 2004
- Tom Petty, "Learning To Fly", Into the Great Wide Open 1991
- Bhi Bhiman, "Have a Little Faith", Peace of Mind 2019
- Bon Jovi, "Bang A Drum", Blaze Of Glory 1998
- Gaslight Anthem, "Stay Lucky", American Slang 2010

- Bon Jovi, "99 in the Shade," New Jersey, 1988, ***Quoted Chapter 22***

- Matchbox Twenty, "How Far We've Come", Single 2007

- Mischief Brew, "Lightning Knocked the Power Out", Smash the Windows 2005

- New Radicals, "You Get What You Give", SCOOBY-DOO 2: MONSTERS UNLEASH, 1998

- Mandisa, "Bleed The Same", Out of the Dark 2017

- Jefferson Starship, Starship, "We Built This City", Knee Deep In The Hoopla 1985

- Prince, "Let's Go Crazy", Purple Rain 1984

- Halestorm, "Here's To Us", Into the Wild Life 2013

goal is to provide accurate and reliable information free of preference, bias, or endorsement. https://psyberguide.org/about-psyberguide/

BetterHelp: An e-counseling site with a solid record, BetterHelp is a safe, private and affordable place to begin working on your mental health. https://www.betterhelp.com

Project UROK:

This project reaches out to teens directly and allows them to engage in the conversation about mental health on their terms in their space: online. It's a safe, welcoming and fun online platform where they can watch and share videos. https://childmind.org/our-impact/project-urok/

Susan's Place Transgender Resources: a peer support website for transgender individuals. The site is intended to be a safe space where transgender people can assist one another, and it has the additional mission of educating the public. https://www.susans.org/

ACLU LGBT Rights:

The ACLU works to ensure that lesbian, gay, bisexual, and transgender people can live openly without discrimination and enjoy equal rights, personal autonomy, and freedom of expression and association. If you are having legal or workplace issues, go to https://www.aclu.org/issues/lgbt-rights

Transgender American Veterans Association:

Founded in 2003, the Transgender American Veterans Association (TAVA) is a 501 (c) 3 organization that acts proactively with other concerned gay, lesbian, bisexual and transgender (GLBT) organizations to ensure that transgender veterans will receive appropriate care for their medical conditions in accordance with the Veterans Health Administration's Customer Service Standards promise to "treat you with courtesy and dignity . . . as the first class citizen that you are." Further, TAVA will help in educating the Department of Veterans Affairs (VA) and the Department of Defense (DoD) on issues regarding fair and equal treatment of transgender and transsexual individuals. http://transveteran.org/

Everyone Is Gay:

This is a collection of voices lending advice and support to Lesbian, Gay, Bisexual, Transgender, Questioning/Queer, Intersex, and Asexual (LGBTQIA) youth, and also offers comprehensive lists of nationwide LGBTQIA resources.

Website: http://everyoneisgay.com

SAMSHA National Helpline

1-800-662-HELP (4357)

TTY: 1-800-487-4889

Website: www.samhsa.gov/find-help/national-helpline

Also known as the Treatment Referral Routing Service, this helpline provides 24-hour free and confidential treatment referral and information about mental and/or substance use disorders, prevention, and recovery in English and Spanish.

Traversing Gender:

Understanding Transgender Realities: This book, written by Lee Harrington, is a solid and approachable manual on transgender issues with an entire chapter of resources. If you're exploring, it's a great read. Take a look on the Zon at https://www.amazon.com/Traversing-Gender-Understanding-Transgender-Realities-ebook/dp/B01ENYNZPA

<u>About The Author</u>

O.E. Tearmann lives in the shadow of the Rocky Mountains, in what may become the Co-Wy Grid. They share the house with a brat in fur, a husband and a great many books. Their search engine history may garner them a call from the FBI one day. When they're not living on base 1407, they advocate for a more equitable society and more sustainable agricultural practices, participate in sundry geekdom and do their best to walk their characters' talk.

Read more and download an exclusive free short story at

aceshighjokerswild.com/read-for-free